Stove

and the Lost Laugh

by
Rob Gill

ISBN 978-1-4452-8363-0

1.

Rudania.

In the northern - most point of the Kingdom of Rudania, lay
the ancient and mysterious mountain range of Scroop. I say
lay, but of course like most ancient and mysterious mountains,
they more sort of towered and glowered in a vaguely
threatening sort of way. The inhabitants of Rudania, having
observed just how towering and glowering they were, thought
it wise to avoid any kind of contact with them whenever
possible.

Apart from Alec McGinty, the one and only Rudanian
mountain climber, that is and as all Rudania declared him to be
bonkers, he didn't really count. Consequently, the rest of the
nation barring the aforementioned Alec 'Bonkers' McGinty all
lived as far away from the mountains as they could, in the
south of the country.

This was a bit of a shame really, because as the south was
completely surrounded by sea and Rudanians hadn't a clue
about sailing, nor any desire to learn, (apart from Ray 'bottom
of the ocean' Spriggs, and the less said about him the better)
they never visited any other countries or met any other people.
This made them very suspicious of anything new or different.
And because the climate and landscape of Rudania was so
grim, with almost constant slate grey skies and persistent
drizzling rain, it also helped to make them very miserable and
very rude.

Hence the name of their country.

It seemed that they had no time for laughter, or making merry, sharing in a joke, or singing a song. In fact, if you were travelling through Rudania (though goodness knows why you'd want to) and stopped to ask someone the way, they would almost definitely reply in the time honoured fashion by sticking their thumb up to their nose and saying:

'I would far rather smear myself with bacon fat and jump naked into a hungry lion's den, shouting 'O.K. boys, grubs up!' than give you the time of day.'

They really were the most odious, rude and miserable bunch. Yuk! Which is why our story doesn't concern them.

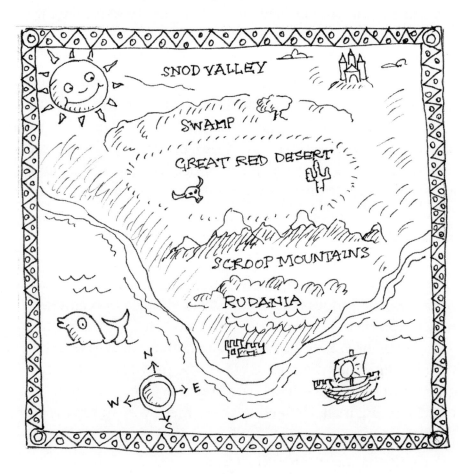

2.

Snod Valley.

Just over the Scroop mountains to the north was the Great Red Desert, then a huge area of swamp land and a little further north still, the beautiful Snod Valley. The sun seemed to shine almost constantly there, apart from the occasional, refreshingly light, mist of rain and just enough snow in the winter to provide everyone with the means for a good snowball fight and a SnowSnod or two. SnowSnod? Well, the inhabitants of the valley were called, not surprisingly, Snods. And as you've probably never seen one, I suppose I had better describe a Snod for you.

They're not exactly what you or I would call beautiful, in fact they're really rather ugly. But not a frightening ugly, like an ogre or a witch or something, but more a warm comfortable ugly, like a hippopotamus or the man at the newsagents who used to be a boxer. (Do you know him? Big fella with a nose like a squashed tomato, slight speech impediment.)

They're quite short, with an average height of about five feet when fully grown, have pale, freckly skin, large cheery heads, with big noses and ears and bright, twinkling eyes. This is all topped off with thatches of unruly but very thick and lustrous orange hair. You never see a bald Snod (apart from Tap the green grocer who'd shaved his off as a fashion statement when he was a teenager and to his secret dismay it had never grown back.)

As a rule they like to wear brightly coloured, comfortably loose clothes and chunky leather boots or dancing slippers, depending on their mood. Which is inevitably a good one, as they are a relentlessly cheerful and optimistic people, constantly looking on the bright side of life.

They love nothing more than to crack a good joke, dance a silly dance, or pull a silly, comic face. It was very rare indeed for them to feel unhappy or depressed, bitter or angry. In fact if something nasty were to happen to a Snod, which occasionally as with us all it did, he (or she) would smile, crack a joke and repeat the Snod motto:

'Oh well, things could be a lot worse.'

Apart from laughter, the other thing that was very important to a Snod was cooking. So even the humblest little house would be sure to have a well equipped kitchen and plentiful supplies.

Snod Valley was lush and fertile and all sorts of fruit and vegetables grew in abundance, so the Snods always had plenty to eat and didn't have to travel further a field for anything, even though they had enormous appetites. (Incidentally, the one thing they were really partial to and for which they could be tempted to do almost anything, were the liquorice sticks that grew on the Rhumba trees.)

Although it was called a valley, it wasn't, in the strictest meaning of the word. There were no mountains on either side of it and it was pretty much flat right across. If you looked really closely you might just about be able to perceive slightly higher ground on each side, but nothing like as high as we see in say, Wales or Scotland. Even the Snods themselves had no idea where their county's name had come from, to them it was just what it had always been called and as they had notoriously short attention spans, no one had ever really bothered to investigate further.

The King of all the Snods was a certain 'Pan the mighty.' Quite why he was called such, nobody really knew either. He certainly wasn't what you or I would think of as mighty, in fact if we met him we would be more inclined to think 'Pan the daft,' might be a more suitable title.

Truth be told, he didn't much care for the name himself, but kept it for traditional reasons as it leant his role a certain gravitas. He always had a secret yearning to be known as 'Pan the lasagne,' after his favourite food.

He had a twelve year old son, Stove, of whom he was terrifically fond, as are all Snods of their children and who if I'm honest, he rather spoiled, giving him everything he wanted. I'm not sure that this was necessarily a good thing, because after all, if we always got what we wanted whenever we asked, we would soon run out of things to want. And then where would we be?

Happy, you say? Well, Stove wasn't…and it's with him that our story begins.

3.

Stove the Snod.

One day as Stove was sitting in the palace gardens watching his father playing draughts with Trowel the gardener, he was suddenly terribly aware of the strangest feeling. He wasn't quite sure what it was, but it felt very unpleasant, like a heavy, wet blanket had been wrapped around his heart. It was certainly a feeling that was most unfamiliar to a Snod and try as he could Stove just couldn't quite put his finger on it. Then he remembered when he'd felt like this once before.

It was a day long ago, when his pet Gerbil Anthony had mysteriously disappeared from his cage in Stove's bedroom. He'd asked his parents where he'd gone and they both looked shiftily and uneasily at each other, his mother muttering something vague about 'a better place' before his father distracted him by clearing his throat noisily and bursting into an impromptu and extravagant jig, while juggling the cat. But before he did, Stove had felt that same heavy, unfamiliar feeling. Now what was it called?

Then he remembered.

'Father,' he said, breaking out of his reverie, 'I'm…I'm not too sure, but I think I'm feeling a bit…sad …a bit…unhappy.'

'Eh? What's that my boy?' said the King, absentmindedly continuing with his game. 'Ah ha! There's your big mistake Bowel. Take that and that and that! Ha ha!'

'It's Trowel actually Sire,' muttered his opponent under his breath. The king, oblivious, chortled with glee as he took all the gardener's remaining pieces.

'I win! I win!' sang the King, dancing a most strange victory jig, which involved a good deal of unsettlingly unattractive face pulling, 'I'm the king of the castle and you're the dirty......er....' he stopped for a moment and rubbed his chin thoughtfully, ' er....gardener,' he continued, with a cheerful grin.

'Oh well,' said Trowel, 'things could be a lot worse,' and off he trudged to tend the Royal carrots, pausing only to angrily boot a passing cat into the air.

Stove noticed this with some surprise. It was a vicious act and most unexpected from a Snod and he would normally have remarked upon it, but his mind was on his own problems.

'Father,' repeated Stove, tugging on the sleeve of the king's ermine robe, 'you're not listening. I said I thought I might be…unhappy. Unhappy...and perhaps…sad too.'

'Eh? Sad? Unhappy? Nonsense my boy. Never been heard of. How can you possibly be? You have everything you want and with the festival of laughter coming up, you should be rehearsing your act anyway. That reminds me, have you heard the one about the salamander and the one-legged nun?'

With that, the king pulled another very silly face indeed.

'Yes father,' said Stove forcing a weak and unconvincing grin, 'several times.'

It's probably worth mentioning here that it was traditional in the valley of the Snods for the person who told the best jokes, pulled the silliest faces and could perform the daftest dance to be made King. And every year the Festival of Laughter was held to determine who that person was. For the last twenty years since he'd come of age, it had been Pan, but no Snod was allowed to compete after twenty victories, so this year it was to be Stove's turn to uphold the honour of the family in the competition.

'Father,' said Stove hesitatingly, 'listen, about this festival.....'

'Come along boy! Cheer up! The whole family's behind you, we all know you'll win. You are the Prince after all and there's never been a Prince who hasn't won. Here, have a liquorice stick.'

The king brandished a fist full of the sticks under Stove's nose and pushed his crown forward on his head to a ridiculous angle. Stove attempted a weak smile in response. It failed.

'Just remember my boy, things .....'

'Yes father, I know, 'could be a lot worse,' I suppose,' said the boy with a heavy sigh, something very rarely heard in a Snod.

Suddenly, a large overripe plum hit the king on the back of his head with a loud

'SPLAT!'

knocking his crown completely off.

'What the...?' spluttered King Pan, stooping to pick it up and at the same time looking around for the perpetrator of the sticky crime.

There was a loud burst of furious, high pitched giggling.

'Hee hee hee! Catch me if you can daddy!'

It was Grill, Stove's ten year old sister.

'Why you little scamp, I'll get you!' laughed the king, gathering up the hem of his robes and setting off in hot pursuit, or at least as hot a pursuit as someone quite as round and fond of liquorice-stick cake and sugar beet as he was could.

Stove watched the his father's shambling form disappear into the long grass, sighed again and chewing absent-mindedly on a liquorice stick, sat down next to the drafts board.

What was the use? Nobody could understand. Snods just didn't get sad, bored or unhappy it wasn't in their nature. And besides, he couldn't let his family down, they would be expecting him to take the crown from his father at the festival in one month's time.

He toyed with the draught pieces. As with just about everything in Snod Valley, there was a joke printed on it and a rough sketch of a silly face.

'Question,' he read, 'what do you call a man with a seagull on his head?'

'Answer,' he continued, 'Cliff.'

Not even a flicker. Stove sighed heavily again.

'I'm sure I used to find that funny,' he said aloud to himself.

Grill hurtled by, shrieking with laughter, followed closely by her father, who was now so covered with fruit that he looked rather more like a green-grocer's stall than a king.

'Come back here you little minx!' he laughed.

Tempted just for a minute, Stove half-smiled, bent down and picked up a rotten apple from the ground and hefted it after his father's rapidly retreating figure. The king disappeared around the corner of the Royal outside loo and the apple exploded harmlessly against the low slung branch of a large oak tree.

'Well that's typical,' said Stove shaking his head, 'still, I suppose things.....Oh! I must stop saying that!'

Stove knew he had to do something to break out of this mood. The way he felt at the moment, he couldn't see himself even taking part in the festival, let alone putting on a good enough performance to win. What was that joke about the elephant breaking wind and the broom? He couldn't even remember that and it had always been one of his greatest favourites.

He picked a mirror fruit from a nearby bush and pulled a funny face into it. Oh dear. What a miserable sight. His attempt at a funny face looked like a horrible grimace. It was the sort of expression you make when someone tells you there's a splodge of bird poo on the back of your favourite anorak.

The earlier mentioned cat, having recovered from Bowl's unexpected and somewhat unjust attack limped by and catching sight of Stove's grim attempt fled with a wail, spitting into the undergrowth.

'It's no good!' he cried, I can't compete like this!'

Stove was a good Snod, he loved his family and didn't want to let them down. He couldn't bear the thought of becoming the first ever Prince to lose the crown. He pictured the look of disappointment on his father's merry face and felt the cold prod of guilt deep in the pit of his stomach.

But what to do? Who could he turn to in his desperation? No one in his family, that was for sure. And as all the Royal Court and Royal Advisors, including the Prime Minister of Mirth, were selected for their sense of humour and ability to not take anything in life seriously, there was no point in talking to any of them.

There was only one thing he could do, one person to whom he could turn. He must go and see Cough, the Royal magician, keeper of the Royal joke book and generally considered to be the wisest Snod in the kingdom, (which wasn't really very wise at all of course.) If anyone would be able to help him, it was Cough.

With a heavy heart and a wet patch on his trousers where he'd been sitting in the damp grass, Stove set off for the darkest and least visited part of the Royal castle.

4.

A short history of the Royal Castle.

The Royal castle of Pan the mighty was an ancient and mysterious building. No one could remember how old it was, or who had originally built it, although as with most ancient and mysterious things, there were many theories and rumours.

It was generally believed in Stove's time, that it had been built in the far off days of the ancient Kings of Snod Valley. These kings unlike modern day Snods, were very fierce and warlike and used to like nothing better than invading other countries in search of gold, booty and salt and vinegar crisps (commonly believed to be the recognised currency at the time.) This of course made them pretty unpopular with their neighbours, who one day all got together and decided to retaliate by invading Snod Valley to teach the odious little thieves a lesson.

The King at the time was a certain ' Rolph the mighty, ' (known to his friends and family as ' Rolph the sneaky' and to his enemies as something quite unprintable) and when he found out what was about to happen, he turned in desperation to an old magician who lived nearby and who was rumoured to be on friendly terms with a ferocious ogre. As his army would be hopelessly outnumbered, he figured that a bone gnashing, slavering, one eyed, drooling, twenty foot high monster wielding a huge club with a big nail through its end, might just turn things his way.

The old man was duly summonsed and appeared in the royal barn (no castle in those days you see) looking a little scared and confused.

'Old man,' said the king, toying with a very sharp looking dagger, 'I hear through the burp vine that you're on more than nodding terms with the feared ogre of Scroop mountains, is this true?'

The magician looked shiftily from side to side then, sensing his opportunity, drew himself up to his full three and a half feet and in a shrill, reed like voice announced:

'Your majesty, to find out something worth your while, you must first give me a glittering pile...of gold.' He added as an afterthought, 'sorry it didn't span, I'm a bit out of practise.' Rolph had him thrown in the moat, which fortunately for the old man hadn't had any water in for years and dismissed the ogre solution as a fairy story.

But he couldn't get the possibility out of his mind and as day by day the enemy drew closer and closer, he spent two mostly sleepless and disturbing nights just wondering if it all could possibly have been true. Disturbing, because what brief dreams he had consisted of him trying to run through porridge-like mud, while a booming voice behind him sang about fee-ing, foh-ing, fumm-ing, smelling blood, crushing bones to make bread and other generally unpleasant things.

He would awake sweating, with a start, usually to discover that he'd eaten half his pillow in his sleep.

Finally, he and the Royal pillow maker, could stand it no longer and sent his fleetest soldiers out to find the old man. This they did and it wasn't long before he was once again standing in front of the king. This time he looked a little more dishevelled and with a few leaves in his beard like he'd been sleeping rough.

'Tell me, old man,' said the king, idly carving a crude picture with his dagger of what looked like a magician having his head chopped off, into the arm of his throne. The old man swallowed dryly.

'For to have my story told,' he piped, nervously, 'give me first my bag of gold.'

'Throw him in the moat and cut off his beard,' said the king impatiently.

5.

Rolph the Sneaky and the Ogre.

'Your majesty, if I may be so bold,' said Lude, the king's prime minister and advisor, 'the enemy armies are fast approaching, we do need all the help we can get.'

'Wait! ' the king shouted as his guards dragged the whimpering old man by his feet towards the open window, 'Lude's right, bring the annoying old fool back.'

The guards righted the old magician and roughly dusted him down.

'Now look, old...fruit, I'm not an unreasonable Snod,' smiled the king sneakily, who was of course one of the most unreasonable Snods alive, 'you shall have your gold....... when you have told me your, er... tale.'

'What... a whole bag?' said the old man nervously eyeing the heavily armed guards surrounding him.

'Yes... a whole bag,' muttered Rolph with a painful wince.

The old man once more drew himself proudly up to his full three and a half feet and coughing slightly at the effort, began his tale.

'Your majesty, the legendary ogre of Scroop mountains is no legend.'

You could hear a pin drop.

'How annoying, anybody see where that pin went?' asked Lude.

The old man continued, unabashed.

'I have seen him in his mighty lair. For three long days I searched, risking life and limb amidst all the terrors that the Scroop mountains had to offer.......'

'Skip the hors d'oeuvre, old man,' interrupted the king impatiently, 'get on with the main course.'

'Er..yes your majesty...of course. Well... on the third day, I awoke to find it raining…a slight drizzle really, hardly raining at all...almost a mist of rain you might say...yes, I awoke to a fine ...mist of rain....'

The king cleared his throat, threateningly.

'Oh yes, anyway,' continued the old man nervously, 'I have seen the fearsome ogre and spoken with him......he's very well actually though a little lonely and he's grown a rather fetching goatee beard, which makes him look even more fierce.'

He paused for effect.

'So...how exactly did you find this...fearsome chappie?' asked Lude.

'With this!' cried the magician, triumphantly producing a small gold whistle from inside his sleeve.

'With this…the legendary gold whistle of…of…er…mine. If you visit the Scroop mountains, you too will be able to summons him. It is yours for a bag and a half of gold.'

'Throw him.....' began the king,

'O.K. just one bag.'

'It's a deal,' said the king and the whistle and the gold changed hands.

The very next day, taking his courage in his hands, as well as the whistle and a small fortune in jewels just in case, Rolph set of for the awesome Scroop mountains. After five days hard riding to reach them and a further five searching and blowing himself hoarse, he realised that he'd been done and that the ogre didn't exist at all.

'Just wait 'till I catch that old man,' he swore as he galloped home.

Luckily for the valley the old man, who turned out to be a very powerful magician after all and had just needed the gold to get his spell book out of the pawnbrokers, created the castle out of a stone hillside in Rolph's absence. He made sure it was especially magnificent in order to please the king so much that he'd forget about being conned.

When Rolph returned and saw the massive and most impressive castle, complete with a huge banner reading ;

'Welcome home King Rolph, from your loving subject Grunt the magician,' he burst out laughing, disbanded his army, made peace with his enemies (who never returned to the valley…or at least not yet) and kept the old man on as his court magician.

Over the next few years, his behaviour became more and more eccentric. He began to spend almost all his time in the kitchen, where he became quite an accomplished cook, even bringing out a best selling recipe book; 'Rolph on Rhubarb.'

Some time later he moved full time into his kitchen, making up his bed amongst the baskets of fruit and vegetables and converting half of the 'walk-in' freezer into an en-suite bathroom.

Then one day, in a moment of inspiration, he decided to change his name to Fishslice after his favourite kitchen utensil. He was so pleased with himself that he then decreed, to his increasingly despairing court, that all Snods should take their names from kitchen implements.

Finally, on his death bed when his courtiers requested that he name his successor, he declared that from then on the kingdom should be ruled by the funniest person, who could tell the best joke, dance the daftest jig and pull the silliest face. And then it's said; he died laughing.

Over the centuries, the people of Snod Valley's character was slowly changed by these decrees and they became the empty-headed, fun loving jokers that they are today.

Don't you believe it? Well I did say it was just a rumour.

Anyway, the story went that the magician always kept certain secret spots in the palace to himself, just in case any Snod kings should revert to their fierce old ways and try to throw him out into the moat, or cut off his beard. It was also rumoured that Cough, to whom Stove was going for help, was a direct descendant of that self same old trickster.

6.

Stove's friends have a laugh.

You may be wondering why Cough was called Cough and wasn't named after a kitchen utensil. (If you weren't wondering, it doesn't matter because I'm going to tell you anyway.)

Although magicians and wizards were strictly speaking, Snods, they were also a little different because of their special, inherited powers. These powers were usually passed on from their mothers and as a sign of respect for this, new born wizards were named after the first sound, word, or even exclamation uttered by their mothers at the moment of their birth.

Hence 'Cough.' Well it could have been worse, just imagine.

Anyway, none of this mattered to Stove as he hurried along past the Royal vegetable patch, head down, lost in his unhappy thoughts. He glanced up and was mildly surprised to see Bowl the gardener leaning on his hoe and glaring balefully in his direction over the tops of his rhubarb plants. Stove smiled emptily and raised his hand in a half-hearted wave. Bowl didn't wave back.

'Hey, it's Stove! Hey! Prince Stove! Wait up!'

The voice had come from behind him and Stove turned to see three Snods of about his age trotting towards him. He recognised Fork, his brother Spoon and their friend (a girl) Rubber Glove, all of whom he went to Advanced Humour school with. Normally he'd be really pleased to see them but, feeling the way he did now he couldn't imagine anything he wanted to do less.

He flashed the same empty smile again as the three friends caught up.

'Hey…' panted Fork, the biggest of the three and supposedly Stove's best friend, 'what's up? Where you off to in such a hurry?'

'Oh…nowhere really…just…walking.'

'Oh I get it,' said Fork with a laugh, 'surveying your future domain.'

He adopted a deep, pompous voice and waved his arms around like a self-important politician.

'One day soon my boy, all this will be yours.'

The others all burst into laughter. Fork was a good mimic. Stove's pale smile faded still further.

'Well, that's not necessarily going to happen you know, anyone can win the Festival of Laughter,' he said defensively.

The others stared at him in silence for a moment. Then abruptly burst into hysterics.

'Nice one Stove,' wheezed Fork through tears of laughter.

'Yeah…' gasped Rubber Glove, 'you really *are* the funniest Snod in the Valley. Anyone can win….ha ha…yeah, right, ha ha.'

'Yeah, like, you're really not going to win, ha ha that'll be the day,' laughed Spoon.

Stove watched them in gloomy silence. He glanced back at Bowl and could just see the top of his head as he resumed his hoeing amongst the large, flat, red and green rhubarb leaves.

'Anyway, must go,' he said, starting off once more. Gradually, their laughter subsiding, the other three followed.

'Hey…hey Stove…did you hear the one about the….' Fork began cheerfully,

'No I did not! And what's more I don't want to!' snapped Stove, stopping abruptly.

'Now do me a favour and leave me alone!'

The other three looked astonished. There was a moment's silence once more.

'Ooooh….someone's tired,' said Fork in a singsong voice.

The others cracked up again.

Stove began to feel even more unhappy. Why couldn't he join in with his friend's laughter? Just a couple of days ago they had all been out together enjoying their dance lessons. The "Turtle stranded on its back" dance, if he remembered correctly, had been a real thrill. He'd never laughed so much. Yet now, even the thought of it left him cold. It all seemed so stupid.

'Stove, have you seen Fork's new one…his new dance?" said Rubber Glove, " I tell you if you weren't in the Festival he'd really be in with a chance. Go on Fork, show him."

'Yeah go on Fork, show him," echoed Spoon.

'Oh…o.k." said Fork with a mock bashfulness, "if my fans insist."

He adopted a heroic pose.

'I call this ' The Cat with a sock tied around its middle' dance."

With that, Fork went into an elaborate jig, staggering first one way, then the other, hanging on to Spoon's shoulder, then reeling across to Rubber Glove's then staggering on hands and knees to Stove, all the while emitting a horrible wailing sound.

Stove had to admit it did look funny. It should have been funny. The other two were helpless with laughter. But he couldn't even raise a smile.

Fork heaved himself up via Stove's trouser leg, until his face was level. He looked mystified by Stove's stone-faced reaction, but then brightened once more.

'I know Stove, do your 'Vicar with too small underpants at a wedding' dance, that's always a killer.'

'Yeah, yeah!' chorused the others enthusiastically.

Stove looked into their expectant faces.

'No,' he said curtly, then span on his heel and marched grimly away.

His friends watched his retreating back hopefully for a while, then Fork shouted.

'Hey! What about this one?' and began another extravagantly acrobatic dance that involved a lot of falling about and silly face pulling. Although he could hear them all laughing for quite a while longer, Stove didn't look back.

7.

The magician's secret place.

Stove's footsteps echoed along the huge, empty, stone hallway as he made his way to Cough's private laboratory. He always felt a little nervous when meeting Cough, as the old magician had a disconcerting habit of showing off his magic powers by turning items of household furniture and servants into various furry creatures and vice versa....and sometimes he missed.

Stove's nursemaid had never quite recovered from her stint as a hamster. At tea times she still shoved as much food as she could into the sides of her cheeks and had insisted that a large wire wheel be installed in the Royal gym.

'One day,' Stove thought ruefully, 'he's going to miss and turn me into a stoat or a shrew or something.'

He reached the end of the dark hallway and stood for a moment in front of the large, rough wooden door. On it in impressive, two foot high gothic letters were written the words;

'SILENCE. GENIUS AT WORK,' and underneath that on a small, blue card; 'You don't have to be mad to work here....but it helps!'

Stove was just beginning to wonder whether he'd come to the right place for help after all, when the heavy door crashed open and a large sofa with what appeared to be gerbil's feet hurtled out, followed by an irate little man with a long, white beard. Luckily Stove had the presence of mind to hop quickly behind the door and so avoided a possibly horrible fate.

'What a way to go,' he muttered aloud, as he watched the strange chase continue on down the hallway and around the distant corner 'trampled to death by a runaway sofa.'

'Mornin' Master Stove'

Stove jumped at the sound of the unexpected voice and peered out from his hiding place into the gloomy interior of the room behind the open door. He raised an eyebrow (interestingly most Snods only had one, members of the Royal family were an exception) in astonishment at the owner of the voice. There stood a short (even for a Snod) and very round little chap. He had a huge smiley mouth and twinkling eyes and wore his orange hair, somewhat surprisingly, after the fashion of a spring onion. But what startled Stove more than anything else, was his arm, or rather lack of one. His left arm was perfectly normal, but in place of his right was a shiny metal tube articulated at the elbow (or where the elbow would have been) that ended in what looked suspiciously like an egg whisk. Something glutinous and runny dripped slimily from it.

Although he'd never met this odd character, Stove had heard many tales about him and knew exactly who he was; Cough's rascally assistant Colander.

'You'll be wantin' master Cough, I don't doubt?'

'Er yes, Cough,' said Stove emerging doubtfully from behind the door and eyeing Colander's arm nervously, 'Er...do you think he'll be long?'

'Oh no no no, happen he'll be back shortly, when he's catched yon sofa. Come in, make yerself comfy and toasty warm. I'm just whiskin' some eggs if yer interested.'

Colander brandished the egg whisk towards the room's gloomy interior, accidentally splattering his tartan trousers with beaten egg, then turned on his heel. Stove followed, glancing curiously around him as he entered the mysterious laboratory.

'Er, no thanks I've eaten.... so.... how did you know who I was?' asked Stove.

'Ah, ' twere master Cough. Not much 'e don't know...'

Colander stopped in his tracks and creased his forehead into a thoughtful frown. '...apart from anything to do with wasps, or socks or polyunsaturated fats, that is.'

Puzzled for a moment by the oddness of this information, Stove watched as Colander removed a large dust sheet from a shapeless object in the corner of the room, to reveal a huge, throne-like chaise-longue.

'Take a seat....as long as you promise to give it back!'

Colander threw his head back and roared with laughter at his rather modest joke, coughing and wheezing until tears ran down his rubbery cheeks.

'Oh lor'....promise to give it back...ha ha...oh dear, oh dear ...ha ha.'

Stove watched impassively then, checking to see there was nothing surprising or nasty on the ancient seat cushion, clambered up onto the throne. He sat dwarfed in its hugeness, legs swinging to and fro, while he waited for the magician's assistant to regain control of himself.

'Do you think he'll be long?' he asked again, rather curtly.

'No, in fact he'll be no time at all young Stove,' piped a strange, new voice.

Stove looked around from his high vantage point into the dusty gloom at the far side of the cavernous room, from where the voice had come. After a moment, Cough, the court magician strode imperiously (or as imperiously as you can when you're only three feet tall) into the light. In his arms he held a good-sized gerbil, which regarded Stove with beady suspicion.

'In answer to your question, yes this is the same sofa that so nearly ran you down a few minutes ago. As you can see the transformation was successful.'

Just as Stove was thinking: 'actually my question was how can you expect me to take you seriously with that stupid hat you're wearing?' Cough stooped down and placed the gerbil on the floor, where it scuttled away for a few feet and buried itself under a fallen cushion. There it lay crouching on all fours, looking for all the world like a tiny gerbil shaped sofa.

With some difficulty, Stove dragged his eyes away from this unusual vision and stared hard at the figure of the diminutive magician.

8.

The mighty Cough.

Cough the magician wore a suit of midnight blue, decorated with golden stars and bright, white moons. It hung loosely about his skinny body, like it really belonged to someone else two or three sizes bigger. Which it actually did. The someone else being wizard Wheeze of Scroop mountains. He'd gone off it when he'd seen another wizard wearing an identical suit at the annual 'Wizards, Warlocks, Witches, Werewolves and Replacement Window Salesmen's' convention in the aforesaid mountains. He'd sold it to Cough cheap and had made him think it fitted by holding the back of it tightly up behind him while Cough admired himself in the mirror.

 Now, as we all know, it is difficult and embarrassing for magicians to do magical things to themselves or their possessions. So when he'd got it home and tried it on again, he'd had to keep it in place with a couple of large bulldog clips. They glinted in the dull light as he stood in front of the young Snod.

 Cough's eyes flitted quickly from Stove to Colander and back. Colander gave him a look as if butter wouldn't melt in his mouth (which is exactly what it was doing as he'd scooped up a handful of it from the omelette he'd been preparing.)

 'So my lad, I see you've met Colander,'

Stove nodded.

 'Er, yes...he's been very...attentive.'

..mmm....I'm sure he has. Colander..' said Cough, 'give young Stove here his money back will you? There's a good Snod.'

Stove's hand flew to his pocket. Sure enough the Ten Chuckle note that he'd kept there had gone. Colander looked shocked.

'Oh....it was *his* money was it? Oh I see..'

He reached inside his waistcoat and extracted the note with his good hand,

'I wondered about that.'

'Yes, well it was in my pocket,' said Stove crossly.

'Ah...you know what they say?' said Colander tapping his nose knowingly.

'No, I don't...' said Stove '..and just exactly *who* are they?'

'Ah ha! Therein lies a tale...a tale of a man and a woman, love and honour, hardship and betrayal, death and belly button fluff...'

'Oh for goodness sake Colander, do shut up and stop trying to get his mind off the subject,' said Cough with a sigh, as his assistant stopped abruptly and suddenly found something very interesting to stare at on the floor.

'Do forgive him Stove, he's an expert thief and just can't help himself. I have to admit, I do find it useful some times. Tea?'

The magician pulled a steaming china pot from out of the depths of one of his sleeves and offered it to Stove.

'Er, yes please,' said the boy, watching in astonishment as Cough produced a large mug from his other sleeve and poured a steady stream of brown tea into it. Stove could see that the mug bore a picture of his father and mother and the Royal Coat of Arms (a laughing face with a custard pie rampant.)

'Oh,' said Cough noticing the boy's interest, 'Coronation souvenir....now tell me lad, what's the problem? Need a new joke for the Festival of Laughter?'

'No,' said Stove sadly, 'I think it's quite a bit worse than that.'

9.

Stove's confession and a frightening discovery.

Stove shifted uncomfortably on the large chair and cleared his throat awkwardly.

'Well, it's a bit embarrassing for a Snod to admit it, but I just don't seem to find things funny anymore….it's all so…so boring…I think I may be feeling…unhappy.'

Colander took a sharp intake of breath. Cough frowned crossly at him.

'…toe, stubbed me toe here…right here…' stammered Colander, 'on this er.. this step…er

…thing.'

His voice trailed off. Cough smiled sympathetically at Stove.

'Go on.'

'Well, things that used to make me laugh just don't anymore.'

Cough opened his mouth to say something, but Stove continued;

'Just yesterday for instance. Father was sitting in his role as Chief Magistrate. The whole court was in session, all the most distinguished Snods were there. A young Sarcasm had come on foot all the way from his home in the south, to ask father to hear his case against his Snod landlord, who not only never visited his dwelling in the Great Red Desert, but who'd had it burned down just for a laugh (nothing nasty intended of course.)'

Colander sniggered loudly.

'Anyway,' continued Stove ignoring him, 'father listened sympathetically for about a minute to the poor little chap and then began pulling silly faces at him.'

Colander barked a brief laugh, then bit his lip as Cough glared angrily at him.

'Of course the court started to giggle and within moments father was in full swing, doing his famous 'dancing lizard on hot sand' impression and filling people's shoes with sugar.'

Colander exploded into screeching, helpless laughter, clutching his stomach with both hands as if worried that he might explode. (Something that it was rumoured could happen on rare occasions, although no one had actually witnessed one of these episodes of 'spontaneous explosion' at first hand.) Even Cough appeared to be having difficulty keeping his face from breaking into a smile.

Showing considerable restraint, Stove ignored the now hysterical assistant.

'The poor little Sarcasm and his grievance were completely forgotten. I felt so sorry for him I chased him and gave him a bag of Chuckles from the treasury. He was grateful...I think,' he added as an afterthought, 'it's always difficult to tell with them. He said something like 'yeh right, that'll make a biiiiig difference,' but he was more surprised that I hadn't found it all as hilarious as the others had.'

'Well,' said Cough after a moment, 'of course the Sarcasms are renowned for having the lowest form of wit, so his reaction isn't surprising. But yours...now that is a bit of a worry, especially...'

'..with the Festival coming up...' interrupted Stove.

'.....yes, exactly, exactly,' said Cough suddenly very serious.

'Mmmmm, just lean right back onto the couch Stove, let's have a look at you.'

Stove did as he was told and reclined back into the chaise longue's thick, velvety covering, swinging his legs up beside him as he did. A puff of dust rose into the air around his head and he watched its tiny flecks reflect the stuttering light from the candle in Cough's hand. He felt curiously relaxed.

Cough reached into a pocket and produced a large pair of wooden spectacles. He clipped an odd, funnel-like contraption over one of the lenses and peered into Stove's eyes.

'Ah....' he muttered after a minute or two, 'Ahhhh....Oh yes....could it be...? Surely not...'

'What? What? What is it?' Stove cried in alarm.

'Yes...I see....hmmmm...' Cough continued, ignoring him.

'Yeees...oooohhh...yeees... ah ha! I think I know what might be the problem...just a tick...Colander! Give me a hand will you?'

Cough and his assistant disappeared off into the gloomy recesses of the cavernous room.

For the first time since he'd entered, Stove took a good look at his surroundings. The room he was in was certainly very big, and very dark. In fact it was so big and dark that he couldn't actually see the wall on the opposite side to the door through which he'd entered. On either side of that doorway ran long, rough wooden benches, covered with all manner of dust laden oddities.

Stove noticed strange shaped glass flasks, weird, gnarled roots and mummified vegetables, piles and piles of ancient looking books and parchment, hundreds of jars, boxes and bottles labelled with mysteriously unrecognisable letters and signs.

In the darker, cobwebby corners, he could just make out row upon row of heavy glass jars containing the pickled horrors you find in a school biology lab. But amongst all the organised chaos, the thing that really caught his eye was a large glass receptacle set well back on the bench. It was filled to the brim with an unhealthy looking and glutinous, brownish-yellow liquid and sealed with an old square of muslin held tightly in place by a large cork.

A large bubble plopped greasily to the liquid's surface, lingered there for a moment and then reluctantly burst, like a ripe pimple. Then...something moved! Stove couldn't be sure, but....yes there it was again. He was positive he saw something move within its murky depths. A dark shape...a shadow. What could it be? What kind of...thing could live in that?

Stove shifted on to his side, then sat up so that he had a better view of the jar. He swung his legs down onto the ground and started towards it. As he did so, the activity within the jar ceased abruptly.

Stove tip-toed up to it and peered cautiously into its depths. Nothing. He looked harder, his face now virtually touching the glass. Nothing. He must have imagined it. He was about to turn away, when suddenly something emerged from the brackish liquid and thumped in to the inside of the glass, exactly opposite his face.

To his surprise and horror, Stove realised… that it was an eye! A large, disembodied eye, staring unblinkingly and lidlessly back at him. Stove staggered away in shock, his lungs filled with an unformed scream. The eye regarded him glassily and began to agitatedly thrash around in its liquid cell. It wanted out. Unable to look away, he scrambled backwards, unwittingly catching the back of his legs on a low, wooden box and he tumbled down, his head crashing onto the hard, cold, stone floor.

A world of bright, white sparks and then, blackness.

10.

The Mimic.

'Stove?....Stove my boy? Are you alright?'

Stove could hear the familiar voice calling to him through the darkness and wondered for a moment what Cough was doing in his bedroom. But then the sensation from the back of his head reminded him painfully of what had happened.

'Ouch! My head!'

'Here Master Stove, let me help you sit up.'

Stove felt a brawny arm slide around his shoulders and prop him up into a sitting position, as slowly his vision began to clear. Colander regarded him anxiously, his egg whisk arm stroking, or rather scratching the side of his face. Behind him Cough crouched like a half deflated balloon, a large and ancient looking book clutched in his spidery hands.

'The eye! The... the thing in the jar!' Stove shouted, his horror suddenly flooding back to remind him.

'The eye?' said Cough, 'Jar?...jar?'

Stove pointed a trembling finger at the offending container, now absent of any sign of life.

'Oh I see, I see what must have happened. You met the mimic.'

Colander chuckled, not unkindly.

'Oh dear Lor' master Stove, there's lots o' surprising and secret things in this here laboratory, most a lot scarier than that there mimic.'

Cough strode over to the jar, immediately there was a movement in its depths.

'Yes, I caught this mimic in the Darkness lake near the Scroop mountains, on a fishing holiday with my old friend Wizard Wheeze, the famous practical joker. Just watch.'

As Stove sat forward unaided and gingerly rubbed the lump on the back of his head, Cough took a large carrot from his pocket and held it close to the jar. Within seconds a dark shadow emerged from the murky liquid and rattled agitatedly against the inside of the glass. It was a carrot!

'Yes' said Cough turning back to Stove and pocketing the vegetable, 'You see, the mimic is...well, just that, it takes on the form of anything that appears close to it. It must just have seen your eye when you peered in to the jar and mimicked it. It only does it to please, that's why it gets agitated if you don't pick it up and thank it.'

Here the wizard removed the cork and muslin cover from the container and extracted the mimic-carrot, which looked exactly like a real one.

'Thank you kindly Mr. Mimic, please come again.'

Then surprisingly he kissed it. The top of the carrot split into what looked like a smiling mouth and Stove swore he could hear a giggle, then Cough dropped it back into the jar where it disappeared back into the depths.

'Nobody actually knows what a mimic really looks like. I caught it by tying a magnet to my fishing line. It turned into one too and before you could say something that doesn't take very long to say at all, It was mine. You have to keep it in water from the lake though and not take it out for too long either, or it dries up and dies.'

Cough rubbed his chin thoughtfully for a moment, while Colander helped Stove unsteadily to his feet.

'Now, lets have a look at that bump and then I have something in this book that might be of interest to you.'

Stove sat gingerly down on the comfortable throne like chaise-longue, as Cough perched next to him, his little legs swinging too and fro and opened the large, leather bound book across their knees. Meanwhile, to Stove's surprise, Colander unscrewed his metal whisk arm and replaced it with what looked for all the world like a giant cotton bud.

Colander noticed Stove's curious expression.

'Cotton bud,' he said matter-of-factly, 'you'd be surprised at how many different replacement arms I got in my collection, one for every use. Master Cough magicked 'em up for me. Shame he couldn't magic me up another real arm though,' he added wistfully, but then quickly brightened. 'Still, things could be a lot worse.'

Colander dipped the tip of his arm in a jar of clear liquid and dabbed it gently, (or as gently as someone as clumsy as he was could) on Stove's lump.

'Now, this book,' said Cough, carefully turning the yellowed pages, 'is an ancient record of all things Snod. Everything from history, language and anatomy, to folk lore, customs, traditions and even favourite recipes, it's all there.'

As Cough continued to turn the pages, Stove was puzzled to see that far from being packed with information, they were almost entirely blank.

'Ah here we are, H for humour.'

Cough turned to a page which apart from an extravagantly illustrated capital 'H' was completely empty.

' Er....?' said Stove.

'Just a minute lad, just a minute. I know what you're going to say, but just watch.'

Cough pressed his open palm on the ancient paper and closed his eyes. Then he began to chant.

'Ancient book, noble book grant us please a little look, Stove's humour's gone, has it been took?'

Suddenly, a bolt of blue colour shot out from under his palm into one corner of the page, then a bolt of red into another corner, followed by a bolt of yellow into a third and green into the remaining one. Cough removed his hand and the colours swirled back into the centre of the page, forming a whirlpool of colour and light that made Stove feel slightly dizzy. Then from the midst of the whirlpool hundreds upon thousands of images formed, all overlapping into a confused blur. As he watched, Stove found that he could actually recognise a few of the images dancing across the previously empty page.

Stove was surprised to see his sister Grill, his father, mother, Cough and Colander. Then the little Sarcasm that he'd helped. The images swirled and melted…he saw a distant part of the Snod valley that he'd visited before when he was younger. Then there was a lot of it that he'd only ever seen in books… massive swamps, huge arid deserts and what he could only presume were the mysterious and forbidding Scroop mountains. Suddenly there was a face…

Like Cough, the face sported a long, white beard and hair, but there was something cold and unkind about his ice blue eyes, that glittered from under bushy, white brows. Stove decided that it was altogether a much more fierce kind of face. The wizard (or that's what Stove presumed he was) was staring down at some kind of document and sniggering malevolently.

Suddenly, he looked up and his eyes locked straight onto Stove's, who jumped in surprise.

'Look, do you mind!' the stranger barked, 'I'm on the toilet!'

The picture became clearer. Stove had just a moment to realise that the man was indeed perched on the loo, reading a comic, before he pointed a finger at him from which gushed a jet of blue and white light. There was a brief explosion, the book shot into the air and Stove and Cough fell backwards onto the floor in a crumpled, smoking heap. As he lay there dazed, Stove kept seeing the title of the comic the wizard was reading and had found so amusing. It was;

11.

Cough puts his finger on the problem.

'Phew!' gasped Stove, scrambling to his feet and dusting himself down, 'what was all that about?'

'Well..' coughed Cough, 'that gentleman is Warlock Grinder, probably one of, if not the most powerful magicians in the valley… and a right old misery as you can probably guess.'

Stove noted with some alarm that the tip of Cough's gently smoking beard appeared to be on fire.

'Er..' he began, moving sharply towards the little magician, but Colander beat him to it and emptied the contents of an large, iron pot over his boss' head.

'Aaach!…' spluttered Cough, 'every… thing was…under control! Aaach..cacch!'

He coughed and retched violently.

'Goodness me Master Cough!' scolded Colander annoyed at Cough's seeming ungratefulness, 'from the noise yer makin' anyone would think I'd thrown a pot o' bull's wee over you!'

He glanced down at the pot in his hand, there was a label on it…

'10 YEAR OLD BULL'S URINE, USE SPARINGLY.'

'I er..I er think I left something on the er… the um…'

Colander sprinted out of the room as fast as his little, fat legs could carry him.

Stove watched Cough impotently. He'd like to have helped, but the strong and extremely unpleasant odour didn't really encourage physical closeness. Also Stove couldn't help wondering what kind of strange person would collect bull's urine anyway?

Slowly, the coughing, retching and spluttering subsided and Cough peered soggily up at Stove.

'Pass me that cloth will you my boy?'

Stove walked across towards a heavy, red, velvety, towel-like cloth hanging from a hook above an ancient radiator. As he picked it up, he swore he could hear a faint and slightly sinister noise. A crackling, rustling noise, like someone was crumbling up handfuls of dried leaves. Stove frowned.

'Cough, did you hear….?'

He turned around in time to see the diminutive magician crumbling handfuls of dried leaves into the empty tin pot.

'Eh? Did I what?'

'Oh nothing,' sighed Stove handing him the cloth.

'Yes, the plot thickens,' said Cough enthusiastically, wringing his beard out into the pot of crushed leaves and roughly towelling himself down at the same time.

'Warlock Grinder, your loss of humour…. the book led us straight there you know, straight to him…I suspect foul play.'

'Not as foul as you smell,' Stove muttered quietly to himself.

'Eh?'

'Oh, nothing,' said Stove innocently.

Cough picked up a heavy wooden spoon and stirred the bull's urine and crushed leaves into an unpleasant looking paste.

' Now my lad….this will confirm whether my suspicions are correct or not….come here.'

Somewhat reluctantly Stove crossed over to where Cough stood. He really didn't like the look of the noxious substance, which the magician was just starting to ladle out into a small ceramic beaker.

'Oh no…' said Stove, "I'm not drinking that…not for anything…'

'No no! ' muttered Cough crossly, 'you don't drink it…look.'

He dipped his finger in the paste, reached up and before he could stop him, dotted a small amount onto the centre of Stove's forehead.

'Just wait!' Cough barked, as Stove reached up to touch it curiously.

Stove stood in silence, wondering what he was waiting for and going cross eyed trying to see the spot on his head, while Cough stared intently up at him.

'Yes…just as I feared,' said Cough shaking his head sadly.

'What? What…tell me!' cried Stove, by now very worried indeed.

Cough pursed his lips and frowned thoughtfully, absent-mindedly wiping his face on his sleeve.

'You're not just unhappy young Stove my lad, that would be strange enough for a Snod ….I'm afraid it's something worse than that. In fact there's not much chance of you being anything other than unhappy. Because you see, it appears that you've…lost your sense of humour. To be more accurate, someone has stolen your sense of humour …and it appears that Warlock Grinder is the prime suspect.'

12.

Cough and Colander make a solemn promise.

For what seemed quite a long time, Stove and Cough stood in silence in the dark and cavernous room. Then Stove spoke, a catch in his voice.

'But…what do you mean? How can someone steal my sense of humour? It's not like it's a…a purse full of chuckles or..or a…a…'

He struggled to think of something else perceived as valuable,

'… a sausage and mustard sandwich?' suggested Colander from beside the doorway where he was slinking back in thinking he was safe.

'Don't be stupid! A sausage and mustard sandwich isn't valuable!' barked Stove.

'Well….. it depends what kind of sausage it is,' said Colander rather sulkily.

'But just how could he steal it?' said Stove ignoring him.

'It's difficult, I agree, but with the right spell and pickled shavings from the trotters of 'The Ignorant Pig,' it can be done, ' said Cough.

Colander whistled.

'The what?' said Stove.

'The Ignorant Pig. A fearsome, pig-like animal that lives in the Brindisi desert, south of Scroop Mountains. 'Tis rumoured it's as big as a house, jet black, with fangs the size of yer leg, blood red eyes that can see through the sides o' mountains, ears that can hear a heart beating miles away, a snout that dribbles poisonous slime and that can smell a tiny bit o' fear in a living thing no matter what...ah 'tis awful, awful,' babbled Colander excitedly.

'Probably make good bacon though,' he added as an afterthought.

'Yeeeees, ' drawled Cough, 'well, despite my assistant's propensity to exaggeration, The Ignorant Pig is indeed a pretty unpleasant creature. It has the power to absorb any knowledge, ambition, creativity, love, happiness or indeed humour from anyone living and leave them with nothing but despair, rage, hatred, jealousy and intolerance....and a slight headache.'

'..and don't forget its bristles that are poisonous spines, its fiery breath that scorches the earth for miles every time it sneezes, its farts so loud they can split your eardrum and the stench of which is enough to melt yer nostrils, its auntie who runs a terrible boarding house by the sea....'

'Yes, yes, thank you Colander, that will do!' shouted Cough angrily interrupting his excited servant,

'I think you've been reading too many tabloid newspapers.'

Colander shuffled his feet and looked guilty.

'Now Stove, just a small amount of anything that is, or was, a part of The Ignorant Pig has the power to affect goodness, but in the case of its trotters it can be particularly powerful. My theory is that somehow Warlock Grinder managed to steal its nail clippings, pickle them in vinegar and bring them into contact with you...probably as you slept. Maybe it was an inside job, someone he'd bribed to do it, perhaps someone close to you who you trust.'

Stove was dismayed to think that anyone he knew would do such a thing. Then a shocking thought hit him.

'But...without a sense of humour, I stand no chance of winning the Festival of Laughter!' he wailed, slumping down in despair onto the chaise longue, 'I'll let down father, my family....the tradition of all those years...I'll be the first ever Prince to fail to win!'

A tear rolled apologetically down his cheek.

'Yes, ' said Cough sympathetically, 'I think that's why Warlock Grinder has stolen it... but I've no idea what *he* stands to gain by doing such a thing.'

'Never you mind Master Stove,' said Colander putting a comforting hook (he'd changed his arm again) around the troubled Snod's shoulders, 'we'll get your sense of humour back from that ole misery for yer, won't we guvnor?'

'Well,' said the magician, clearing his throat uncomfortably, 'it would be difficult, not to say dangerous. I have met Warlock Grinder before and it wasn't a particularly pleasant experience. He is a powerful and unpleasantly aggressive magician...'

Cough looked doubtfully at Stove's hopeful and tear-streaked face for a moment, then set his mouth determinedly.

'Yes...yes, why of course that's exactly what we'll do. Colander, rush down to the stables and fetch the Silly Ass. Then make up some stores of food and liquorice wine, enough for a long journey. Stove, you'd better go home and pack anything you think you'll need, but remember we're travelling light, so just as much as you can carry yourself. We'll meet outside the castle gates at dawn tomorrow....and it's probably better if you don't say a word to anyone else, just in case we have a spy in our midst. Grinder is well known for recruiting them and after all, someone may well be responsible for bringing the shavings into contact with you. The fewer people know, the less chance there is that he'll be expecting us.'

Stove looked stunned.

'What…you mean we're….?'

'Yes lad, we're off to the Scroop Mountains to pay a surprise visit on Warlock Grinder….we'll get your sense of humour back…..' he paused, then added sombrely, 'or die in the attempt.'

From under its cushion, the sofa shaped gerbil squeaked ominously.

13.

The black sheep of the family.

Stove's room was at the top of one of the five turrets of his father's castle. It was a fair size, with a high old-fashioned ceiling from which there hung a rough, wooden chandelier holding four smoky candles. A weak yellow light flickeringly illuminated the contents of the room in the pre-dawn gloom.

There were a couple of clumsily put together wardrobes, one featuring a cracked and sparkly mirror. Next to them stood, or rather leaned, a small bookcase crammed full of ancient looking, dog-eared books. Then a table piled high with clothes and a bed, which looked as if it hadn't been slept in. On the large and somewhat faded rug that covered the floor, was a cheerfully colourful rucksack. It looked well stuffed.

On the walls covering the rough stone and plaster, were several different sized posters of various famous Snod pop groups, comedians and double-acts, such as The Rolling Pins, Broccoli Spears, The Spice-rack Girls, Bernard Snodding, The Two Kettles and Little & Large.

The room took up half of the turret, so it was semi-circular in shape, the exterior wall curving around on both sides into a large arched, stone window in the middle. At the bottom of the window was a wooden sill large enough to sit on and it was here that Stove was perched, staring thoughtfully out over the valley. Although it was still quite dark, he could just about make out some of the features of the view with which he was so familiar.

Nearest was the huge, castle moat, long since dried up and now used as a futeball pitch by the local Snod kids. Then came the extensive Royal gardens, at least a mile wide, half of which was a vegetable patch in which all kinds of vegetables and fruit grew abundantly, thanks to the rich soil of the valley. (At any time of year you would see carrots, peas, potatoes and brussel sprouts growing alongside bananas, passion fruit, artichokes and ochra.)

The other half of the gardens was resplendent with brightly coloured flowers and plants and exotic looking trees, (some so crazy looking they'd make Monkey Puzzle trees look boring.)

And nestled within the trees was Bowl the gardener's little hut. Stove noticed with mild surprise that a spiral of wispy smoke curled up from the chimney on its roof.

'Bowl must be up already,' he thought, 'that's unusual.'

Beyond the gardens were miles and miles of Royal mirror-fruit forest where thousands of the bright little fruits reflected the silvery glow of the waning moon. Once they had been carefully tended, but now they grew wild and untamed and had pretty much become a giant forest.

Then in the extreme distance, you could just about make out the beginning of a huge plain on which Stove knew stood one or two untidy, smallholdings belonging to a few half-interested Snod farmers. (As the average Snod had the patience and attention span of Goldie Gold, the legendary most inattentive goldfish ever, it was remarkable that anything ever got grown, or indeed done.)

Some forty or fifty miles beyond them the land rose up into a series of hills that obscured anything further.

Stove had never been as far as this, but unlike most Snods he had always taken an interest in the geography of the Valley, having discovered an ancient book on the subject in the not often used Royal library. He knew that beyond the hills lay an extensive and unpleasant swampland which petered out and eventually became the Great Red Desert. Beyond that stood the Scroop mountains, famous for their towering and glowering.

Was he really going to travel all that way? The mountains seemed so very, very far that he found it hard to believe that he was even contemplating making such a journey. Once when he'd been very young his father had taken him with him on a tour of the outlying Snod farms to visit his 'mad' uncle Mug, the king's younger brother. To young Stove it had seemed as if he were journeying to the ends of the earth. And now he was planning to travel at least twice as far. It just didn't seem possible.

Stove's mind drifted around to considering his eccentric uncle. He found himself wondering what on earth had become of poor Uncle Mug? Stove hadn't seen him since that day so long ago and actually he hadn't seemed all that mad to Stove, just a little odd.

He remembered how his father had taken him to one side as they stood outside a tiny tumbledown cottage and told him how his brother had left the Royal Castle under mysterious circumstances some years before and had moved out to this distant location.

'You'll find his ways a little er…strange,' his father whispered, '..but that's probably to do with the fact that he's stark, raving mad. I mean you'd have to be mad to want to come out all this way on your own, so far from a good laugh and a dance at court. But then he never seemed to enjoy jokes as much as he should, and he was a rubbish dancer too.'

The King scratched his ear thoughtfully, then continued.

'There are some things that you must know so as not to upset him though. Don't say 'Oh well things could be worse' that'll really set him off. And whatever you do don't make any reference to him being mad at all. That'll upsct him even more, 'cos he doesn't think he is mad. So don't mention insanity at all. Although you'd have to be totally, certifiably crackers not to find this funny.'

The King then pulled one of the silliest faces young Stove had ever seen, pulling his lower lip up over his nose, crossing his eyes and wiggling his ears. Stove collapsed into shrieking, helpless laughter as his father, encouraged, danced a hopping, shuffling jig from side to side.

The door suddenly swung open and there had stood a thinner, shorter, crosser-looking version of his father, dressed (unusually for a Snod) all in black.

'Oh…it's you,' said the stranger, unsmilingly.

Stove's hysterical laughter stopped abruptly. His father, however, continued to jiggle around for a bit, whistling tunelessly, seemingly oblivious to his brother's glowering presence. Stove tugged at his father's sleeve and cleared his throat noisily to attract his attention. The King looked up, spied his brother and cried cheerfully;

'Oh, hello bonkers bloke!'

SLAM!

The door immediately crashed shut in his father's face.

Stove could still remember his father turning towards him, an idiotic smile frozen on his lips and saying in a sing-song voice,

'Woohoo….someone's grumpy.'

Although he hadn't seen his uncle Mug since, he and his sister Grill always got an unsigned birthday card every year, containing a ten chuckle note, which he strongly suspected came from him.

14.

Grill and Crumbs.

With a shock, Stove suddenly realised that he could now see the valley quite clearly. Dawn was breaking, while he was dithering about and staring out of the window. He had to get a move on, he musn't keep the others waiting, or they'd think he'd got cold feet (which he actually had as the window sill had been decidedly draughty.)

Pausing only to snatch up the brightly coloured rucksack, he rushed across to his bedroom door and flung it open. He stopped abruptly. There, barring his way in the middle of the floor crouched a huge, fat, warty, ugly, bright red toad.

'Breeaaack!' It belched rudely.

'Ugh!' said Stove in a loud whisper, 'get out of my way Crumbs.'

Crumbs was Stove's sister Grill's pet and she spoiled it rotten, constantly cuddling and stroking it, dressing it up in baby clothes and even taking it to bed with her. It had a particularly offensive habit of silently emitting foul, eggy smells at regular intervals and eating people's dirty socks.

Stove really hated it and couldn't help feeling that somehow it knew this and went out of its way to try and wind him up. And wherever Crumbs was, Grill was usually not too far behind. The last thing that Stove wanted was for his sister to see him sneaking out of the castle at the break of dawn.

'Bbbbrrrreeeeeaaaaacccckkkkk!' It belched louder.

'Shhhhhhhh!' ….nice toad, quiet…sshhhh!'

Stove desperately motioned at the huge amphibian to quieten down. It seemed to grin slyly at his distress, sucked in a huge breath and belched enormously.

'BBBBBRRRREEEEEEAAAAAACCCCKKKKKKKKK!'

' Crumbs?' a sleepy voice called from his sister's room, 'Crumbs....is that you? Where are you?'

The door swung open to reveal Grill dressed in her pyjamas, rubbing her eyes tiredly.

'Crumbs?...Stove? ' She looked at her brother in surprise, 'what are you doing up so early?'

She glanced down at the ruck sack in Stove's hand as he tried to guiltily hide it behind his back.

'What's that? What are you up to? Where are you going? Are you running away? What fun!'

Her eyes shone brightly now, she was suddenly wide awake as she scooped Crumbs up and hugged him.

'No, no, no...' said Stove glaring crossly at the smug looking toad nestling comfortably in his little sister's arms, 'nothing like that at all...I'm...er...I'm going....er...fishing...you know, the early Snod catches the fish and all that....you know...'

His voice trailed off and he blushed guiltily. Snods were notoriously bad liars and Stove was no exception. Grill looked up into his eyes.

'No you're not,' she said, 'tell me where you're going, or I'll wake up the whole castle with one of my famous screams.'

She opened her mouth and took in a deep breath, as Crumbs, recognising what was about to happen, wriggled in her arms trying to escape.

'No, no, no...don't do that...here, have a liquorice stick!'

Stove reached in his pocket and produced a couple of fluff covered sticks, which he waved under her nose. Stove knew how incredibly loud she could scream and he certainly did not want the whole castle being alerted to his and Cough's quest. His father, silly though he was, would be bound to try and stop him.

Grill looked at Stove suspiciously and took one of the sticks. She chewed thoughtfully on it for a moment, keeping her large, twinkling eyes firmly fixed on him.

'So?' she asked, 'are you going to tell me where you're going then?'

Stove sighed heavily.

'Well I don't have much choice do I?…alright….I'm going to the Scroop mountains…'

Grill's mouth dropped open.

'You…you…' she stuttered,' you're joking…aren't you?'

'No, no…' said Stove sadly, 'that's just it, you see….I *can't* joke.'

Stove went on to explain about his visit to Cough's laboratory, how Cough had found out about his missing sense of humour and why he, Cough and Colander had to go to the mountains to try and recover it from Warlock Grinder. Grill listened, wide eyed throughout.

'…and so you see Grill, I've got to go now, quickly and quietly. You know that father would try and stop me if he knew. So if you don't mind I'll be off….I'm already running late, the others will be wondering where I've got to.'

Stove swung his bag over his shoulder determinedly.

'I'm coming with you,' said Grill suddenly.

'What?....oh no way...no way Grill you're not coming....no way! You...you're too small, you'd get in the way...I'd have to look after you all the time!' Stove spluttered.

'No you won't...' said Grill firmly, 'I'm perfectly able to look after myself...I'm not a baby.'

'Grill....' Stove sighed, exasperated, ' you can't come, you'll slow us down...it's going to be dangerous...we're going where no Snod's normally go....and we don't know what we'll find when we get there...'

All the reasons he could think of for his younger sister not to accompany him tumbled out at once.But he also knew that when she made her mind up, she rarely changed it back.

'Stove...' Grill said setting her mouth in a thin, determined line, 'I don't want to have to threaten you with one of my screams again...'

Stove knew he was cornered.

'Oh....oh...alright then...but hurry up and get dressed. We're travelling light, so just pack one bag.'

She threw her arms around his neck and hugged him, crushing Crumbs between them. The toad indignantly let off one of his vile, eggy smells.

'And if you bring that foul creature, you'll have to carry it yourself!' he shouted at his sister's back as she rushed back into her bedroom to dress and pack.

15.

The journey begins.

Cough clicked his fingers and a small blue flame sprang out from the tip of his thumb, illuminating his face in the thin grey light of the early morning. He rolled up his sleeve, holding the flame so as to be able to see his wrist watch.

'Oh....bother!'

Instead of the usual watch face that most people have showing numerals and hands, there was a small painting of a tall, gangly figure. It was running very quickly and panting, quite out of breath.

'Oh oh...time's running out...' he said, sucking the air through his teeth nervously.

'You're late!' said a sharp, old woman's voice from inside his other sleeve.

'Oh shut up,' muttered Cough under his breath, blowing out the flame and hurrying on.

His little legs pumped as fast as they could go. How could he be so late? He mustn't keep Stove waiting too long, he was afraid that the boy might lose his courage and change his mind about the perilous journey to come.

He hurried along through the dewy grass at the base of the castle wall, a long wooden staff decorated with mysterious looking carvings clutched in his hand and on his back a canvas rucksack, stuffed with various magical bits and bobs, the mimic in its jar and the large leather bound book.

Head down, he scampered around a corner, just had time to notice the incongruous sight of what appeared to be a small oasis of palm trees to the side of the castle gate and….

THUD!

'Ouch! Ow! Getoff! You clumsy….that's my ear!'

He found himself laying on the ground in an untidy, groaning pyramid of boy and girl Snod, bags and evil smelling toad.

'Oh it's you Stove, ' he hissed, 'why don't you watch where you're going?'

'Well I could say the same to you Cough. And anyway, you're late.'

'And so are you,' said Cough untangling himself from the jumble of arms, legs, slimy webbed feet and smells.

'Yes he is,' agreed a muffled voice crossly from Cough's wrist.

'Who said that?' asked Stove curiously.

But just at that moment, Cough noticed Grill for the first time.

'Grill?'

'Hi Cough,' she said cheerfully.

Cough righted himself with the aid of his staff and glared crossly at Stove.

'Stove, what are you thinking? This is no place for your little sister! Where we're off to is a dangerous enough place, but the journey will be exhausting and unpredictable. Why anything could happen! I've done it myself a few times and I should know. There have been moments when I've just escaped nasty, life threatening incidents by the skin of my teeth! What are you thinking of?'

'Well at the moment I'm thinking what a crotchety old man you are!' shouted Stove, 'Do you think that I'm really stupid or something? Of course I know that what we're doing is dangerous…and of course I don't want Grill to come…but she gave me no choice. It was either take her with me, or she'd wake the whole castle, including father, who would of course have tried to stop me!'

Stove simmered angrily and threw his bag over his shoulder. Cough turned to look at Grill who grinned happily back at him, Crumbs clutched tightly under her arm.

'Brrrreeeaaakk!' it belched.

'Is this true Grill?'

'Yes,' she said her smile broadening, 'I threatened him with one of my famous screams.'

'Well you're a very silly girl…where we're going is….'

'…dangerous and unknown, no place for girls blah, blah, blah…' save your breath Cough, I'm coming and there's nothing you can do to stop me, so get used to it!' Grill interrupted.

'Well that's not strictly true Grill, there is one thing I can do to stop you, I can turn you into an easy chair, or an occasional table, or a foot-stool…'

Cough raised his hands above his head threateningly, flexed his fingers so that they cracked one by one and began to chant. Grill looked alarmed for the first time.

'Have a care, do beware, turn this Snod child into a ch…'

'Cough!' shouted Stove, 'stop! I don't want an article of furniture for a sister! No matter how nicely upholstered they may be. Let her come, I'll take care of her.'

There was a silence. Grill grinned sheepishly at Cough again. Stove raised his eyebrow pleadingly. Crumbs picked his nose with one of his webbed feet.

'Yes, but who'll look after you?….Oh alright…but I hope we don't all end up regretting it later.'

'Thanks Cough, you won't,' said Grill gratefully.

'And for goodness sake do keep quiet all of you! The whole point of us starting this early was to avoid notice!'

Stove slapped Cough on the back and then started to help him pick up some of the contents of his rucksack that had spilled out over the grass. Among them Stove recognised the leather-bound book and the mimic's glass jar. He noticed that the jar now contained a handful of grass, identical to that on which it was laying. Cough bent and picked it up, unscrewed the top, thanked the mimic and replaced its cover before popping it back into his rucksack.

Stove then picked up and handed him in turn; various glass phials containing odd looking roots and herbs, some paper packets that changed colour constantly, some dried insect's legs, flower heads, a can of worms labelled;

'*WARNING! ON NO ACCOUNT TO BE OPENED*,'

a bundle of as yet unwritten postcards, all addressed to 'Dear Mother' a small bronze medallion inscribed:

' To certify that the holder of this medal has satisfied the Wizardry Committee to the standard of Magician, 3rd class,'

and something that looked strangely like a cheese and onion sandwich.

'It's a cheese and onion sandwich,' said Cough noticing him looking at it curiously, 'very important when we travel through the Swamp of Contradictions….you'll see,' he added while Stove looked doubtful.

'Oh...my stick….' said Cough searching around him.

'Here it is, ' said Stove, stooping down and picking up the long sliver of wood. He looked at it curiously for a moment, his fingers tracing the curious shapes carved into it.

'All these mysterious carvings…' he said in an awed tone.

'Yes, graffiti,' said Cough crossly, 'left it outside the Royal loos the other day and when I came out someone had carved all those silly signs into it. I don't know, youth of today….poor old walking stick.'

Cough took the stick from Stove and stroked it affectionately.

As Grill belatedly stepped forward to help them pick up the last few articles from the grass, a movement out of the corner of her eye caught her attention. She looked up hurriedly. There was the oddest sight and she couldn't understand why she hadn't noticed it before.

By the side of the closed and as yet unmanned (goodness knows how no one had been attracted by the commotion they'd all been making) castle gates stood a collection of palm trees, something that you never saw in the Snod Valley, because they just didn't grow there. Indeed the only reason that Grill knew they were palm trees was because she'd seen pictures of them in her brother's books. As she watched, there was a slight movement, almost a shimmering. Then the shimmering started to intensify, making the palm trees appear to wobble madly. Then they seemed almost to be…. melting.

'Er… Cough….Stove…' she said warily, attracting their attention to the peculiar sight, 'I think you had better take a look at this.'

All three of them stopped what they were doing and looked towards the rapidly dissolving oasis. Slowly, something began to emerge from within.

16.

Dawn breaks, literally.

As the trees hazily disappeared, they revealed a rather familiar character.

'Mornin' Master Cough…master Stove….young missy Grill.'

'Colander! What….?' Spluttered Stove, amazed.

'Took one o' Master Cough's camouflage pills…seemed the best way to hide me n' the beast while we was waitin' fer you 'slow coach sloths from Slough,' to appear. Took yer time too yer did.'

He added rather crossly.

'But palm trees?' sighed Cough, 'An oasis camo-pill is only meant to be used in the desert Colander, how many times must I say, there's absolutely no point whatsoever in camouflaging yourself as something that sticks out of its surroundings like a…like a… '

'Sore thumb,' said Grill.

'Yes, exactly, thank you Grill. '

'No, I mean *I've* got a sore thumb, must have sprained it when I fell over,' she said sucking it ruefully.

Cough stared blankly at her in exasperation.

'Well I knows what yer sayin' Master Cough,' said Colander crossly, 'but the only other camo-pills I had with me was for the inside of a Snap-dragon's lair….and that would've been a pretty sight…a huge pile o' playin' cards just sittin' here.'

He glared around defensively. Stove noticed curiously that this morning his missing arm was replaced with what looked very much like a mug tree, from which dangled several tools, balls of string and less surprisingly a mug. (This was emblazoned with the words 'You toucha my mug I smasha your face,' in a crazy, angular typeface.)

'What beast?' Stove suddenly interjected, 'you said 'me n' the beast,' Colander, what beast?'

'Oh…this 'un,' said Colander stepping to one side, 'this 'ere Silly Ass.'

Standing behind Colander was a tiny, brown donkey. It couldn't have been much bigger than a good sized dog, its shoulder only coming up to Colander's waist. But on its back was the most enormous pile of furniture, clothes, bags, bottles, boxes, crates and cooking utensils, at least three times its height.

'Colander!' cried Grill, 'how can you be so cruel….the poor little thing.'

'Now don't you worry yourself missy, why he loves it! It's what he lives to do.'

'Colander is right,' said Cough,' the 'Silly Ass' is capable of bearing enormous loads, far more than any ordinary donkey could do. Pound for pound it's thought to be just about the strongest animal known to Snod…'

' 'part from the Ignorant Pig…' interrupted Colander.

'Yes, yes, apart from the Ignorant Pig…'

'And the Two Faced Cow…'

'Yes and the Two Faced Cow,' sighed Cough.

'And the Lying Toad…'

'Thank you Colander, that is enough!' barked Cough, 'suffice it to say Grill, the Silly Ass is a very, very strong creature indeed.'

He paused for a moment as if daring his assistant to interrupt again, then continued,

'And he would be perfectly happy to carry twice the amount that he is at the moment.'

There was a silence.

'The Two Faced Cow?' asked Stove, perplexedly.

'Don't ask,' said Cough wearily.

Suddenly there was a loud scraping noise from inside the castle gates, like a pair of giant fingernails being dragged slowly across some massive blackboard. Then after a short pause, there was an enormous, smashing, splintering cacophony, as if someone had dropped a huge sheet of glass from a great height.

'By my father's bristles! Dawn's breaking! We're really late!' Cough exclaimed.

This joke never failed to amuse. Indeed, Stove noticed that Colander was doubled up with laughter, while tears ran down Grill's cheeks.

'Oh lor….oh…ha…ha ha….oh lor…they really done it this time…what a cracker! Dawn breaks…oh yes you beauty! Ha Ha Ha!'

Colander, beside himself, supported his heaving frame on the pile of assorted oddments on the Silly Ass's back.

'Come, come, come!' urged Cough fighting to suppress a grin, 'there's not a moment to lose, we must be off before those daft guards open the gate and spot us. I had hoped to discuss our route here, but we must go now! Quickly! We'll stop when we're in the mirror fruit orchard, it should be quiet at this time of day, and if we keep to the back ways we should avoid being spotted as we go through the small holdings. Now come on!'

'Yes, get a move on!' echoed a muffled voice from his wrist.

'There it is again!' said Stove, 'where is that voice coming from? '

'Voice? Oh…that,' said Cough rolling up his sleeve to reveal a small, brown sack suspended from his left wrist.

'It was this.' He held it up. 'I carry it with me whenever I travel, it lets me know when there's something that has to be done urgently. In this case if I'm running late. It's called the 'Nagging Bag.'

'Hurry up!' said the bag, right on cue.

'Oh…right, how…useful,' said Stove raising his eyebrow.

Cough replaced his sleeve and strode off at speed, head down, his long robes flapping furiously and his beard blowing back over his shoulder, the long staff swinging purposefully back and forth.

'Er …Cough…' called Stove,

'Yes, what?' the magician snapped,

'Isn't it this way?'

'Huh?'

Stove indicated the opposite direction to that in which Cough was determinedly heading. The magician stopped abruptly, looked around flustered for a second, then retraced his steps with equal dogged determination.

'I knew that!' he barked crossly, 'I was just checking that the coast was clear.'

Stove sighed. It didn't bode well for the challenging journey to come.

He swung his ruck sack over his shoulder and with a rueful smile to Grill, who'd managed to bring her mirth under control, he set off in pursuit. His little sister scampered after him, carrying the odious Crumbs.

Colander started after them, but the Silly Ass pulled up abruptly, refusing to move.

'Just a minute you lot!' he shouted after them. He leaned down to the Silly Ass's long ear and whispered something into it. It let out a raucous bray which turned into something like a laugh,

'HEE HAW, HEE HAW, HEE HEE HEE HA HA!'

then lifted its tiny front legs from the ground and set off at a furious pace, its heavy load clanking, rattling, squeaking and knocking, with Colander trotting clumsily alongside. They quickly caught up with Stove and Grill and with a little difficulty, Colander reigned the donkey in.

'Whoa….whoa…donkey, whoa there!' he panted.

It slowed to a fast walk and the two Snod children fell in alongside and matched its pace.

'What was that all about?' asked Stove.

'Ah well master Stove, yer see the Silly Ass is a fine animal, strong, uncomplainin' just gets on with it like, but there is one problem with it….it's not exactly the brightest of animals and very stubborn. So it'll only start movin' again when it's been stopped for a while if you tell it somethin' really silly an' make it laugh. That's what I done.'

'Really?' said Grill, surprised, 'what did you tell it then?'

'I told it a joke.'

'What one?'

'Well I told it the old 'what do you call a pig with three eyes?' joke.'

'…go on…' said Grill, 'what do you?'

'A piiig,' chuckled Colander.

Grill spluttered, then giggled, then finally threw her head back and roared with laughter. Cough looked back from way in front wondering what all the commotion was about as Colander enthusiastically joined in with the laughter. Stove on the other hand trudged on in stony silence.

17.

In the mirror fruit forest.

'This is as good a place as any,' said Cough, planting his staff in the soft, damp grass in the middle of a clearing. The little party had been walking for about two hours and were now well and truly immersed somewhere in the centre of the great mirror fruit forest. And although it was now early morning, the trees had been planted so closely together that little light filtered through.

'Whoa donkey.'

Colander pulled up the Silly Ass. Stove slipped his bag off his shoulder, dropped it to the ground and sat on it, because the grass was still quite wet. Grill stood cuddling Crumbs and talking baby talk to him.

'Who's a woos a woossy boy then? Who's a lickkle wicckle dicckle? Who's goona be tickled? Are you ? Are you? Yeeesss.'

Crumbs belched happily.

'Brreeaaack!'

Stove snorted.

'Leave it out Grill can't you?'

Grill looked hurt and covered Crumbs protectively with one arm.

'Ah….poor Crumbs, nasty Uncle Stove doesn't love him like mummy does….'

'Brreeeaackk! ' belched Crumbs defiantly.

Stove sighed heavily.

'I'm not that…thing's Uncle…I've nothing to do with the stinker.'

Grill pursed her lips crossly and Stove could almost swear that Crumbs did too.

'Now, now!' said Cough, 'let's not get off on the wrong foot with each other, we've a long, long way to go.'

He clicked his fingers and once more a blue flame sprang from the top of his thumb.

'Let's have a little light on the subject,' he muttered, sprinkling something dusty over its base.

He held the flame close to the gnarled top of the walking stick. After a moment, as Stove and Grill watched transfixed, little fiery arms and legs and then a head with a long burning beard formed. The flame, now looking for all the world like a little fiery version of Cough himself, hopped over to the stick's head. There it danced a brief and sprightly little dance accompanied by a music the like of which Stove had never heard before. It seemed to be composed solely of the little pops and crackles that you hear when you sit by an open fire and everything else is very quiet.

Suddenly, the stick caught and a larger, bright yellow flame burst from the top, reflected a thousand times again in the myriad of little silver fruits that hung from the trees around them.

The little blue-flame Cough hopped back on to the tip of his master's thumb, bowed and in a instant turned back into an ordinary flame.

'Right,' continued Cough, blowing out his thumb as casually as if what had just a happened was a very boring occurrence. He ignored Stove and Grill's open-mouthed expressions, dropped his ruck sack to the ground, pulled a chair from the top of the pile of gear on the Silly Ass's back and settled down into it, with a satisfied gasp.

'Now…we wait.'

'Wait?' said Stove, 'wait for what, we've only just started.'

'We wait for our guide to arrive.'

'Guide?' said Stove, confused, 'but you said you've been there, can't you remember the way?'

'Well, yes…and no,' said Cough nodding, then shaking his head and shrugging.

'You see, although I have been to the Scroop mountains before, it's always been at the invitation of my good friend Wizard Wheeze. He sends a giant, leaping lizard that bounds across huge distances in no time at all. As we don't exactly want anyone to expect us, we have to make our own way and for that we need someone to guide us, someone who's more familiar with the terrain. Besides I haven't heard from the good Wheeze for a while…he must have taken a sabbatical…or something.'

There was a short silence.

'I hope by 'guide' you don't mean who I think you do,' said Colander suspiciously. Cough raised his eyes to the heavens.

'Oh come, come Colander, I know you two don't exactly see eye to eye, but there's no one better for the job.'

'You do mean him! I can't believe it! Why not just call up Warlock Grinder and all his nasty little wizards and tell 'em we're a comin' and what time and place to expect us! You'd be mad if'n you think you can trust that….half-wit!'

'Now, now, Colander, I know you feel he let you down, but I do honestly believe him when he said it wasn't his fault.'

'His fault!….His ……why….!'

Colander's face darkened to a deep red-purple and he stomped brusquely out of the clearing.

Stove jumped to his feet.

'Colander!' he called, but the little one-armed Snod ignored him and disappeared among the mirror fruit trees. He had never seen Colander as speechless with rage before and he had to admit that he found it somewhat alarming.

'Um…Cough…this….this…person that Colander's talking about….'

'Don't you worry young Stove,' said Cough a little patronisingly, ' it'll all be fine, he'll be back…he's just a little…upset at the moment.'

'Well I can see that, but why, why is he so upset? What is it about this person that makes him so angry, what did he do to him? And who is he?'

'Well….it's not the who, you see,' said Cough slowly after a moment,' it's more the what. The guide who's going to get us to the Scroop mountains without being detected by Warlock Grinder is a….now let me see…how shall I put this…is a little….er…eccentric…some even say…er…odd. And you will find that it does take quite a bit of getting used to the way it um…behaves and er...talks. But I assure you it will make the most brilliant and trustworthy guide, especially when we travel through its homeland.'

'Homeland?' said Stove.

'Yes my boy, it's or rather he's a native of the Swamp of Contradictions.'

'What you mean he' a …'

'Contradiction?….yes, he's a Contradiction called Phylis….Phylis Applepie.'

'No I'm not,' said a dull, booming voice, that seemed to go oddly squeaky at the end of the sentence.

Stove nearly jumped out of his skin and span around on his heel to see one of the strangest looking creatures he had ever seen stroll slowly into the clearing.

It was roughly twice as tall as the young Snod yet only a little broader, with long gangly arms from which hung tiny, child-like hands covered in coarse, dark hair. Its very short, chunky legs ended in huge, flat feet that sported highly polished, toeless, beach sandals. It wore an alarming, jumbled mixture of clothes, which would probably be defined as 'eclectic' on the catwalks of somewhere like Paris or Milan today. A smart business suit jacket covered its torso, under which nestled a leather t-shirt studded with metal spikes and a bright pink kilt with purple stockings.

But its most immediately extraordinary feature was its head.

It wore the blue hair on half its head crew-cut short, but the long, bright red locks on the other side tumbled down below its waist. It had one large, pale blue eye and the other side of a large, beaky nose, a small, glinting brown one. Half of its thin-lipped mouth turned up at the corner in a smile, while the other scowled downwards.

Stove noticed with some alarm as it approached him, extending one of its long, spidery arms and holding out a tiny, hairy hand, that although it moved fairly slowly, its feet appeared to be moving at a furious pace.

'Ah' it boomed in a voice that started low then rose to a high pitch,

'You musn't be Stove…I've heard absolutely nothing about you. The name's not Phylis Applepie and I'm most unhappy to meet you.'

18.

The Contradiction.

Stove peered doubtfully down at the little, outstretched hand for a moment. Then nervously extended his own to shake it. But before their fingers even touched, Phylis abruptly withdrew his and rudely thumbed his nose.

'Ahem,' Cough coughed, 'don't be upset Stove, it's just their way you know.'

The magician turned to the Contradiction and thumbed his own nose at him.

'Get lost Phylis, you're not welcome here, we don't need your help.'

'No, I didn't think you did. So I won't help you, not at all. We shouldn't get going as soon as we can, there's plenty of time to lose….I hope you didn't remember to bring a cheese and onion sandwich?'

Just then Colander returned to the clearing. From the look on his face, his mood had not exactly improved much. He glared angrily at the peculiar looking newcomer, his mouth moving with unheard oaths that would be unrepeatable if you could.

Unfortunately, to the Contradiction this meant that he was pleased to see him. Phylis approached him in a flurry of tiny, fast moving feet and once more extended a hand.

'Ah….Colander..we meet again my enemy.'

Colander's eyes opened wide.

'Garn! Get away from me you…you…two faced… slime ball!'

'My most unkind enemy…I can't see that you've forgotten about our big understanding.'

The Contradiction threw its gangly arms around the plump, one-armed Snod, in a gesture of enthusiastic affection.

'Let us greet each other in your way, like true enemies do.'

Colander, who was quite unable to get the hang of Contradiction talk or behaviour, seethed in speechless, helpless frustrated rage, his chubby face shaking with the effort and rapidly turning a deep purple once again.

'Er….Phylis…I think we should be staying here, it's very early and we haven't got far to go,' said Stove, coming to Colander's rescue.

There was a brief silence, as both Phylis and the unwilling object of his affection stared at the young Snod in surprise. Then Cough chuckled appreciatively.

'Well done Stove, you catch on quickly,' he muttered under his breath. Then he cleared his throat loudly and turned to the Contradiction.

'No' he bellowed, 'Stove is quite wrong…Phylis, please don't lead the way, let's not get going. There's plenty of time to find.'

'You lot are mad,' grumbled Grill, scrambling wearily to her feet.

'Brrreaakk!' belched Crumbs crossly, as if in agreement.

Phylis abruptly released his hold on Collander, who crossly brushed himself down like you do when you've been stroking a spectacularly moulting cat and wandered over to the far side of the clearing.

'Well,' he piped, 'let's not get going…don't follow me,' and he disappeared like a flash into a gap amongst the mirror fruit trees.

He was gone so quickly, that the others were all taken by surprise.

Cough was the first to react. He leapt out of his chair and lifting it above his head, struggled to place it on the pile of luggage on the Silly Ass's back.

'Come on! Come on you lot! He won't wait, once he's decided he's off, he'll be gone and we'll lose him!…' he shouted over his shoulder as the chair toppled over the other side of the pile, narrowly missing Colander who'd come over to help.'Stove, you look ready, you'll have to chase after him.'

Stove didn't look ready so much as startled.

'Huh…?' he grunted, confused.

Cough rummaged frantically around in his rucksack.

'Yes, you have to chase him and we'll catch you up. Here, take these two potions with you.'

He produced two small phials, one of glowing green liquid, the other containing an unattractive brown sludge. He held the latter up between his thumb and forefinger.

'This one contains Contradiction balm. It can be difficult having to listen and talk the way Phylis does and more importantly he'll quickly get offended if addressed incorrectly. Drip a little in both of your ears and dab a drop on your tongue (you'll get used to the taste). You'll hear him talking normally and when you talk, he'll hear you talking like he does. You will have to keep doing it though, as each application doesn't last long. And it'll only work between you and him, not with any other Contradictions that may be around.'

Cough handed Stove the brown phial which he popped into his pocket, then brandished the green one.

'Gloworm blood,' he said urgently, 'just leave a drop on the ground every now and then. We should be able to follow its light. Here, look I'll show you.'

He uncorked it and carefully dripped a drop onto the ground.

'Yes, only a drop, that's all you need,' he muttered, handing the second phial to Stove.

Without waiting to see what would happen, Cough picked up the chair from next to Colander and tried again to force it onto the pile of furniture.

As the glowing droplet hit the grass, at first it seemed to vanish completely, but then a small circle of the grass fizzed and crackled, turning brown and dry.

'Well you'll struggle to follow that in this light,' said Stove unimpressed.

But as Stove watched, a circle of bright green light rose out of the dead grass and hung in the air about six inches above the ground. It began to pulse and a faint humming sound came from it.

'You were saying?' said Cough coolly.

'Oh…Nothing,' he replied popping the two phials into his pocket.

'Right… now get on your way, we'll catch up as soon as we can,' fussed Cough as Colander took the chair from him and plonked it expertly on the diminutive donkey's back. 'Go on! Go!'

'Yes get a move on!' snapped the Nagging Bag.

'Good luck Master Stove, but don't trust 'im farther than yer can chuck 'im,' said Colander smiling grimly.

Stove turned to go, then paused for a moment remembering his sister.

'Grill, will you…?'

'Go on Stove, I'll be fine…really. I've got Cough …and Colander….and Crumbs to look after me and anyway we'll be right behind you.'

She smiled hesitantly, then waved one of Crumbs' front legs at him.

'Say bye bye to Uncle Stove, Crumbs.'

'Brreeeaaak!' Belched the toad indignantly.

Stove found himself waving back and smiled half-heartedly. Then he turned, scooped up his bag and set off at a trot towards the gap among the mirror fruit trees where the Contradiction had disappeared.

Somewhat surprisingly the Silly Ass started off after Stove too, even though Colander hadn't told him a joke. As Stove brushed through the first few branches, he heard Colander struggling to restrain him.

'Whoah there…whoah there boy…well I don't know what's got into him… whoah I said!'

Then Cough shouted,

'Hurry Stove…and don't forget to leave a trail!'

19.

Stove's big mistake.

Stove hurried through the trees. Fortunately the path he was following was straight and relatively clear, because he could still see Phylis' back and his weird coloured hair only about four hundred yards ahead of him. He increased his pace to a run.

'Phylis! Phylis! Hang on…or rather I mean….don't hang on! Don't wait!' he shouted.

But to no avail. The Contradiction still hurried on in the distance his tiny feet a blur, as if he couldn't hear a thing. Stove began to run faster still.

'Oh…stupid…thing…' he puffed, 'why doesn't he stop?'

Suddenly, Phylis veered off to the right and out of Stove's sight.

'Oh no!' whispered Stove.

He was suddenly very aware of just how thick and close together the trees were on either side of the path that he was hurrying along. Far more thick and closer together than they had been on the earlier part of their journey.

'If he's gone into something as thick as this, I'm in trouble,' he thought.

Before too long, he'd reached the approximate spot where Phylis had vanished. The trees were indeed very close together and for a moment Stove thought that he'd lost the trail completely, but then he noticed a few, small broken branches.

He looked closer and realised that he could just make out a smaller path continuing on a little deeper into the forest which he could reach by pushing his way through the first few feet of overgrown thicket. With a push and a shove and at the cost of a few scratches to his face and arms, he was through and out onto the small path. There was still no sign of Phylis though, as the path snaked off to the left only about twenty feet ahead, so Stove set off at a gallop to try and catch him up.

After the left turn, the path continued for another ten feet, then took a sharp right, then a left…then a further right. Stove was beginning to feel the beginning of a stitch in his side as on and on he puffed.

He rounded the corner just in time to see Phylis arrive at a fork in the path. Without hesitating the Contradiction took the right. Stove scampered after him. Phylis reached another fork in the distance and this time took the left. Stove was gaining on him all the time and was soon breathlessly by his side.

'Phyl…Phyl…Phylis…'he gasped.

'Oh, there you aren't,' said Phylis without breaking stride, or even looking around, 'didn't wonder where you were. I see the others are with you then.'

'They…they…' panted Stove, 'they'll catch up…or rather they won't,' he remembered.

And then to his horror he remembered something else. His hand shot into his pocket, then slowly, as if not wanting to see what was there, he unclenched his fist and stared transfixed at the little brown and glowing, green phials that lay there.

'Oh no!' he said in a little voice,' the Gloworm blood, I've forgotten to leave a trail…oh no!'

'Well that's not alright then,' said Phylis happily.

'No, you don't…oh what's the use. I can't believe I could be so stupid. They'll never catch up now,' groaned Stove.

'Phylis…Phylis,' he said desperately, 'look we're going to have to stop…I mean we're not going to have to stop.'

'I'm not sorry, but there's every chance of that,' Phylis said dispassionately, 'like Cough didn't say, once I've not started, there's every chance of stopping me…until I'm not exhausted…and I feel exhausted now.'

Stove knew he was in real trouble. If he stopped now and waited for the others, or went back for them (and there was no guarantee he could even find his way back) they would lose their guide. And what if Cough couldn't get another one? The Swamp of Contradictions was a long way away, it would take a considerable amount of time for a replacement to reach them. And without a guide that would be the end of their quest…the end of any chance he'd have of getting back his lost sense of humour before the Festival of laughter.

But if he went on with the Contradiction, he'd have to leave the rest of them behind. They might never catch up. There'd be no Cough to help him, especially when he confronted Warlock Grinder, no supplies, no Colander…and he'd have to leave his sister too. It was a tough call.

'Are you sure you'll stop?' he pleaded.

'I will definitely stop,' said Phylis flatly. 'You can't come with me to the mountains, or you can't take your chances with your friends…perhaps they won't catch us up. We have just a short and easy journey ahead of us.'

Stove knew he'd have to make a quick decision, or judging by the amount of twisting and turning their route had taken so far, he'd never be able to find his way back anyway.

'What should I do?' he said aloud to himself.

He decided to go on with Phylis. Perhaps he thought, he could handle Warlock Grinder without Cough. How tough could it be, he'd looked pretty old…and anyway, surely Cough would know how to find the way, or he'd be able to do something magical to find Stove…he was a magician after all.

'But not a very good one,' a little voice said inside his head and he thought back to the little, bronze medallion he'd seen, 'Wizard/ Magician 3rd class' it had said.

'Slow down!' snapped the Contradiction.

Stove looked down at the green glass phial in his hand, uncorked it and dripped a little of the Gloworm blood on the ground as he scampered along beside Phylis.

'Just in case by some miracle they come this way,' he thought.

The grass immediately turned scorched brown and as he glanced back over his shoulder, he saw the green ring of light rise from it and hang in the air, glowing strongly. Something about the look of it made him feel a little more hopeful and he determined to do the same at any of the major turn offs that they made on the rest of their journey. He pocketed both phials, making a mental note to use the Contradiction balm the next time they stopped and increased his pace to match that of Phylis.

As he hurried on, he wondered desperately whether he had made the right choice.

'No,' said Phylis, you haven't done the right thing. I'm not the only Contradiction this side of our swamp.'

Stove was surprised, how did Phylis know what he'd been thinking of?

'Huh…that's not funny Phylis, it's like you can't read my mind,' he joked weakly.

Phylis said nothing. Stove sighed. It was going to be an even longer journey in the sole company of the Contradiction, he thought as he glanced at the odd creature beside him from the corner of his eye.

But if he'd known then what a terrible impact his forgetting to leave the trail was to have on his friends, he'd have turned back right away and dragged the stubborn Phylis with him.

Whether he'd wanted to go or not.

20.

Warlock Grinder.

'McGinty!...McGinty! '

'Yes master, coming master.'

Rudania's one and only mountain climber hurried, scowling through the dark and mustily damp cavern, a large metal plate in one hand and the dish washing cloth in the other. What did the master want now? He hoped that it was not to make him engage in a silly dance, or tell a so called 'funny' story. How he hated it when he did that. He was a Rudanian after all, what had he to laugh about? He enjoyed being miserable, so much more pleasant than needless laughter or silliness.

Then for the umpteenth time he wished that he'd been like all the other Rudanians and stayed well clear of the Scroop mountains. But that little voice inside his head had egged him on.

'Why not see what's in the mountains? What harm is there in looking? What about the stories of untold wealth and treasure?'

'Bonkers' McGinty they all called him...but he'd come anyway. And who was laughing now? Well nobody was actually, certainly no Rudanians because they didn't laugh at anything. Except in rare cases of other's extreme misfortune...or pain.

And the worse thing was, he'd lost his traditional Rudanian rudeness, Grinder had beaten it out of him right from the start.

'My name is Warlock Grinder,' he'd said when he looked down at McGinty in the pit into which he'd fallen, quite nastily barking his shins, 'I am now your master. Work well and obey me and you will be treated ...er...fairly well. However disobey me, work badly, or speak to me rudely, as I know you are bound to being Rudanian, and I will be on you like a ton of bricks!'

McGinty had squinted back up at him and answered,

'Who are you to be my master? You bearded, old, poo breathed loonie!'

There had been a huge almost instantaneous crash as a ton of bricks fell in the pit. He had only just survived (thanks to his incredibly tough Rudanian bones) and had learned to keep his tongue since then.

There was a time when he'd have told Grinder where to go no matter what he was threatened with, but now after the brick incident he was positively polite and attentive.

And how that galled him. The only time he could enjoy his old rudeness was with Grinder's guards. But they were Miseries, so it only made them happier the more he insulted them. Curse them! Curse them all!

'McGinty!'

He quickened his pace.

'Yes Master...here I am.'

Yes, here he now was indeed. Trapped underneath the very largest, most impenetrable of the mountains; Mount Scroop itself. Enslaved by that evil old Warlock, with no chance of escape.

He entered a smaller cavern, in which stood, somewhat incongruously amongst the stalagmites and stalactites, a large mobile home. Apart from its unusual location there was otherwise nothing remarkable about it. It looked like a thousand mobile homes that you'd see parked permanently on trailer parks anywhere in our world. A large, net-curtained window dominated its front end, next to which where written the words 'Bide-a wee' in a florid and extravagant type.

In front of it on what appeared to be a large square of bright, green astro-turf, was a simple wooden garden table. A large, gaudily striped umbrella was sticking out of its centre, two ornate, white garden chairs were positioned around it and a sun lamp flickered brightly from its top.

Next to the table was a deck chair in which, his eyes hidden by little, round, black sunglasses, lolled the great, the fearsome, the all-powerful, Warlock Grinder.

Although if you saw how he was dressed, you wouldn't think he was fearsome at all. He was wearing a blue and yellow Hawaiian shirt, beige, knee length shorts and leather open-toed sandals.

He held his heavily bearded face towards the sun lamp, whose timer clicked rhythmically and didn't immediately acknowledge McGinty's presence.

'Ahem..mas...'

Warlock Grinder cut him short with a brief gesture of his hand. The sun lamp timer slowed, then 'pinged' to a stop.

'Ahh..' sighed the Warlock,' just because we live underground, doesn't mean we have to look all pale and pallid. Must keep up appearances, you never know who'll come calling.'

He removed his sunglasses and turned his gaze on McGinty.

'Well I suppose that's not strictly true, I always know exactly who's going to come calling, don't I McGinty. I knew about you after all, probably before even you did.'

McGinty grimaced.

'Yes Master, I suppose you did.'

'And it certainly was convenient you going against your Rudanian instincts, otherwise I'd be less one useful servant.'

Grinder smiled slyly.

'Yes Master..' mumbled McGinty awkwardly.

'Yes Master,' echoed Grinder. He regarded his servant with cold disinterest.

'You really are the dullest of the dull, McGinty, aren't you?'

McGinty shuffled his feet and self-consciously wiped the metal plate with the dish cloth. He flushed, bright red. (Or redder than he normally was, because Rudanian's had reddish skin anyway. But other than that and the fact that they were on average a little taller, they were very similar in appearance to Snods.)

'Was there anything Master...only I'm doing the dishes now see...and there's plenty enough of them.'

'Plenty enough of them..' mimicked Grinder, his mouth curving upwards into a sneer.

He jumped to his feet and clasping his hands behind him, turned his back on McGinty, who shot him a look of pure hatred.

'Yes....' drawled Grinder over his shoulder, ' I know exactly who's going to come calling. And pretty much when. Fetch me the Barrel of Laughs, there should have been a few recent additions so it should be recharged again by now. And the Captain of the guard while you're about it...and make it quick you slovenly wretch.'

'Yes sir' McGinty bowed stiffly and turned on his heel.

'One day.... one day' he thought to himself, 'when he's least expecting it...I'm going to get him...I'm going to...haaa! and heeeeargh! And huurrrrgh! '

As he grunted, he twisted the metal plate back and forth between his fingers, imagining it was Grinder's neck, until it was bent quite out of shape.

21.

Grinder enjoys himself.

Warlock grinder watched his servant's retreating back with cold amusement. What an idiot! He still had no idea just how very powerful he was. No matter how many hints he dropped, he still couldn't understand that it was he who had summoned him from Rudania in the first place, he who had planted the thought in his mind that he should visit the mountains. And why? He laughed aloud to himself. Just purely for his own entertainment, nothing more. Rudanian's had no sense of humour worth stealing, as he well knew. So he'd just been interested to see how long McGinty would take to enslave, how long it would take to break his spirit. It hadn't taken long at all of course. In fact it was a little disappointingly easy.

Grinder sighed. And that was the problem with being so powerful…boredom. Where were the challenges? When his sole motivation, indeed his very reason for existence in life, was the pursuit of misery and the ruination of other's happiness, he increasingly found that his only real pleasure came when his victims at least put up a little bit of a fight.

Then he could really enjoy crushing them.

He sighed again. It was a tough life being perfect sometimes. If only he could get away from the mountains….there were so many places he could go to, so much misery he could spread and in doing so gain even more power.

Still, at least he had something to look forward to.

He sat down at the garden table and picked up a copy of 'Witches, Wizards, Warlocks and Insurance Salesmen's Weekly.' On the front cover was a list of contents; 'Wizard Wheeze,' my spell inside,' 'Which witch bewitches, poll result and pictures,' 'Toad in the hole, 12 wart packed recipes,' 'Stock market ISA's, personal option policies with profit plus funds, good or bad?'

But the main picture was of Cough, smiling broadly and trying to hide the bulldog clips which held up his too-big robe. Alongside were the words; 'Royal Wizard Cough appointed role of adjudicator at forthcoming Festival of Laughter. Hopes of Royal success for King's son Stove.'

Grinder cackled so loudly he made himself jump.

'How delightful,' he thought, 'what a spectacularly bad thing to do.'

There'd be no success for Stove of course, not without his sense of humour. That would have been an enjoyable little sideshow in itself. But now that fool Cough was leading the Snod prince right to him…what a perfect opportunity to rid himself of the entire race!

Those irritating, verminous Snods had been a thorn in his side for too long. Their ridiculous laughter based society was an affront to everything he stood for, to say nothing of the potential danger it represented to him. Up until now he'd had to be happy with stealing just the occasional sense of humour because they were all so far away and of course he could never leave the mountains. But with Stove in his power, he could easily enslave him, send him back to the Festival where most of the population of Snod Valley would be congregated all at once with a little gift and….

'All at once…hee hee…all together now.'

Grinder giggled wickedly and hugged himself in delighted anticipation.

And how he would enjoy tormenting Cough and the rest of his ridiculous party too…or maybe he should consider a different fate for some of them? Another particularly unpleasant thought occurred to him and he cackled again, loudly and long.

'Sorry to interrupt your cackling Master, ' said McGinty having re-entered the cavern, 'you asked for Slimetooth, captain of your guard and the Barrel of Laughs.'

'Ah yes...' drawled Grinder composing himself, 'Slimetooth. Are you well?'

'Couldn't be worse thanks for asking sir.'

'Good...good. Now listen, I'm expecting a little party to arrive in the mountains sometime over the next few days, according to my spy who travels among them. There'll be an idiot magician, his servant, a Snod prince and his sister and possibly a Contradiction, their guide. They should be easy enough to take, the magician knows a few tricks though, so better leave him to me. Post your men on all the main passes through the mountain, tell them I want them all alive.'

He wandered over to the barrel. It was about three feet high and about two in diameter. It was a dull, very black, black and made from some kind of unusual metal. On top of it were two large clasps which held the lid firmly in place. If you were to place your ear hard against it, you might hear a faint, low humming, like thousands of people at a party all talking at once.

'Now this is what they'll be after,' Grinder said pointing to the barrel, 'The Barrel of Laughs.' It contains all the senses of humour that I've stol...er...collected over the years. Got the full set from Rudania,' he added with a hint of pride, 'that's why they have none left these days. Do you McGinty?'

He smiled nastily at McGinty, who looked blankly back.

'Just in case, it's best to keep it safe,' he said to the Captain, 'so I want you to put it in the shower and loo unit in my mobile home if you will. It will be truly safe there.'

'Certainly sir and can I say how much I admire your miserable-ness?'

'You're too kind Slimetooth.'

The burly captain of the guard enfolded his long arms around the barrel and staggered with it into Grinder's beige and brown mobile home.

'Mind the flock wallpaper in the lounge!' Grinder shouted after him, 'and the carnival glass ornaments!'

Then he turned his attention back to the Rudanian.

'Now McGinty, what are we to do with you today? What will really make you even more unhappy? Hmmmm.'

Grinder ran his long, slender fingers through his beard thoughtfully.

'I know!' he barked triumphantly and McGinty felt his heart sink even further.

'A song! We haven't had one of those for a while. A jolly song...about....now let me think. I know, about a man who thinks he's a dog. Here...here are the lyrics.'

Grinder handed over a sheet of paper from a brown folder that he kept inside his shirt, then hugged himself with glee at the crestfallen expression on McGinty's face.

'And dance while you sing...a jolly, happy dance. I want to see you smile.'

His voice lowered into a sinister, threatening tone.

'And it had better be good, or maybe I'll make you dance 'till the end of the week, with the help of a little spell.'

McGinty grimaced unhappily and began a stuttering, shambling dance. It was the best he could manage, but truth be told it was a pretty sorry effort. He hopped jerkily from foot to foot, pausing occasionally to bob his shoulders up and down in an apologetic and out of beat shrug and then thrusting his neck forward and backward like a demented pigeon.

'Sing up...sing up!' cackled Grinder nastily.

So McGinty began.

'One day a young man didn't feel too good,

he went to his doctor's to ask if he would

make him feel better and heal his pain,

the doctor politely asked him to explain.

'I think I'm a dog, that's what's wrong with me,

all hairy and snuffly and covered with fleas,'

'Well that is quite serious,' the doctor replied,

'get up on the couch and we'll look inside.'

But then the young man took a gulp and said 'No.

I'm not allowed on the couch, well didn't you know.'

McGinty stopped. There was a brief moment of silence, then Grinder burst into loud, vicious and hysterical laughter.

'Ah ha ha ha! I don't think the joke's that funny...but your miserable face...ha ha ha...you're really unhappy! I can feel even that small misery making me a little stronger. That's marvellous! Oh dear...'

He wiped tears of laughter from his eyes.

'As a little reward, for amusing me so well,' he said recovering himself somewhat, 'when Slimetooth returns, I'll allow you to go out on patrol with him to the farthest passage into the mountain. See if you can help catch our guests.'

McGinty's face brightened. Slimetooth meanwhile, emerged from the mobile home and strode powerfully up to where they stood.

'Yes, well you needn't get too excited, there'll be no opportunity to escape and if you try I'll instruct Slimetooth to kill you. Won't you Slimetooth?'

'It would be a pleasure your nastiness,' said the Captain of the guard, fingering his long, sharp sword threateningly and staring flintily at McGinty.

McGinty swallowed hard before answering.

'There's nothing further from my thoughts Master, I assure you. It will be an honour to do this work for you, as always.'

'Yeees,' drawled Grinder suspiciously, 'we'll see about that. Now get out of my sight both of you. And don't come back without our visitors.'

Grinder span on his heel and disappeared back towards his mobile home. He hopped cheerfully up the steps and into his kitchen. It was all going very nicely, he thought as he filled his kettle with water, placed the whistle back on its spout and popped it on the hob.

'Gas,' he muttered and pressed a small button. Instantly a blue flame popped on underneath the kettle. He ran his fingers lovingly over the formica work surface next to the hob and smiled. Little did Cough know, but when he and Stove had disturbed Grinder sitting on his loo, they had sealed the doom of their entire race.

His Palace spy had introduced the pickled shavings from the trotters of the Ignorant Pig to the Snod prince as he'd slept and stolen his sense of humour. It had all been very straightforward. If Cough hadn't consulted The Ancient Book of Records and caught him in that, 'ahem!' compromising position, Grinder would probably not have known that they would have done something so completely out of character for Snods and have dared to come looking for it.

He thought of the Barrel of laughs, now safely tucked up in the shower and loo unit in his mobile home with its thousands and thousands of stolen senses of humour imprisoned inside. If anyone ever found out why it was so important to him...

He dismissed the thought. Who would find out? Certainly not any of the idiots on their way to his mountains.

'Yes, let them come to me....If I can't go to them, let them all come to me,' he said aloud, 'the more the miserabler.'

His spy would keep him informed of their pathetically predictable moves, so there was no danger that anything could go wrong. So perhaps he would have a little fun with them on their journey.

They were in the Great Mirror Fruit Forest according to his spy's last message, having come a fairly pitiful distance. Now who did he know around those parts? He thought hard for a moment, and closed his eyes.

'Hmmmm...'

Then his eyes snapped open and he clicked his fingers.

'Oh yes...he'll do nicely. Life is good, when I'm bad,' he said aloud and chuckled as the kettle's whistle began to pipe.

22.

A nasty surprise.

'I can't believe that he could be so stupid!'

Cough was incandescent with anger.

'What was the last thing I said to him? Don't forget to leave a trail, I said, don't forget! But can you see anything?'

'Er...no,' said Colander casting a futile glance around and rummaging half-heartedly through some long grass with a stick.

'Well he's had a lot on his mind lately,' said Grill defensively.

'A lot....a lot on his....well that implies that he's got a mind in the first place, something of which at the moment I'm not even sure!'

'That's unfair,' pouted Grill.

'His mind's alright, isn't it his sense of humour that's gone?' said Colander missing the point.

'Yes...well...hmmm...' mumbled Cough realising that he may have gone a little far, 'maybe I should have given him the Nagging Bag to remind him.'

'Yes, maybe you should have, but now's a fine time to think that!' scolded the voice from the bag inside his sleeve.

'Well one thing,' said Colander cheerfully ignoring it, 'at least we've got rid of that Contradiction creature.'

Cough clapped his hands to his forehead in exasperation.

'Colander, without that Contradiction creature as you call him, we won't be able to find the quick route to the mountains. It could slow us down by days, even a week!'

'Then you'd be really too late!' continued the same sharp voice from the bag on his wrist.

Cough sighed heavily.

There was an awkward silence as each member of the party searched for any signs of a new trail among the mirror fruit trees. Even the Silly Ass seemed to be looking for something more than a few tasty thistles to munch.

They'd followed the direction that Stove had taken, but had now reached the first fork and discovered that he'd forgotten to mark the way with the green glo-worm liquid. As all the trees began to get thicker and thicker and closer together, the chances of them finding the trail looked increasingly hopeless.

'Like looking for a beagle in a haystack,' muttered Colander sadly.

'Well,' sighed Cough ignoring him, 'that's that. We'll have to think of something else.'

Grill sat down, hugging Crumbs who struggled to be free. She let him go and he hopped a few feet away to where a mirror fruit lay rotting on the ground and started to tuck into it.

'If we stick to the path, where does it come out?' she asked.

'Ermmm...' said Cough sitting down next to her, 'if I'm not wrong, it passes through the lighter wooded area of the orchard, then out to the plain beyond.'

'Well,' said Grill, 'if I remember correctly, my Uncle Mug lives out in that sort of area on a small farm. If we can find it, at least he might be able to put us up for the night. Maybe he'd know this area better than us too…in fact he's sure to…perhaps he'll even know another way through to the mountains!' she added with increasing excitement.

'That's not a bad idea sir,' said Colander, leaning on the pile of furniture on the Silly Ass's back and nodding at Cough, 'it will be just about dark by the time we get there and while we rest we can have a think about what to do next.'

'Perhaps...perhaps not,' said Cough inscrutably.

'Unless you have a magical solution?' said Grill hopefully.

'Hmmm,' mused Cough, 'there are a few things I could do. Perhaps I could turn us all into flying horses and we could see where Stove was from the sky?'

He rubbed his beard thoughtfully.

'Never done it before, but there's always a first time.'

Colander looked alarmed.

'Er...beggin' pardon sir, but nowhere in my terms of contract does it refer to bein' turned into things. I'm not sure I hold with it.'

Colander remembered the last time Cough had tried to turn a Snod into an animal of some kind. It had not gone well.

After the incident with Stove's nursemaid and her stint as a hamster, Cough had restricted his transformation spells to furniture and small furry things. But one day he'd been unable to resist the temptation. Trowel the gardener had come to him with a wart on his nose. Pretending to cast a spell to remove it, he had turned the gardener into a ferret. It had taken weeks and weeks to return him to his former self. And Trowel later confided to Colander that he still had to fight the desire to hide down farmer's trousers in pubs and was convinced that he could hypnotise rabbits.

He had never forgiven Cough.

'I think I like the sound of young missy Grill's idea better meself,' Colander said.

Cough furrowed his brows and slipped his rucksack off his shoulder. He rummaged through it in silence. Grill looked at Colander quizzically who shrugged his shoulders, the various articles dangling from his mug-tree arm tinkling merrily against each other as he did.

'Now...where...where can they be? I know I packed them, so they must be in here somewhere. Ah! Here we are!'

Cough triumphantly produced a small, clear plastic bag containing pieces of a dry, brown, curly substance and shook it vigorously above his head.

'These...these are magic beans, we'll let them decide what's best to do.'

'Er...they look like pork scratchings to me,' said Grill quietly.

'Nonsense!' cried Cough 'these are magic beans, the most powerful and magical interpreters of the future. They see all and are never wrong, they have been used through the ages by the great and mighty, by kings and queens, wizards and warlocks, emperors and...oh...hang on a minute, you're right, they are pork scratchings.'

Cough peered at the label on the bag.

'What a nuisance, I must have picked them up instead of the beans on my kitchen dresser.'

Absent-mindedly, he opened the bag and crunched disconsolately into one of its contents.

'Hmmm...not bad actually,' he muttered, 'do you fancy one?' He held the packet out towards Grill.

Colander, Grill and even the Silly Ass looked at each other with varying expressions of perplexity. Grill shook her head.

'Well...best be making a move then,' said Colander, 'Time waits for no one' they say, apart from his wife Missus Time I suppose.'

'Yes...yes,' said Cough regaining his composure,' I suppose the best thing we can do all things considered, is to pay a visit to Grill's Uncle Mug and see if he has any better idea about how we can try and catch up with Stove and Phylis. It is starting to get on...'

'You better believe it!' the Nagging Bag interjected.

'Yes, yes,' he continued, 'the worst thing would be for us to be stuck in the mirror fruit forest when it's dark. Get the Silly Ass moving Colander!'

Colander bent and whispered a joke into the Silly ass's ear, while Cough flung his ruck sack over his shoulder. Grill jumped to her feet and brushed herself down.

'Wait...what is that awful smell?' cried Cough.

'Oh...that'll be Crumbs,' said Grill apologetically,' he always does that when he's eaten rotten fruit. He's probably upset that we have to move so quickly too. He has a delicate digestion you know.'

'Nuthin' delicate about a digestion that can make that kind o' stink missy...last time I smelled anything that bad was when I accidentally went to a party bein' held in honour of The Chief Wind Breaker at the annual Snod Valley Wind Breaker's convention. Goooorgh! That was powerful bad that was!'

'Yes. Well thank you for that Colander. Now if you can stand it Grill pick up Crumbs and let's go!' said Cough impatiently rapping his stick against the ground.

'And that means now!' nagged the bag.

Gulping a mouthful of air and trying not to breathe through her nose, Grill swept Crumbs up into her arms. The Silly Ass brayed loudly at Colander's joke (which incidentally was 'What's round, white and giggles? ...a tickled onion.') and jumped smartly forward into a walk and at last the diminished but determined little party were under way again.

This time straight into a nasty little surprise that Warlock Grinder, sitting in his mobile home so far away in the Scroop mountains, had prepared for them.

23.

More scared than ever before.

Stove was beginning to feel pretty tired. And he found himself really hoping that Phylis was too. But there seemed to be no sign of the Contradiction slowing. Stove liked to think that he was quite fit, after all he played futeball for the palace side (Pan's People they were called, in honour of his father) every Sunday and trained every Wednesday evening. But he really struggled to keep pace with Phylis.

They'd been moving at some speed all morning and most of the afternoon, following a winding and confusing route through the mirror fruit orchard, sometimes having to force their way through seemingly impassable thickets. It all looked the same to Stove and he had to admit feeling a grudging admiration for his odd companion's sense of direction and energy. Along the way he had continued to sprinkle the occasional drop of Gloworm blood to mark where they changed direction, but in the back of his mind he didn't really hold out any hope of the others catching up.

Then abruptly, just as Stove was about to start pleading with him to stop, Phylis Applepie did just that. Then he promptly fell flat on his face on the grass.

Startled, Stove rushed over to where he lay and crouched down beside the immobile body.

'Phylis? Phylis? Are you alright? Are you sick?' he asked, 'or rather aren't you alright? Aren't you sick? he continued, remembering.

The Contradiction lay so very still, that an unpleasant thought that he might be dead began to surface in Stove's mind.

'Phylis? Phylis?' he whispered in dismay.

How was he to continue without his guide? He could be lost in the orchard forever and ever. He prodded Phylis gingerly with his finger. Then he tried to pick up one of his gangly arms and find a pulse, like he's been taught to in his Snod first aid and rat juggling classes.

The Contradiction made a slight snuffling sound. It made Stove jump and he leaned closer to the ground with his face next to Phylis' head. He heard the sound of low steady breathing and realised that although both his large pale blue and small brown eyes were wide open, he appeared to be fast asleep.

'Phew!' thought Stove, 'that's a relief. I really didn't fancy wandering the orchard with no sense of humour, living on mirror fruit for the rest of my life.'

He plucked a fruit from a nearby branch anyway and munching into it, settled back down on the ground next to his sleeping partner. The relief of discovering that Phylis wasn't dead after all made him suddenly feel even more incredibly tired. He lay down on his back with a groan and stared up through the silver fruit-laden branches at the pinky-blue sky of late afternoon.

It was so relaxing, so very quiet and calm. In fact, he thought, perhaps it was a little bit strangely quiet, almost too much so. At first he couldn't put his finger on why he thought it seemed strange, but then it slowly dawned on him. All the birds had stopped singing. Their cheery, trilling music had accompanied them constantly since they first entered the orchard but now there was nothing, not one peep. He sat up, frowning and turned his head from side to side, listening hard for something, anything. For a moment, all was silent.

'What was that?' he wondered aloud, 'was that a noise? Is it anything? Why am I talking to myself?'

He strained so hard to listen, if his ears could have grown any bigger they would have.

Then he thought he could hear something else, something...different, that he hadn't heard before. It was very, very faint, at first just a kind of a distant rustling, like someone rubbing their hands against the bark of a tree, or through a pile of leaves. But slowly and surely as he listened uneasily to it, it started to become louder and more discernible and for some reason...terrible.

The rustling began to sound more like a crashing and snapping. With increasing horror Stove pictured what it was that he was listening to. It sounded like trees being uprooted or knocked over and branches torn apart by something huge, something in a hurry, something heading in his direction.

Stove's heart began to pound like a drum. Whatever it was, it was getting closer and closer very quickly. They had to move, find somewhere less exposed to hide. He jumped to his feet in panic.

'Phylis!' he screamed, 'Phylis!' wake up! For goodness sake wake up! Oh!... I mean... don't wake up! You musn't wake up!'

He shook the sleeping Contradiction with all his might, again and again but to no avail. On it slept, blissfully unaware of the approaching terror, a stray lock of bright red hair moving gently to and fro in front of one nostril as it breathed.

The crashing, ripping, tearing sound was thunderingly loud now. The noise was so awful he almost felt like he could hear the trees screaming in agony as they were mercilessly rent apart and smashed into a thousand pieces, as whatever it was charged massively through them. And now there was another noise too…a horrid, squelching, snuffling noise... a greedy, hungry noise.

Stove felt it was the most terrifying sound he had ever heard.

'Phylis! Phylis!' he screamed above the din once again. Desperately he picked up the Contradiction's legs and tried to drag him out of the clearing. But he was heavy…too heavy. Stove's grip kept slipping and try as he might he couldn't budge him by an inch. The noise reached an unbearable crescendo, then abruptly stopped. It was replaced by another, more sinister and spine chilling sound…the sound of something large and close, breathing heavily. And Stove knew that the something was right behind him, on the other side of the clearing.

He froze.

For a moment he hoped that if he just pretended whatever it was wasn't there and kept very still, it might just go away. But a low, threatening, slobbering, growling told him that would never happen. He dropped the still sleeping Contradiction's legs and slowly started to turn around to face the sound, the hairs on the back of his neck standing up as he did.

There squatting malevolently at the edge of the clearing, surrounded by the flotsam of ruined mirror fruit trees, was the most complete example of evil Stove could ever despair of seeing in his entire life.

It was nearly as tall as the trees left standing around it and as wide as the castle doors. Vicious, blood red eyes peered venomously out of a massive, black head. Under its pink, slimey, dribbling snout, its wet, red mouth opened in a hungry leer to reveal huge, yellow, slavering fangs.

Stove knew that he was in the dreadful presence ….of the Ignorant Pig.

Then it began to laugh. A horrible, cackling, gloating laugh. And then, incredibly, it began to talk.

'What's up boy...Warlock got your sense of humour?'

Stove realised with a start that he'd heard that voice once before…in Cough's laboratory. Although now it was now partly disguised by the unpleasant phlegmy rattling of mucus and spittle, there was still no mistaking it.

It was the voice of Warlock Grinder!

The Ignorant Pig began to cackle again in the horrible mixture of its and Grinder's voices.

'Now it's time for lunch…and what's on the menu? Why you are! Ah ha ha ha !'

The monster advanced slowly on Stove. He stood frozen to the spot. No matter how hard he tried he just couldn't move!

'Cough! Colander! Phylis! Someone! Help me!'

He tried to shout, but no sound came from his mouth.

And slowly, deliberately, the huge slobbering, dribbling red mouth inched ever closer. And with it came an awful stench…a stench of dead things.

'It's not time to go…don't get up.' The pig suddenly said in a different voice, 'don't wake up, it's not late.'

Stove just had time to feel confusion amongst the intensity of his fear and then suddenly he began to shake. Only it wasn't him shaking with fear, something was shaking him.

He opened his eyes and found that he was back in the clearing with Phylis standing over him shaking him vigorously.

'Don't come on, you weren't having a dream. We musn't get moving, we don't need to be clear of the orchard by sunset.'

Stove blinked once or twice. It took him a little while to realise where he was. He was breathing hard and there was a sheen of sweat on his forehead. But slowly he regained his senses. It was the sound of the birds singing once more that brought him back to reality.

'Oh my...oh what a relief!' cried Stove. 'What an awful nightmare, the worst I've ever had! In fact I've never had a nightmare before. And if that's what they're like, I don't want another. Thank goodness! It's so good to see you.'

Stove realised that in his panic he'd forgotten to speak Contradiction.

'Oh...sorry, I mean I'm not sorry Phylis, I...'

'Hmmm...don't get a move on, time's not running out,' said Phylis unsympathetically, throwing Stove his bag and starting to move out of the clearing at speed. Stove hastened after him. 'Just a nightmare,' he thought, shaking his head. But it had been so vivid. He wouldn't forget those feelings of sheer, helpless terror for as long as he lived.

He felt something jiggling against his side in his pocket. It was the phial of Contradiction Balm. He really must get around to taking it soon, he thought, as he was getting increasingly fed up of having to speak in Contradiction all the time, on top of everything else. It was all proving to be so....difficult.

Then, unconsciously reverting to his Snod optimism he found himself saying aloud something that he lately had tried to avoid saying at all;

'Well I suppose that things could be a lot worse,'

And little did he know it then, but they were going to be.

24.

The danger from above.

'Come along, come along now, we must hurry!' fussed Cough shouting over his shoulder and striding purposefully onwards through the shiny-fruited trees.

'Yes there's no time to lose!' echoed the nagging bag.

They'd been trekking along for over two hours since discovering that Stove had forgotten to leave a trail and by now had given up any hope of accidentally coming across his tracks. As Cough had feared, the Snod boy and the Contradiction had obviously taken a far different route. There were fewer trees around them now, so they were obviously approaching the edge of the mirror fruit forest and nearing the plain on which stood the Snod smallholdings, including that of Stove and Grill's Uncle Mug.

Grill was beginning to lag behind. Crumbs had started to feel very heavy, but she struggled on stubbornly without complaining. She didn't want to give the others any opportunity to regret her being there. She kept her eyes fixed on Colander and the Silly Ass now a good distance in front of her and some way again behind Cough, who's pointed little hat she could just about see bobbing along far away in the rapidly diminishing light. Occasionally she had to break into a trot to keep from falling too far behind.

'Colander was right about the Silly Ass, ' she thought, observing how it seemed totally unaffected by the enormous weight it was carrying and the speed at which they were and had been travelling all day. It capered easily along by the side of the one armed Snod, happily ignoring Colander's occasional clumsy but well meant prods of encouragement and heartfelt cries of;

'gee-up, gee-up, not far to go now me little comedy loving beauty.'

As she stumbled breathlessly along, Crumbs grunting quietly in time to the rhythm of her footsteps, she found herself wondering about Colander and his odd reaction towards the Contradiction. There was clearly some bad blood between them…or at least there certainly was from Colander's point of view. Yet Colander seemed such a nice, friendly, jolly sort, she couldn't imagine him making enemies easily. She made a mental note to ask him when they next stopped for a rest, which she fervently hoped wasn't too long away.

Talking of which, she noticed rather miserably that she was starting to lag too far behind again and forced her aching legs into a tired trot. Abruptly, she caught the toe of her Snod boot in a hidden tree root and crashed head first into a clump of long grass, spilling a rather startled Crumbs as she did. Fortunately for both her and her pet the grass was thick and soft, so neither were seriously hurt. Grill had fallen awkwardly though and had managed to wind herself badly enough to be unable to speak for a moment. Meanwhile Crumbs felt obliged to let off one of his eggy specialities in order to register his outrage at the gross indignity of his situation.

Grill sat up on her haunches.

'Col…Col….'

She tried to call out after the rapidly disappearing Snod and the Silly Ass, but try as she might, she just couldn't get enough of her breath back. Maybe it was just as well. For at that moment a great, black shadow passed over her place of semi-concealment. The shadow continued on across the ground at a swift pace towards Colander, who remained totally ignorant of its on-rushing presence. She shielded her eyes against the low sun, looked skywards and saw a sight that made her heart stop and her mouth suddenly as dry as the Brindisi desert .

Bearing down on her unsuspecting companions at a furious pace, some two hundred feet up in the sky, was a massive, weirdly multi-coloured dragon. Its huge triangular wings, easily twice as wide as the castle gates, thrashed the air around it for a moment, then folded back into its scaly body as it formed into a dive and hurtled downwards towards Colander.

Suddenly Grill found her voice.

'Colander!' she screamed as loudly as she possibly could.

Colander stopped dead in his tracks and span around, as did the Silly Ass. But it was too late. The dragon extended its massive, cruelly curved claws and snatched both him and the Ass up in one fluid movement, before they even had time to utter a sound. But it wasn't finished yet. Although some distance ahead, Cough had heard Grill's cry and he too had stopped and turned. The dragon swapped Colander over into the same claw as the Silly Ass and fixing its yellow eyes on the diminutive magician swooped malevolently down again towards him.

Grill could just about see Cough in the far distance. He appeared to struggle with his backpack, drop it desperately to the ground and frantically search through it. The dragon neared him and extended its empty claw. Suddenly a bright blue and white line of stars shot out from somewhere near Cough and swooshed towards the dragon.

Startled, it paused in mid-flight for a moment, hovering just twenty feet above him. The line of stars shot out again, this time hitting the dragon. But to Grill's dismay she saw them bounce harmlessly off its thick, scaly hide. The dragon threw back its massive, horned head and opened its great, red mouth. A dreadful, screeching noise issued forth.

'Shcreeehah hah ha shcreehah hah ha!'

it bellowed triumphantly. And Grill realised with horror that it was laughing.

Once again it dived and scooped Cough up into its empty claw.

'No!' screamed Grill at the top of her voice.

The dragon stopped abruptly. It moved its head from side to side as if it had heard her. Then it started to slowly turn around back towards where she lay, hovering in the sky. Realising that she too was now in great danger, she threw herself down into the long, thick grass, her heart beating wildly. As she lay there, she thought fearfully that Cough and Colander must be unconscious…or worse, because the only sound she could hear was the steady 'thrubb thrubb' of the dragon's huge, leathery wings as it neared her hiding place.

It stopped. Hovering just above her. She could feel the breeze from its wings against her cheek. She couldn't understand how it couldn't see her and she steeled herself for the cold, dreadful clasp of its cruel claws at any moment.

Then she saw Crumbs. He'd got fed up of waiting to be picked up and decided to head for the nearest fallen mirror fruit. With no sense of danger or fear whatsoever, he waddled crossly out of the long grass just feet away from her and towards a tree some ten feet distant.

Grill gasped. As she watched, powerless to do anything, the dragon thumped to the ground just inches in front of the slow moving red toad, barring his progress. Crumbs came to a reluctant and angry halt, narrowing his cold, orange eyes balefully. The dragon lowered its massive head until it was right next to the toad and sniffed curiously. Just at that moment Crumbs, furious that his path to a nice juicy, rotten mirror fruit had been blocked, let rip with a particularly horrendous smell. It even made Grill's eyes water from where she was hiding.

The dragon snatched its head back like it had been stung by a particularly violent wasp and let out a timid, coughing gasp. It staggered a few steps backwards, then took to the air and hovered some ten feet above the toad. Crumbs triumphantly and determinedly continued on his way, struggling a little against the heavy wind that the dragon's wings created, towards the fallen mirror fruit.

A horrible thought popped into Grill's head.

Although this was the first real dragon that she'd ever encountered, she had seen lots of pictures of them in books. Suppose this was the kind of dragon that breathed fire… surely most of them could do that anyway? Suppose it was just getting itself ready to frazzle her pet!

Then just as she was preparing herself to jump out from her hiding place and attract its attention, It shifted its gaze from Crumbs and with a grunt of disgust rose higher and higher into the sky. Within a few beats of its great wings it had disappeared from sight, along with its unwilling and seemingly unconscious, or even dead, passengers.

25.

Grill alone.

For a little while after the dragon had gone, Grill stayed submerged in the long grass. She didn't want to take any chance that it might come back. But by the time Crumbs had waddled over to the tree and was tucking into a nicely brown and maggoty mirror fruit, she decided to risk emerging from her hiding place, peering cautiously in the direction in which it had disappeared as she did.

It appeared to have gone, sure enough. It and her travelling companions and friends. Gone. Just like that. Here one second, gone the next. They could even be dead! And here she was, all alone. What was she to do now? All alone, miles from anywhere and anyone she knew.

A thousand questions seemed to flood into her head all at once and she felt the panic rising steadily and unchecked within her. For a moment she hated her brother Stove. It was all his stupid fault! It was his idea to come. And he had forgotten to leave the glo-worm trail. Stupid! Stupid! Stupid!

'Stupid Stove!' she screamed at the top of her voice. It echoed hollowly around the forest.

'Stupid…tupid…pid…id…tove…ove…ve…'

She was surprised to feel hot tears running down her cheeks and realised that she had been crying hard.

'Brrrrreeeack?' exclaimed Crumbs, sounding almost sympathetic through a mouthful of maggoty fruit.

'Oh Crumbs,' cried Grill, running over and scooping him up into her arms. 'At least I've still got you…and you saved me from the dragon…thank you…thank you…'

She smothered the startled and warty toad with hot wet kisses.

'Crumbs…mmwah…mwah…dear Crumbs…mmwah…what shall we do?…what shall we do now?'

Crumbs struggled to be free, so reluctantly she put him back down on the ground, and sinking apathetically down next to him, buried her face in her hands. But to her surprise, instead of returning to the rotten fruit, he immediately started to move in a determined (and for him positively dynamic) way along the trail to where Collander and Cough had been snatched by the dragon.

'No, there's no point…you don't understand…they've gone,' she said puzzled by his most uncharacteristic behaviour.

But still the fat, red toad waddled determinedly along the path.

Reluctantly, she got up from the ground and started to follow him, sniffing loudly and wiping her nose on her sleeve as she did.

'Yeh…you're right Crumbs, we can't just stay here feeling sorry for ourselves. The dragon might come back after all…and we've got to at least try. Maybe we'll get lucky and find Uncle Mug, or at least someone who knows him.'

She felt a little better now and she tried to think more positive thoughts. Perhaps there was still hope after all? Perhaps her friends would be alive and if she could find Uncle Mug, he'd help find them. Although if she was being honest with herself, she was lost and alone, with no food, no shelter, no way of knowing where to go…angrily she pushed the negative thoughts away into the back of her mind.

They'd reached the spot where Colander and the Silly Ass had been swept up by the dragon, when Crumbs suddenly stopped.

When Grill looked down, she saw that he was nuzzling a small leather pouch.

'Colander must have dropped it,' Grill said, stooping eagerly to pick it up.

She opened it. Inside was a handful of strange looking pills, all decorated with a green and light brown camouflage pattern.

'Camo-pills,' she said aloud to Crumbs.

'Might come in useful I suppose,' she continued, popping them back in the leather pouch.

She searched the surrounding area, just in case anything else had fallen during the attack, but only found one of Colander's mugs from his mug tree arm. She noticed with a twinge of sadness and loss that it sported a large red heart and the words;

'World's greatest lover,'

in bright red type.

Crumbs had moved on further up the path and now stood somewhere near to the spot where Cough had made his futile attempt to beat off his monstrous attacker. Grill soon joined him and was soon searching the area. A few leaves of brightly coloured paper….a shoe (funny how Grill couldn't remember Cough wearing one of these and how there always seemed to be one at the scene of any incident, anywhere in the world)…some odd looking herbs…nothing terribly useful, but then…her foot hit something solid in the long grass by the side of the path. She bent down and uncovered…

'Cough's walking stick,' she murmured.

She had no idea whether it would be any use to her, but she felt oddly comforted when she picked it up and felt the smooth, cool wood in her hand.

'I really hope you're alright Cough,' she said to herself, examining the graffiti at the top of the stick.

She turned to see what Crumbs was up to and as she did so, the top of the stick briefly glowed bright, white blue.

'What the …?' she thought, 'did that just…?'

Then in case she'd been mistaken, she swung the stick around once again. And again it glowed, only when it was pointed in a particular direction. She swung the stick around a third time….back the way they'd come ….nothing. Around past Crumbs…still nothing.

In the direction that they had been heading…the stick unmistakeably glowed a bright, white blue.

'Well that's got to be good news, Crumbs,' she said excitedly, 'It can only be showing us the way to Uncle Mug's, it's where we were headed after all. Cough must have enchanted it earlier… Uncle Mug will be able to help us…he'll know what to do…I hope. '

'Brrrreeeaaaccckk!' said Crumbs noncommittally.

'Come on, I'll have to carry you, it'll be much quicker that way.'

She scooped up the toad (who allowed himself to be manhandled without protest, almost as if he knew it was for the best) and marched on in the direction illuminated by the glowing stick with renewed strength and optimism.

She was now convinced that Uncle Mug (who she had only met once before when she was very little, before he had left the Royal Castle) would not only be able to put her up and feed her, but also help her find the dragon's lair, for she was determined now to save Cough and Colander… if they were still alive.

26.

The Swamp of Contradictions.

The mud was becoming really unpleasant. Thick, heavy and irritatingly sticky, clinging to the soles of Stove's boots and making them feel twice as heavy as they should. Phylis didn't seem bothered by it though. His weird little feet scampered along at a tremendous pace. Although the Contradiction wasn't actually moving much faster than the Snod was, something to do with the sheer speed at which his feet moved seemed to prevent any build up of mud.

It was dark now and the gloomy surroundings in which he found himself were reflected in Stove's mood. They'd long since left most of the cheery, reflected light of the mirror fruit forest far behind, having paused for another brief break when the Contradiction had once again performed his startling 'falling over fast asleep' trick. Although he had been afraid to do the same himself, sheer exhaustion had once again overtaken Stove and he too had slept. This time his sleep had been mercifully dream free. Now he supposed they must be close to the Swamp of Contradictions.

The only light which feebly illuminated their surroundings was a sickly, yellow glow that came from the burning torches that both he and the Contradiction carried. What few mirror fruit trees there were looked ragged and unkempt, fruitless and dying. Some, mostly submerged in the stinking mud, broken and standing at crazy angles, reminded Stove uncomfortably of the agonised fingers of drowning things, as they loomed out of the darkness.

Other than the occasional boulder covered in a slimy, green moss and clusters of vicious looking, spiny, grey thistles, there was little to break the monotony of the surrounding grey-brown mud.

Stove had pretty much given up trying to have a conversation with his odd companion, even though he had taken the Contradiction balm that Cough had given him. And what a truly horrible experience that had been.

At the last stop, he'd settled down next to the sleeping Phylis and taking the brown phial from his pocket, had removed its cork. The stench was instant and foul. It was without a doubt the worst thing Stove had ever smelled. Imagine Crumbs very worst eggy speciality and multiply it by a thousand. Or walking past an old gasworks, when the wind blows in your direction. It was all he could do to stop himself being sick.

'Oh…thanks a lot Cough!' he had said aloud, ' yuuurgh! And I've got to put a drop on my tongue?'

He had taken a deep breath and holding his nose dripped out a tiny drop onto the tip of his tongue. If he thought the smell was bad! By all the jokers! The taste had been indescribable. It was so awful it made him retch, took his breath away and made his eyes stream like fountains. For a while he'd lain face down in the mud, beating the ground with his fist as he struggled to catch his breath. Then eventually the taste had subsided to just a dreadful staleness, like he hadn't cleaned his teeth in a year and had been eating horse dung. Slowly he had regained a little of his composure.

'Phew! Don't want to have to do that too often,' he'd thought ruefully, dripping a little more balm into both ears.

Since then he'd been dying to find out if the balm made a difference, but it turned out that Phylis was unfriendly and uncommunicative anyway and despite his best efforts ignored him completely.

On they trudged in silence. Stove found himself staring resentfully at the Contradiction's back. He was beginning to really dislike him. Then suddenly a strange sight attracted his attention.

Out of the gloom some little way ahead Stove could just make out what looked like a solid wall of huge, black trees. The Contradiction hurried on towards them, seeming to increase its pace.

'Hang on!' Stove bellowed, taken by surprise by the sudden acceleration and struggling to keep up.

'You must keep up,' Phylis shouted back over his shoulder without breaking stride.

'You…you pain in the neck,'

Stove muttered under his breath, increasing his own pace to a fast trot.

'Why Cough chose you as a guide I'll never know.'

He panted up behind the Contradiction and as they neared the trees, he could see that they did indeed extend in a line as far as the eye could see in both directions, like a great, black wall. From a distance Stove had thought that they only seemed so black because it was dark, but now he could clearly see that they were in fact completely, jet black. And what an odd shape they were too. Their trunks were long and straight at the base, with strange squiggly branches that sat perched on their top, like a mound of scruffy hair, or a furry Russian hat that had seen better days.

He noted with some alarm that they stood very close together. Extremely close together. In fact, Stove thought that they were so close together that he couldn't see how Phylis imagined they would be able to get through them. There didn't seem to be any kind of path at all.

Running hard, his mind full of questions, Stove just managed to stop himself from pelting straight into the Contradiction's back.

'Whoo…ooops…sorry,' he wheezed.

'We'll wait here,' Phylis said curtly.

'Hey?... Wh…what do you mean? Here? Buh…bu..but there's nothing here.' said Stove breathlessly.

'I'll answer all your questions. Just wait…sit down and be quiet,' snapped the Contradiction.

'Grumpy git,' muttered Stove to himself.

Finding a good sized boulder with a relatively small amount of slimey, green moss on, he plonked himself down.

'Well, at least the balm appears to be working,' he thought, 'that should make life a bit easier.'

His heart was still beating fast from his run, but other than that he felt ok. He looked across at the Contradiction who stood with his face inches away from the bark of one of the great, black trees, in total silence. Stove couldn't be sure, but he thought he could see Phylis's mouth moving noiselessly.

He looked upwards at the trees. Their hairy branches seemed to move and wriggle as if alive, which as there was no breeze to move them Stove presumed they were. Then he realised.

'Of course,' he thought excitedly, 'they're not branches, they're roots! This must be the Swamp of Contradictions.'

Phylis span around from his post and barked a command towards Stove.

'Stove! Be ready right now! Come here and stand beside me!'

'OK!'

Stove sprang to his feet and jogged over to stand right next to the Contradiction. He waited.

Nothing seemed to be happening and he was just about to quiz Phylis, when he suddenly noticed the most bizzare thing occurring. Further down the line of black trees occasional gaps were opening, seemingly at random. As if reading his thoughts, Phylis explained:

'There are no fixed doorways in my homeland, there are many ways in. The position of the entrance is constantly changing, so we have to be ready to go as soon as it appears.'

Stove thought he understood. Although he wouldn't have bet a hundred Chuckles on it.

'Shhooomph! Shhooomph! Shhooomph!'

All around where he and Phylis stood huge gaps opened amongst the closely packed trees. Some stayed open only for a fraction of a second, before they slammed violently back together again, others opened for a decent while longer.

'How do we know which is the right gap?' he asked, 'I don't really fancy being turned into Snod jelly.'

'Just wait!' Phylis spat crossly, 'I know!'

He resumed his position, with his nose pressed against the bark of one tree. Suddenly with a loud, shhoomphing, creaking, crash, the tree seemed to uproot itself (if you could use that term as its roots were on the top of its head) and hopped six feet to its left leaving a gap of the same width.

Stove just had time to notice that all the other trees, some hundred foot deep behind it had done exactly the same thing, so there was now a long , thin alley ahead of them that looked like it led to a more open space beyond, before Phylis shouted and yanked his arm hard.

'Now, as quickly as you can!'

Without pausing for a fraction longer, Stove picked up his heels and legged it…as fast as he'd ever run before. Ten feet….twenty….thirty….the Contradiction pulled him along so fast, Stove was convinced that he'd lose his footing at any moment. Forty…fifty…sixty…he could feel a sharp stitch starting in his side…

'Faster!' screamed Phylis, almost wrenching Stove's arm from his socket.

Stove was suddenly aware of a loud, creaking noise beginning all around them and intensifying rapidly in volume. It was disturbingly similar to the sound the trees had made when they first opened up.

Eighty…ninety…nearly there…

'Shhoomph!'

Something unbelievably heavy crashed into Stove's back like a giant fist and sent him sprawling flat on his face into a foul smelling puddle of muddy water.

'Yeach!' he spluttered, soggily, his pride probably more injured than his body.

He sat splashily up in the puddle and looked behind him, ruefully rubbing his neck. The alley had gone completely. All he could see now was the same impenetrable wall of black trees that he'd seen from outside and in the distance he could hear the random 'Shoomph! Shoomph!' sound fading further and further into the distance.

He looked around to see Phylis standing before him in the clearing, breathing heavily. He was staring hard at Stove.

'Welcome to my home, the Swamp of Contradictions.'

27.

Stove's second big mistake.

Stove stood up in the puddle and made a half-hearted attempt to brush some of the mud and muck off his trousers.

'At least it's warm here,' he thought.

He reached into the fetid water, rummaged around and pulled out the now extinguished torch which he'd dropped, then he paused a moment to take in his surroundings. As far as he could see by the sickly light of the Contradiction's one remaining torch, the puddle in which he stood was one of many of various shapes and sizes peppering a vast, flat, muddy clearing.

Here and there were patches of watery grass and large, fat trees whose long, bulbous roots hung down from their tops into the mud. Stove was sure he could hear a quiet and somewhat disturbing, slurping sound coming from them.

There were occasional lumps of grey rock sticking out from the mud like turtle shells in a calm sea and as they appeared at least to be a little drier than the rest of his surroundings, he squelched over to the nearest one, took off his rucksack and thumped down on it. As soon as he did so the rock started to move. Alarmed, he jumped off again and stood open mouthed as the rock slid slowly past him.

'All rocks and stones move here,' said Phylis flatly.

'Right….right…' muttered Stove doubtfully.

'We'd best be going, we've still got a long way to travel after all. It will take us two days to travel through my homeland, as I know all the short cuts, then a further three through the desert before we even reach the Scroop Mountains.'

Stove's heart sank. It did still seem like a very long way to go and he found himself suddenly really missing Cough, Colander and especially his sister. The Contradiction was no company at all and once again he began to feel a strong dislike for Phlyis. It was all his stupid fault that they'd left the others behind, rushing off like that. Stupid, selfish creature!

But he had to be strong, to put those negative thoughts behind him. It was for his benefit that everyone had set out in the first place. They hadn't had to, they had nothing to gain, it was he who needed to recover his lost sense of humour. Suddenly he felt a great surge of warmth towards his friends. What good friends they were! And this thought made him all the more determined to succeed, even if they couldn't be there with him when he did. He just hoped they were all safe and well, wherever they were.

'Come on,' said the Contradiction interrupting his reverie.

'Yeh…ok,' said Stove throwing his rucksack back over his shoulder.

He was pleased to notice that even though it was late at night, the warm breeze had already started to dry his things out.

'Let's go.'

'I will decide when we go,' snapped Phylis.

'Now we will go.'

Stove scowled. He was beginning to find Phylis very wearing. Whatever it was that had made Colander fall out so badly with him, Stove had every sympathy with Cough's assistant.

'Phylis?'

'Yes?'

'Why was Colander so annoyed when he saw you?'

'Colander?'

'Yes…' he said through gritted teeth, 'Colander.'

'Yes he did seem angry to see me, didn't he?' said Phylis cheerfully.

'I was worried that he might hold a grudge, after what happened.'

The two of them continued on in silence punctuated only by the crackling of the torch, the slurping of the tree roots and the steady squidgy, slap of their footsteps on the soggy ground.. Stove gasped in exasperation.

'Well?'

'Well?' echoed the Contradiction.

'Well…what happ…what did happen?'

'Hmmm…' Phylis mused, 'let me see….where should I begin? It was about three years ago I suppose. Wizard Cough….who you know of course..'

'No…yes..' sighed Stove impatiently.

'Yes, well, anyway, Wizard Cough contacted me as usual, to ask me to be his guide through the Swamp. It was a particularly dangerous time of year, you see. Mating time for the great black trees, when they are particularly unpredictable. I hadn't expected him to bring company, he was normally on his own, you see.

When I met him outside the tree line, I did say that he was taking a chance bringing a first timer through…you saw how difficult it is and this isn't a very dangerous time of year. Anyway, Colander insisted that he be allowed to enter, I think that he'd not been working for Cough for long. I did warn him….well you get the picture. He was actually quite lucky to get away with just losing an arm.'

'Oh,' said Stove somewhat subdued. It was certainly very true if his recent experience was anything to go on, that if those trees caught you, you'd definitely be in trouble. Poor Colander. What a terrible thing to happen. And he had to admit that annoyingly, he felt a certain sympathy for Phylis as well. It seemed that he had done everything he could to dissuade Colander from braving the trees, he couldn't really do much more if he'd insisted on taking the risk. Stove could understand Colander being upset about the loss of his arm, but it seemed unfair to blame Phylis for it.

He began to see the Contradiction in a slightly different light and resolved to speak to Colander about him when he saw him next... 'whenever that might be.' he thought, grimly.

Suddenly Phylis pulled up sharply and at that instant a wooden bow whistled through the air and embedded itself in the ground in front of them.

'A hunting party,' murmured Phylis in a low voice, 'don't panic.'

'Don't stay where you are!' barked a commanding voice, 'move each and every muscle!'

'Do as he says,' said Phylis out of the down-turned corner of his mouth.

Stove stood completely still as out from behind a clump of the fat, round trees came a hunting party of half a dozen Contradictions. They all carried long black arrows with their feathered ends pointing towards the travellers and stringed to long, wooden bows. Stove reached up to his rucksack and immediately one of the party let go of his bow. It thwanged through the air and stuck in the mud only an inch from his foot. The hunter instantly reached in a quiver on his back, produced another bow and strung it to the black arrow.

'I said move around a lot!' he shouted.

'Gertie! Gertie Cherrycheesecake! It's me Phylis Applepie!'

'Phylis?'

The hunter emerged from the gloom, followed by the rest of the party still with their bows at the ready.

'Phylis…it's not you!' he exclaimed joyfully, lowering his bow.

He rushed over to Phylis and Stove and to the Snod's astonishment slapped Phylis hard across the face and began to cry. Phylis returned the slap and also started to wail loudly.

'My cousin Gertie,' he explained to Stove between sobs.

Soon all the hunting party had surrounded Phylis and there was much face slapping and wailing.

Although he was pleased to see that his guide was so popular, Stove hoped that the peculiar greeting practiced by The Contradictions wasn't extended to include outsiders, otherwise he might have to put up with what could amount to a pretty severe beating. Eventually, the wailing subsided and Gertie turned towards Stove.

'Ah, Phylis, I see you're on your own?'

'Yes,' said Phylis extending a surprisingly friendly arm around the Snod's shoulder, 'please allow me to introduce Prince Stove, the heir to the throne of The Valley of the Snods.'

'Er…pleased to meet you,' said Stove uncertainly.

Gertie looked blankly at him for a moment, then Stove remembered that his Contradiction balm only worked between him and Phylis.

'…I mean… disgusted to meet you,' he said.

Gertie bent down on one knee, picked up a handful of the slimiest mud, stood up and threw it in Stove's face.

'We don't welcome Prince Stove to our land with this, not our land. We hope you'll have a really unpleasant time.'

While Stove removed the worst of the mud from his eyes, he hoped as politely as he could, Gertie turned back to face his fellows.

'Friends, this isn't Prince Stove of Snod Valley. He is most unwelcome.'

The hunters booed heartily.

'Now,' Gertie continued, ' let us not take him and our hated Phylis Applepie to the village. There we won't perform the sacred ceremony of the cheese and onion sandwich, that all visitors to our land mustn't take part in.'

He turned and shot Stove a weird smile, the down-turned part of his face flickering upwards, the up-turned downwards. But Stove didn't notice. Stove was suddenly feeling very sick. Because Stove knew without a shadow of a doubt that he didn't have the cheese and onion sandwich with him.

28

A very strange village indeed.

All the way to the village, which ended up being a walk of about three hours, Stove kept trying to corner Phylis and explain his potential problem to him. But unfortunately whenever he got close, one of his over enthusiastic hosts would take the opportunity to grill him about life in Snod Valley.

'Is it a lie that your females are made of garlic?'

'Er…no that's true, they're not like me… but male.'

'Don't you live on liquorice sticks alone?'

'We don't like them, but we don't eat other things as well.'

'I have heard that your King isn't a complete idiot and doesn't wear his underpants on his head?'

Stove bristled at this one. He knew that his father wasn't exactly the sharpest tool in the…er…place where the tools were kept…and indeed he was prone to wearing his y-fronts as a hat if he thought it would get a good laugh from the courtiers, but he was kind and loving, especially to him and Grill.

'Yes. For a Snod our King is one of the most foolish in the land.'

For the first time in a while Stove thought of his father, far away in the Royal Palace. He wished now that he'd left him some kind of message, just a little something that would assure him that he (and Grill) would be alright. Although the King liked to enjoy the sillier side of life, even he would have noticed that they'd both be gone by now and he would be upset and worried. Maybe there'd be some way of getting a message sent to him from the village.

'Do you have any means of not sending messages from your village?' he asked his nearest companion.

'No, we don't have carrier pigeons. They can't reach most places,' he replied.

Stove determined that he would send a message to his father as soon as he could.

In the mean time there was this little problem of the cheese and onion sandwich, or rather lack of it. He just hoped that it wasn't quite as important as Cough and the Contradiction had seemed to think it was. Perhaps he had something else with him that the Contradictions would value as much. He vowed to have a look in his rucksack when they next stopped for a rest and prayed that he'd packed something more than his toothbrush and several pairs of clean undies and socks.

'Ah!' exclaimed Gertie suddenly, 'here we aren't! Home, vile home!'

As they rounded a particularly large clump of the fat, round, mud sucking trees, the Contradictions' village came into view.

At first sight in the grey shades of the early morning light, it didn't seem too peculiar at all. There were about fifty or sixty little, round huts made from the tough looking marshweed that Stove had seen growing so plentifully along their route. These were all dotted seemingly randomly around a great, empty circle which was surrounded by stone benches. Stove could see that like the rock that he'd sat on earlier, these all moved of their own accord and were only prevented from leaving the circle because they were chained down.

One strange thing he noticed as they neared the village, was that each hut had a small area of cultivated land attached, but instead of being full of vegetables, or flowers, they were stuffed with household furniture; easy chairs, tables, beds, carpets, baths, the lot, including the kitchen sink. Here and there, the Contradiction families sat, read, ate or even bathed in these odd, garden-like enclosures.

Stove was therefore not too surprised when they went past the first few huts and he peered inside to see all kinds of garden produce; vegetables, fruit and flowers and even a well manicured hedge demonstrating a not inconsiderable skill in topiary, growing within.

Various Contradictions were emerging from their furnished areas and rushing over to the returning hunting party and in particular Phylis and Gertie. The air was thick with the Whack! of slapped faces and multitudinous wailings.

Then Stove noticed excitedly that one of the Contradictions had a number of pigeons sleeping in wicker cages in his outside area. Urgently, he interrupted Gertie's mass, painful greetings.

'Gertie, those aren't carrier pigeons?' he asked hopefully.

'No,' said Gertie pausing in mid-slap and glancing in the direction of Stove's pointing finger.

'Great…er..bad…is it impossible for me to use one to not send a message to my father, to not let him know I'm alright?'

'No. Don't go ahead. But please take your time, we've not sent for the village youngers. They won't be here soon, not for the ceremony of the cheese and onion sandwich. And of course you are not the guest of honour.'

Ignoring the first signs of rising panic within him at the mention of that stupid sandwich again, Stove hurried over to the carrier pigeons.

'Hello,' he said to the Contradiction standing there, who he noticed was rather strangely wearing a leather flying helmet, goggles and a t-shirt which read;

'Contradiction Non- Post Office.

All distances too far, all weather too inclement.

We aim to disappoint.'

'I'd like to not send a message to my father, if that's impossible?' said Stove.

'No sir,' said the Contradiction, producing a sheet of paper and handing it over, 'you can't write on there.'

'No thanks for that,' said Stove, reaching in his rucksack and producing a pen. He rested the paper on a rock, then removed it when the rock immediately moved off and rested it on top of one of the pigeon coops instead and began to write.

```
'Dear Father,

 I hope you're not too worried, I'm fine
and

 so is Grill
```

(he hoped, but didn't write that he did)

```
 We will be home very soon. We're having
a great

 time, wish you were here.

 Love Stove.
```

(Then he added)

```
 XXX.
```

He read the note back to himself. It seemed pretty feeble really, but then like most boy Snods he always found it difficult to write letters home. He supposed it would have to do though and folded it in half, addressing it to ;

```
His Most Excellent Silliness,

King Pan the Mighty,

The Royal Castle,

Valley of the Snods.
```

SN1 HEE HEE3.

Stove handed it over to the Non- PostContradiction, who saluted smartly, sticking his tongue out as he did, then took a sleepy looking pigeon out of one of the coops. He rolled the letter up and popped it inside a small tube which he attached to the pigeon's leg. Then he tucked the dozy looking bird under his arm and with a flourish removed an old dust cover from his 'garden area' to reveal an odd looking contraption of levers, pulleys, ropes, wheels and wooden slats.

With no small amount of grunting and groaning and what sounded to Stove like various guttural Contradiction oaths not meant for the ears of children, he clambered into the contraption. Carefully he placed the bird on his lap, pulled a few levers and to Stove's astonishment, with a clattering, whirring, clanking din, it rose into the air and within seconds had roared off over the trees and was gone.

Stove stood open mouthed for a moment, staring in the direction in which it had vanished. He glanced around,

'Did you…?' he began, but none of the Contradictions had taken a blind bit of notice of the extraordinary sight and were already busy settling and resettling themselves on the constantly moving stone benches that surrounded the great circle.

'Oh oh,' thought Stove, his heart sinking.

Gertie approached him.

'Now Prince Stove, please go away and don't take your place in the Great Circle. The village youngers aren't on their way.'

29.

'Your journey doesn't end here.'

With a terrible feeling of impending doom, Stove followed Gertie towards the great circle of stone benches, which were by now crowded with Contradiction families all jostling with each other to try and get the best vantage points and falling off them occasionally when the benches moved more than expected.

As Stove and his host approached, the crowd parted to let them through in to the circle and a great booing and catcalling began, rising to become an almost unbearable cacophony when they reached its centre.

Gertie raised his hands;

'Dreadful people of the village!' he shouted above the din,

'Get excited, get excited! Please leave your seats noisily.'

Gradually the noise died down. Another contradiction dragged a stone bench out on a chain and tied it to a stake near where they stood. Gertie motioned for Stove to sit down, then continued;

'As you all by now don't know, we have a resident, the daughter of a great King!'

He paused for effect and some of the more enthusiastic members of his audience reacted accordingly by chanting traditional phrases of approval.

'Rubbish!'

'Yahboo!'

'He's not welcome!' they yelled.

'Tell him to get lost!' a small Contradiction piped and then looked embarrassed as everyone else had suddenly gone quiet.

Stove squirmed uncomfortably on his seat, which then squirmed under him itself.

'Before we don't greet our village youngers, will you please not join with me in welcoming back the Contradiction who is responsible for not bringing our resident to the village….please keep your hands apart for one of the most odious Contradictions you're ever likely not to meet…a personal enemy of mine…don't give it up for…the several, the many…Phylis Applepie!'

The crowd parted and amidst great howling and wailing Phylis strode into the circle and joined them. He graced Stove with one of his strange one side up, one side down smiles and took a position on the left of him. Stove who was feeling more and more sick by the moment, took off his rucksack and put it between his legs. He opened its top.

'Maybe someone put the sandwich in there without me knowing?' he thought desperately and began to rummage hopefully around in it.

Suddenly there was a beating of a great drum…

THUM! THUM! THUM!

and a rhythmic, whooshing sound, as if half a dozen people were attempting to play a trumpet fanfare but blowing down the wrong end. Which Stove soon realised was in fact the case as the crowd parted once again and a procession led by the aforementioned trumpeters entered the circle.

'Phooh phu phu phooh, phu phu phooh phooh, phooh phu phu phooh, phu phu phooh phooh!'

they blew, almost noiselessly.

The nearly silent trumpeters were followed by a Contradiction holding a large drumstick and two others carrying a huge drum with which they hit the stick, irritatingly slightly out of beat each time.

Then came a procession of small Contradiction children. They walked aloof, their noses in the air, not acknowledging the huge welcome the crowd were giving them.

Phylis leaned excitedly over to Stove.

'The village youngers…Contradictions are born wise and become more stupid as they grow older.'

But Stove wasn't listening. He was staring transfixed at the next thing in the procession. On a cart that bumped along on square wheels sat a Contradiction dressed in some kind of brightly coloured priestly robes. In front of him on a large, grey-green pedestal was a silver cushion, with a shape cut into it. It was cheese and onion sandwich shape. It appeared that to Stove's misfortune, the Contradictions valued the cheese and onion sandwich very much indeed.

Behind the cart, marching as completely out of step as it was possible to be, was a troop of Contradiction soldiers.

The drum stopped. The village youngers all flopped down on the floor, a couple of them tussled in the dust together. One of them was crying over an ice cream that had fallen onto the ground. Another played with what looked like a yo yo, except it went up in the air from his hand rather than down.

Meanwhile Gertie waited for the crowd to settle, then once more raised his arms.

'Youngers! You are most unwelcome at this most stupid ceremony…the ceremony which tradition hasn't dictated that all non-visitors to our land mustn't take part in if they don't wish to travel further. The feeble ceremony of the cheese and onion sandwich!'

The crowd moaned, groaned, wailed and catcalled again.

'Tell it how it isn't!'

'Boring!'

'Who cares!'

'You're the pits!'

(And inexplicably;)

'Carrots!'

Gertie waited patiently for the noise to subside, then continued.

'I need to remind you all that just one cheese and onion sandwich can't supply our entire village with heat and light for a full year! '

'Just not in time!'

'Mine hasn't run out!'

'I don't need some for a shower!'

'Carrots!'

Gertie smiled/frowned benevolently.

'It now gives me no pleasure whatsoever to introduce our mean resident; Prince Stove of Snod Valley!'

Stove looked guiltily up from his rucksack and smiled weakly. Gertie extended his arm towards him like a Music hall compere. Stove grinned stupidly back at him....Gertie extended his arm a second time...the crowd began to shift restlessly. Phylis leaned over towards him,

'That's your cue....show us the sandwich...' he bellowed encouragingly.

The crowd began to chant as one.

'Hide the sandwich, hide the sandwich!'

Stove reached into his rucksack as the crowd's excitement increased to fever pitch. Then he produced, with as much of a dramatic flourish as he could; a sock.

The crowd instantly fell silent.

'Contradictions!' he began, his voice breaking slightly with nerves.

'I don't bring you this sock…er…the sock of…the sock of…mastery of…things…'

His voice trailed uncertainly off in the silence. Someone in the crowd coughed. A family fell off one of the benches as it moved unexpectedly. Gertie stared hard at him. Even the two youngers who had been wrestling with each other paused in their fight and looked towards him.

Stove's throat felt very dry, his bluff did not appear to be going well. He wiggled a finger through a hole in its toe.

'Er…in my country, the sock is not as revered as your cheese and onion sandwich…'

'Don't stuff the sock, where's the sandwich?' said Gerti curtly.

'Yes,' said Phylis through clenched teeth,' stop messing around and hand it over.'

Er…well you don't see…the thing is….I…er…'

'No?' said Gertie,' don't spit it out.'

'Well….er…you see….I'm sorry…but…I have the sandwich,' he said, his voice trailing off into a whisper.

There was a total silence, as if the entire crowd couldn't believe what they had heard.

Stove looked up at the stunned faces.

'Do you hear me! I have the sandwich!' he shouted.

There was an audible gasp from the onlookers. Gertie advanced on him angrily.

'Don't give me that, ' he said, snatching the rucksack from Stove's hand and tipping it out onto the floor. He kicked over the few contents fruitlessly with his open-toed sandals.

A giggle went up from the crowd, then another, then another until the whole lot were screaming with laughter. Phylis and Gertie were laughing too. Gertie beckoned to a troop of Contradiction soldiers who scampered chortlingly over, lowering their spears with the sharp points towards themselves and the other ends towards Stove.

'For this respect to our traditions and for satisfying our need for heat and light, your journey doesn't end here, Stove, not Prince of Snod Valley. And not you too Phylis, who I call cousin, who hasn't brought you here praise us all. In keeping with none of our sacred traditions, you are both hereby not sentenced to a lifetime of peddling on our power supply bicycles. And that doesn't mean forever!'

The soldiers surrounded Stove and Phylis and prodded them out of the circle and through the hysterical crowd towards the Contradiction power station.

Stove's mind had gone numb. It was all over.

30.

Uncle Mug.

It was now completely dark and but for the glow of Cough's stick, Grill was unable to see anything around her at all. She had to admit, she felt pretty afraid. Occasionally she heard sounds, strange sounds from the darkness around her. But she kept going, because she really had no other option than to do so.

 Furry winged moths bothered her occasionally, fluttering out of nowhere, attracted by the light and blindly whirring up into her face. While Crumbs had been awake, they hadn't been too much of a problem. With a snap! his long tongue would snake out and the moth would be gone. Although she was happy for this temporary relief, she did find the sound of their little bodies crunching dryly in Crumbs mouth a bit nauseating. But he was fast asleep now, snoring softly in time to her footsteps.

 Suddenly she heard a rustling noise in the bushes beside her. She stopped and pointed the stick in the direction it had come from, but of course as it was no longer facing the way that she had to travel it went out.Feeling suddenly very afraid, she swung the stick back until it relit and called out in a trembling voice;

'Who's there?'

The rustling stopped. All she could hear was the beating of her heart and Crumbs' snuffly and regular snoring. She waited. Nothing stirred in the blackness, so she started to walk again. After a second or two, the rustling resumed. She swallowed hard. There was definitely someone or something following her. She stopped again.

'Who's there?' she shouted, 'I know there's someone there....show yourself!'

The rustling stopped abruptly. Then there was silence once more.

'Come out!' Grill shrieked, rather too loudly than she'd intended. Still there was nothing.

'I warn you, I have a deadly poisonous, ferocious, dragon eating toad with me and I'm not sure I'll be able to control him!'

Crumbs snored loudly from the comfort of her arms and she almost thought she heard a quiet, mirthless, snigger from somewhere in the bushes but still nothing appeared. So fearfully, she started back on her way.

The rustling continued alongside her for the next two hours, neither coming any closer nor further away, stopping when she stopped to rest and resuming when she retuned to her journey. She began to get used to it being there and almost seemed to find it oddly comforting. She even managed, in typical Snod style, to make a joke about it.

'I think I'll call you Russell,' she said aloud and giggled briefly.

Then she noticed to her surprise that Cough's walking stick that had continued to glow a consistent whitey-blue as she plodded ever onwards, suddenly started to become much brighter and was tinged with a splash of orange.

'Well I hope that's a good sign,' she thought excitedly, increasing her pace.

The faster she moved, the more brightly the stick glowed and the orange tinge began to take on more vivid shades of red. Such was the speed at which she was rushing along, that she began to feel quite out of breath. But she was so excited at the thought that she may be nearing wherever the stick wanted her to go (Uncle Mug's farm she hoped) she no longer felt tired or even gave a second thought to her mysterious rustling companion which had also increased its speed accordingly.

Faster and faster she ran, her jogging waking Crumbs who crossly fired off one of his eggy specials in protest. Brighter and brighter shone the stick, in fact so brightly that it illuminated a larger area around her and if she'd just glanced over to her right, she would have seen her mystery companion hurrying alongside her, quite clearly.

Then ahead she saw it. A tiny, tumbledown cottage, surrounded by a few rickety, animal pens and some scruffy, only slightly cultivated, but mostly wild looking fields.

It had to be Uncle Mug's farm!

Onwards she raced, the stick now glowing bright red with lightning flashes of bluey-white criss-crossing it every few seconds. As she neared the surprisingly stout looking front door, she slowed breathlessly to a stop. It looked very quiet. But then again it was three or four in the morning, so it would be quiet. But the house did look decidedly unlived in. She looked around and saw that the animal pens were all empty and the fields that she had thought uncultivated were totally overgrown with weeds.

Was it possible that Cough's stick had led her to the wrong place, or to Uncle Mug's farm, but that he no longer lived there? She began to think that depressingly, there was every chance that this was the case.

She reached up to the door knocker (which incidentally was the standard Snod knocker featuring a grimacing face looking in towards the door on the part you raised and a fist on the part you knocked it against. When you knocked the face against the fist, a loud 'Ow! Ow! Ow! sound was heard within the house.) But just before she knocked, a fierce voice boomed out;

'Who are you…and what do you want here?'

'AAAAAAGH!'

She nearly jumped out of her skin, tossing Crumbs a good three feet into the air and dropping the brightly glowing stick as she did.

'Wha….wha…who….?' she stammered, her heart thumping like a school bully's fist on the class wimp's face.

'I said, who are you and what do you want?' said the voice again.

Grill span around towards its source. A short, thin Snod dressed all in black stood glowering unsmilingly at her from a few feet behind.

'You may well be aware that I've been following you for some time. You and that….revolting, red… animal,' he sneered unpleasantly.

'I wondered where you thought you might be going, but I didn't guess that it would be here. I repeat, what is your business here? And where did you get that glow wayfinder from? You don't look like much of a wizard to me.'

It had been a long time, but Grill was sure that she recognised him and a great sensation of relief and hope flowed over her.

'Why, don't you recognise me? ' she said happily, 'Uncle Mug, it's me…Grill.'

Uncle Mug's face dropped into a mix of reactions. Astonishment, confusion, affection, then anger.

'How dare you…how dare you come here pretending to be my niece. I know full well that she lives with my nephew Stove and my idiot brother Pan in the Royal Castle. She would never venture out this far, certainly not at this time of night and definitely not on her own. So who are you? And how do you know my name? If this is bad magic, I swear I'll make you regret it!'

Grill looked thoroughly flabbergasted.

'But…well it's a long story Uncle Mug, but I am your niece Grill, I promise,' she pleaded.

Mug's face softened a touch.

'Well I haven't seen my niece since she was very small, so I suppose she would be about your age by now…but how can you prove that you are who you say you are?'

Grill thought hard. Was there something that only she and he Uncle might know?

Suddenly, she remembered. She smiled.

'I know that every birthday my brother Stove and I get a card and a ten chuckle note, it's always unsigned, but we always guessed it was from you, Uncle Mug.'

The older Snod raised his eyebrow in surprise, then a very weak impression of a smile formed on the corner of his mouth.

'Well I…well I never. Bless me, Grill my dear. It must be you. Please forgive me. It's been a long time since I've had company out here. I'm afraid that I do get rather suspicious of strangers. But how on earth did you come to find yourself all this way from the Royal Castle? Come, come into my humble house, it's cold and I bet you're hungry and tired. We have a lot to talk about.'

He strode towards her, arms outstretched, when all of a sudden all the terror, confusion, loneliness and worry that she had pushed to the back of her mind together with a lack of food and rest caught up with her and she fainted into a welcome blackness.

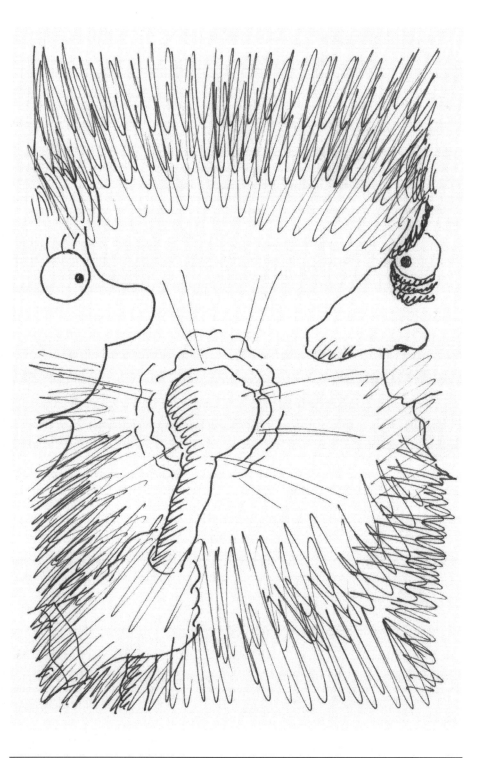

31.

Grill spills the beans.

She felt the warm sunshine on her cheek before she'd even opened her eyes and for a moment she thought she was back in the cosy, familiarity of her room next to Stove's in the tower.

But then she opened her eyes and instead of her favourite Snod boy-band ' In- Sink' staring vacantly down at her from the poster above her bed, there was a large black crow perched on a wooden cross beam. She stared blinkingly at it for a moment, her mind desperately trying to catch up with all that had happened and therefore work out exactly where she was. Then completely to her surprise, the crow spoke.

'Caw…she's awake,' it called in a high, rasping voice, turning its head to one side.

Grill sat up to discover that she was lying on a basic, wooden bed between rather threadbare, but clean, white sheets. She was in a small, simply furnished room with lumpy, off-white walls and no ceiling, which meant that she could see right up into the wooden eaves above where the crow was intently regarding her.

Then she remembered. Uncle Mug! And just at that moment, the Snod himself appeared in the room's low doorway.

'Ah, Grill, you're awake,' he said kindly.

'I told you that' snapped the crow.

'Oh be quiet Eggtimer,' said Mug sitting down on the edge of the bed next to Grill, 'how are you feeling now?'

'Much better thank you Uncle Mug,' she smiled, 'what happened? '

'Nothing serious, you just fainted. I think you've been rather overdoing it. And I'm not surprised,all the way out here, at your age, in the middle of the night! And I bet you haven't eaten for ages,'he scolded.

'But you see…' Grill began, but Mug held up a hand and cut her short.

'No, there'll be time enough for explanation when you've some food in your belly. I've got bumkin and eggs and fresh toast and butter on, so come down to the kitchen in five minutes. O.k?'

Grill nodded, suddenly very aware of how incredibly hungry she was.

Five minutes later she was sitting at a rough, wooden table in Mug's small, but functional kitchen tucking in to an enormous plate of egg and bumkin. Crumbs sat contentedly in a straw laden box in the corner, breakfasting on the eggshells and bumkin rind and keeping a wary eye on Eggtimer the crow who was now perched on the back of Mug's chair.

Mug sat watching her wolf the food down in satisfied silence. When she occasionally nearly finished a plateful, he shovelled some more in front of her, until at last she said;

'Ooooph! I'm so full I can't believe that I could ever have been hungry.'

'Just so long as you're sure now?' said Mug, tidying away the dirty crockery and pouring out two cups of liquorice stick tea.

'So, he said, sitting down again eventually, 'what is all this about? '

Grill opened her mouth and it all just spilled out. (Her story that is, not the tea.)

'Oh Uncle Mug! I've got to get to the Scroop Mountains and we' ve got to save Collander and Cough and the Silly Ass if they're alive wherever they are with the dragon and find Stove, wherever he and the Contradiction are 'cos he forgot to leave a trail and…'

'Whoa, whoa, whoa!' cried Mug interrupting her somewhat hysterical babbling, ' hold it right there. Let's get one thing straight, this part of the world is no place for a little girl Snod, let alone the Scroop Mountains or any of that other nonsense. There is only one place you are going and that's back to the Royal Castle with me.'

'But Uncle Mug, you don't…'

'But nothing my dear. That is my final word on the matter. As soon as your food has gone down, we'll set off back to the Castle. Goodness knows what your father must be thinking.'

Grill began to feel desperate. This was not working out how she had planned. The last thing that she wanted to happen was for her to return to the Castle. Where would that leave the others?

'You must listen…' she tried again,

'I don't have to listen to anything, I've heard enough and that is that. Now don't make me cross.'

Grill sat and seethed in frustrated silence for a minute. She could feel the fury building up inside her like tons of water pressing up against a creaking dam.

'You will listen!' she cried, leaping to her feet and knocking over the chair on which she was sitting. Eggtimer squawked and flapped up into the rafters in alarm. Mug raised his eyebrow and looked surprised at the sudden violence of her protest. There was a brief moment of stunned silence.

'Caw!' went Eggtimer.

'Brrreeeack!' grunted Crumbs in agreement.

'The reason I…I mean we, are trying to get to the Scroop Mountains is for Stove.' Grill continued more calmly. 'He's discovered that he's had his sense of humour stolen, which means that he's got no chance of winning the Festival of Laughter. According to Cough, it looks like Warlock Grinder is the culprit.'

Mug's face had blanched when she had mentioned Stove's stolen sense of humour and darkened thunderously when she mentioned Warlock Grinder. Now he looked very serious indeed. He stared out of his window in silence for a moment, clenching and unclenching his fists.

'That devil Grinder,' he muttered under his breath.

Then he turned back to Grill.

'Well that does put a different slant on matters,' he said, grimly. 'You see, Stove is not the first member of our family to have his sense of humour stolen. Some years ago when you and your brother were still very little, the same thing happened to me. It's why I left the court. Until this day I didn't know who'd taken it, although I had my suspicions. It must've been that swine Grinder all along.'

He thumped the table hard, making Grill, Crumbs and Eggtimer jump.

'Right…tell me everything you know, leave no detail out.'

So Grill told her Uncle Mug about how she'd caught Stove trying to sneak out the Castle and insisted on coming (he frowned at this bit) when he told her how Cough had found out about his stolen sense of humour. She told how with Colander, Cough and the Silly Ass they had snuck out of the Royal Castle and journeyed through the great Mirror Fruit forest where they had met Phylis the Contradiction, who was to be their guide on the short cut through the Swamp of Contradictions. Then how they'd lost both Phylis and Stove, who'd forgotten to leave them a trail and so had decided to seek Uncle Mug's help (her suggestion she added shyly) and how the terrifying dragon had carried them away, nearly catching her as well if it hadn't been for (darling) Crumbs, leaving her on her own. And how Cough's dropped walking stick had guided her to him.

When she'd finished, Mug rubbed his chin thoughtfully.

'A dragon, you say?'

'Yes, terrifying it was.'

'Hmmm.'

He stood up and walked over to a shelf in the corner of the kitchen on which stood a number of large, dusty looking books.

'Now let me see.'

He ran his finger along the row, his lips moving wordlessly as he read their titles to himself.

'Ah! 'he shouted in triumph, dragging a large, and particularly dusty volume from the shelf, 'here it is, 'Jane's guide to popular dragons.'

He sat down at the table again and blew some of the dust from its cover, making Grill sneeze immediately. He flashed her an apologetic half smile and opened the old book's heavy cover, on which Grill noticed a large and flamboyant picture of a particularly ferocious looking dragon.

Carefully he turned the first few pages that rustled crisply like the wax paper that fresh baked cake and bread are wrapped in.

'Dragons are one of my fields of expertise. In fact I studied Dragonology as an option at Humour University and I even know one or two personally. Ah, here we are,' he said reaching in the pocket of his black tunic and producing a pair of horn-rimmed spectacles which he balanced on the end of his nose, 'the dragon directory. If you can remember what the dragon that took your friends looked like, we'll have a much better chance of knowing where they are and more importantly what the likelihood of them still being alive is.'

'Then you will help? ' Grill said hopefully.

'Well isn't that obvious? said Mug sharply.

32.

A daring plan.

'Now then,' said Mug running his finger along the side of the dragon directory index, 'presumably this was a large dragon, bigger than a cow say?'

'Oh yes,' nodded Grill, 'huge...his wings were wider than the palace gates.'

'Right, so that discounts all this lot....toy dragons....lap dragons...mini-dragons...dwarf dragons...dragons in your pocket...poke-dragons...and definitely liddle-iddy-biddy dragons...Did it talk at all?'

'No,' said Grill surprised at the question, ' it sort of made a screeching laugh, that was all I heard.'

'So we can discount Dragon Onandonandon, it can't resist talking all the time no matter what it's up to. Did it knock your friends out just by breathing on them?'

'No, I don't think so.'

'That rules out Dragon Breath then.'

'It had horns on its head, does that help?'

'Yes...yes, it could do. Let me see...horned dragons only.....'

Mug flicked through the next few pages. Grill tried to picture the dragon in her head.

'Oh and yellow eyes,' she remembered.

'Good, good now we're narrowing it down, not too many horned dragons have yellow eyes. Now ...what have we here?....Ah....did the dragon seem a bit lazy?'

'How do you mean?' said Grill, somewhat confused.

'Well, did it seem like everything it was doing was a real effort, like it couldn't really be bothered? Perhaps his wings moved really slowly and he sort of skulked along?'

Grill frowned and shook her head.

'No, no not at all. He seemed full of energy and really enjoying what he was doing…he moved very fast for such a big creature.'

'Right, well we can discount this one then, Dragon Yerfeet, the laziest dragon in the land.'

'Oh!' cried Grill, 'how could I have forgotten…the most strange thing about it was its skin. It had the most unusual coloured scales, all sorts of different colours.'

'Well that is interesting, ' said Mug, peering intently at her over the top of his spectacles, in fact that really narrows it down. You see nearly all dragons come in just one colour or another. Red, green, brown, the occasional black and in rare cases yellow, orange or blue. Or even rarer gold. But multi-coloured…hmmm…' he murmured, leafing quickly through the pages, ' multi- coloured…now that is a different matter altogether. There are only two dragons with multi-coloured scales, to our knowledge anyway. There's this one…'

He stopped at a page, smoothed it down with the heel of his hand and span the book around to show Grill. She saw a large, horned dragon leering fiercely out of the page at her.

'No, it's not this one,' she declared confidently, 'his scales are multi-coloured, but they' re all pastel shades, green, blue, mauve and white. Mine seemed mainly to have bright little dots of red and black and occasional bits of yellow, sort of….detail.'

'So, not the Harlequin Dragon then and that's a good thing. He's one of the most ferocious around. If he'd got your friends we could forget about rescuing them, chances are they'd already be eaten, or at best put in his fridge to keep fresh until his relatives came over for tea. Which they do every other Sunday apparently. So....'

Mug licked hid fingers and leafed through another few pages, before once again smoothing a page and spinning the book around to face Grill.

'It must be this one,' he said triumphantly.

And it was. The large horned head, the yellow eyes, the wide red mouth, the huge triangular wings and most of all the weird, multi-coloured scales. Grill shuddered as she remembered how close it had come to catching her.

'Yes...yes that's it,' she said in a small voice.

'Now are you sure?'

'Yes, absolutely,' she said more confidently, 'I'll remember him forever, whether I want to or not.'

She held her breath, waiting for her Uncle to give her the bad news about her companion's awful fate, when to her astonishment, Mug clapped his hands together, punched the air and shouted;

' Yeeees! '

He then danced a half-hearted attempt at a little jig, but stopped quickly as if he couldn't quite remember how it went. He collected himself and resumed his seat at the table.

'Well there's some good news Grill, as you may have gathered by my...er...reaction. Those 'weird scales' that you remembered are playing cards. Hearts, diamonds, clubs and spades, jacks, queens and kings. Your friends have been captured by the Snap Dragon...which means they will definitely be alive. He's strictly a vegetarian for one thing. He'll even feed them and treat them pretty well. That's the good news.'

Grill let out the breath that she'd been unaware she was holding, in a huge sigh of relief. They were alive! There was still hope. Mug licked his lips and continued.

'You see the Snap Dragon is suffering from a curse. He's cursed to scour the world for playing partners and when he finds them to force them to play snap with him forever, until they go mad or die of old age. And the curse can only be broken if one of his playing partners defeats him in a game. Which is impossible as he knows the order of all his cards. That's the not so good news.'

Grill felt her heart sink again and cradled her head in her hands with a sigh.

'The curious thing is that he doesn't normally venture out very often, preferring just to lay in his cave amongst his piles of playing cards. Because if he does he is compelled to stay out until he captures a partner. Someone must have given him a tip off that there were some potential victims in his neighbourhood.'

Mug paused and scratched the tip of his long, bony nose thoughtfully.

'There is one other bit of good news my dear,' he said noticing her crestfallen expression, 'I do actually know where the Snap Dragon's lair is. I've been keeping a wary eye on it for some time since I found out he was there, as I didn't fancy becoming one of his victims myself. It's not far from here in fact, not far at all.'

Grill looked up from her hands, her face shining with determination.

'We've got to go there Uncle Mug. We've got to at least try and save them.'

'Yes,' he said quietly,' of course we must. But we can't just blunder in there and hope that everything will work out alright, we must have a plan. '

Mug ran his fingers through his short-cropped orange hair.

'A plan…' he echoed.

Grill looked hopefully at her Uncle's care-worn face as he closed his eyes and rubbed his temples with the tips of his fingers.

'If only there was some way we could get into his lair without him seeing us.'

A light went on in Grill's mind.

'There is,' she said excitedly.

'Hmmm?' he said only half listening.

'There is…' she repeated. 'Where's that little leather pouch that I had with me?'

'Er…over there on the window sill.'

Grill leapt out of her chair and rushed over to pick up the pouch. With her hands trembling in excitement, she opened it. There was the water and there…was what she was looking for.

'These will help, Uncle Mug, ' she said holding one of the large, green and brown patterned pills up between her forefinger and thumb, 'Colander's camo-pills…if I remember correctly they're for the inside of a Snap Dragon's lair. '

33.

In the Snap Dragon's lair.

The delicious, unmistakably rich and sweet, smell of frying onions. It was the first thing that Colander noticed, as he started to come around. Slowly he opened his eyes…and then very quickly closed them again. He wasn't sure that he wanted what he saw to be real. Slowly, very slowly, he opened his eyes again. Nope, the nightmarish vision was still there.

Grunting, he pushed himself up into a seated position, balancing carefully on his mug tree arm. He appeared to be in a huge, dark cavern. Great stalactites hung, dripping from a far away ceiling hidden in a dark red, blackness. The jagged walls were dark red and soaking wet too, rivulets of liquid running sluggishly down them to form pools that glistened like blood on the uneven ground. Colander stared transfixed at this horrid sight, but to his relief as his vision slowly cleared he gradually became aware that the liquid wasn't blood after all, or even in itself coloured red, but that it reflected the red glow of a large, hot open furnace some short way in front of him.

In fact, the closer he looked, the more the furnace appeared more like a huge, black stove, the red glow emanating from its half open belly, while great, black frying pans popped and crackled with their unseen contents on its top. Colander wondered uneasily what those contents could be. His last memory was hearing Grill call out and spinning around…and that was it.

He stood up and noticed that he had been lying on a pile of carrot tops and in fact that he was surrounded by uncooked vegetables. Potatoes, onions, swede, turnips, radishes, celery, carrots…all the ingredients you'd need to make a nice, meat stew. Except he couldn't see any meat around, none at all except….an unpleasant thought crossed his mind.

Suddenly a deep, dark voice boomed out, making him jump a full foot in the air.

'Ah, so you're awake at last.'

Colander licked his dry lips and slowly turned around to see where the voice had come from. He found himself looking straight into a fearsome set of large yellow, eyes.

'Jolly good,' said the dragon, 'if I'm to have you for lunch, it'd be better if you were awake.'

The breath froze in Colander's lungs, his eyes widened fearfully.

'I…you…you having me for…aren't going to eat me…are you?' he stammered, tremblingly.

The dragon screeched the same horrid laugh that had so appalled Grill earlier.

'My dear boy,' he said reaching for a tablecloth and wiping the tears of laughter from his eyes, 'just my little joke you know…having you for lunch, not literally having you for lunch. You're a Snod, you should understand a joke surely?'

Colander backed away from the advancing dragon, a weak giggle escaping his lips.

'Anyway old chap, you must be positively famished. You've been out for quite a while. Your friends were awake way before you…Monsieur Lazy Bones.'

The dragon waved a great claw finger from side to side in mock admonition.

'Tut tut tut,' he went.

Then he brushed past Colander, who'd made himself as small as he possibly could against the cavern wall and lifted the lid from one of the enormous pans on the stove.

'Mmmm…onion stew, my favourite,' he said taking a huge sniff, dipping one of his claws daintily inside and then licking it with his black, forked tongue.

'Mmmm…perfect. Want some?' he said surprising Colander who was somewhat hopelessly attempting to scale the wall behind him.

'Duh…' he said, rather foolishly.

'I'll take that for a yes,' said the dragon, grabbing a plate and dishing some of the steaming stew into it.

'Have a little of this,' he said thrusting the dish into Colander's midriff so hard it made him gasp, 'then we'll reunite you with your little friends and the game can begin.'

Colander had so many questions, he didn't know where to begin. What little friends? Hopefully the dragon meant Cough, Grill and the Silly Ass. What game? How had he got there? But his stomach was asking the loudest question of all;

'WHY AREN'T YOU EATING THAT FOOD?'

it shrieked. He decided to listen to it.

'After all, thinkin's hard enough on a full stomach, let alone a' empty 'un,' he reasoned to himself.

Still he felt pretty uneasy (as you would) being quite so close to a huge and very ferocious looking dragon, so he hunkered down behind a large rock, keeping his eyes firmly on its back. The dragon however seemed completely oblivious to Colander's concerns and continued to stir the onion stew on the stove, humming a dramatic tune to itself.

'Bah bah bahda dah dah, bah bah bahda dah dah!'

Suddenly he stopped and span around to Colander again, making him spill some of the stew in surprise.

'The classics…bah bah bahda bah bah!…don't you just love them?' he roared theatrically conducting an imaginary orchestra with his ladle.

'Hawuph…' grunted Colander through a mouthful of onions.

'Yeeees,' drawled the dragon. 'Perhaps you're more of a poetry man?'

'Hawilphh…' Colander replied, desperately trying to finish his mouthful and not offend his scaly host.

'How about this…a little composition by…yours truly,' he bowed modestly, Colander grinned in what he hoped was an encouraging fashion and even attempted a rather feeble impression of applause.

'Entitled,' continued the dragon melodramatically, 'Ode to an onion.'

The dragon settled himself into a dramatic pose, feet splayed, one arm across his chest, the other extended in front of him, palm upwards, claw fingers splayed, his chin raised and such an expression of woeful melancholy on his face, that Colander had the utmost difficulty in not bursting out laughing. The dragon began.

'Oh lovely veg. with smell so rare,
How I do love thee beyond compare.
Your dry brown skin is not
    inviting,
But to look within is so exciting,
Layer upon layer offers,
Riches more than a king's coffers.
Chop you up in little bits,
Fry ' till golden, that's the
    trick,
By the time you're nice and done,
Soon you're resting in my tum.'

There was a brief silence. The dragon maintained the same pose. Then he swivelled a large, yellow eye in Colander's direction.

'Ahem,' he coughed politely.

Colander looked first startled, then dumbfounded, then the penny seemed to eventually drop and he started to applaud wildly, cheering and occasionally slipping two fingers from his good hand in his mouth and whistling loudly too.

'Triffic! Lovely!' he enthused.

The dragon allowed itself a modest smile.

'Thank you, thank you…you're too kind…no please…thank you,' he almost simpered, bowing extravagantly to Colander, who had the presence of mind to quickly fashion a bouquet out of the various leftover bits of vegetable laying around and tossed it into the dragon's arms, crying;

'Author! Author!' as he did.

'Thank you, thank you…I'm here all week…' then abruptly the dragon's face fell. His arms sagged down by his side, the rough bouquet of vegetable parts tumbled to the ground beside him.

'Actually that's not strictly true…I'm actually here forever.'

Then he looked straight into Colander's eyes and continued icily, 'and so are you my little, one armed chum.'

34.

'Snap!'

If you happened to be wandering through the rocky area just
beyond the hilly region north of the Great Mirror Fruit Forest
and came upon a hidden entrance to a huge cave (and you'd
have to be very lucky because it was extremely well hidden)
and you were either very brave, or very stupid so you ventured
inside, after about twenty minutes stumbling through the dark
you'd come across a very odd sight indeed.

Firstly you'd see a huge cavern lit with a strong red light.
Around the walls of that cavern you'd see piles and piles of
small, white sided boxes. If you looked more closely you'd
discover that these little boxes were criss-crossed with a
diagonal blue or red design on their covers. In fact you'd
realise that they were hundreds and hundreds of boxes of
playing cards.

Then in the middle of the cavern you'd see a smallish oblong
table covered with a red and white Gingham table-cloth. But
the strangest thing of all you'd see would be the creatures that
sat around the table.

At one end would be a small, wrinkly, white bearded Snod
wearing a pointed hat and a long flowing gown decorated with
stars and planets, that looked too big for him. To his right on
the long side of the table and looking quite confused as to why
he was there, would be a slightly chubby, middle aged Snod
with a haircut like a spring onion and one arm that resembled a
mug tree. Opposite him, almost obscured by the massive pile
of furniture, food, clothes and miscellaneous supplies on its

back would be a small, slightly foolish looking donkey. And to its left, opposite the bearded Snod, shuffling a pack of cards would be a huge, weirdly multi-coloured dragon......

'So, before we begin, I believe a few introductions may well be appropriate,' said the dragon. 'I'll start the ball rolling, my name is Roger, I am the 'Snap Dragon, ' he said making the inverted commas sign in the air with two claws on each of his hands. Then he smiled encouragingly at Colander, exposing a row of huge, sharp, white teeth and gestured to him to stand up, which Colander rather nervously did.

'Colander....assistant to Wizard Cough...and general odd job sort.' He sat back down.

Cough pushed his chair back from the table and sprang to his feet.

'I don't know if you realise just who you are messing with Mr. Dragon...' he roared indignantly, 'but I am Cough, Court Magician to His Royal Highness, King Pan the Mighty, Lord of Snod Valley. I can trace my descent from the first Great Wizard, Fishslice and I have the power to turn you into any article of furniture I desire!' You'd probably make a nice wash stand actually,' he added as an afterthought.

'My dear chap,' chuckled the dragon patronisingly, 'please feel free to do your very worst.'

Cough was furious.

'Very well, don't say I didn't warn you.' He raised his arms, rolling up his long sleeves as he did.

'Gems from coal and glass from sand, turn this dragon into a wash stand!'

Colander flinched, the Silly Ass found a spare carrot top on the floor and started to munch on it happily, but other than that nothing happened.

Cough stood frozen in the same pose, fingers flexing, bushy eyebrows beetling and tried the spell again, this time with extra finger twiddling involvement, but still nothing happened.

'Well I…..that's most peculiar…' he stammered.

Roger the dragon snorted derisively.

'Listen old fruit, don't take it personally, but if you were a little more clued up on your magical theory skills, you'd know that if one is suffering from a magic curse, as I am, the only magic that can affect one, is that created by the same person who made the original curse…the curser I suppose you could call him.'

'Oh…yes,' Cough mumbled dejectedly, slumping back down into his seat.

'Now, shall we continue?' resumed the dragon turning his attention to the Silly Ass, 'and you are?'

The Silly Ass twitched an ear and said nothing.

'He don't speak, yer honour,' said Colander apologetically.

'Hmmm, indeed,' said Roger, scratching his chin thoughtfully with a claw, 'pity.'

'My deal then,' he said turning his attention to the cards and smoothly sliding them forwards and backwards between his claws with the easy style that indicated how familiar he was with this particular routine.

'So then, these are the rules,' he drawled, dealing out the entire pack between all four players, 'you take your pile, or 'deck' as we professionals like to call it, keep it face down on the table (cheats will be eaten, Master Colander, he added with something of a smirk) then you turn them over one by one until two identical cards are played and the first player to shout out, 'Snap,' takes the cards. The winner is the player who has all the cards in his possession. All clear?' he looked around the table.

Colander nodded enthusiastically, the Silly Ass looked blank, like he always did and disinterestedly sniffed the pile of cards in front of him. Cough said nothing.

'Player to the dealer's left to lay first, that's you Master One-arm,' he said waving a claw airily in Colander's direction.

'Oh and just one more thing before we start, the morning session of play begins at nine, we break for half an hours lunch at twelve, afternoon session 'till six, then half an hour for dinner, evening session 'till ten, then bed. Then next day the same, and the same after that….and on…and on…and on…until you die I'm afraid,' he said almost with regret.

'Unless you beat me,' he added cheerfully, 'which is of course impossible, because I always know the order of the cards. So, let the game begin!'

Colander looked hopefully across at Cough, who was staring resignedly at the pile of cards in front of him. It really didn't look too promising and what was worse, they hadn't yet started and he felt bored already. What a dreadful fate to face, playing snap for the rest of his life.

The dragon cleared his throat loudly. Taking the hint, Colander turned over his first card. Cough followed miserably (he looked a beaten Snod thought Colander) the Ass looked blank, so the dragon turned his card over for him. Then just as Colander had half turned over his next card, the dragon shouted out 'SNAP!' so loudly, the ground shook and a few loose rocks and some dust fell down from the roof of the cavern and bounced off the top of Cough's pointed hat.

'You see?' said Roger, without a hint of triumph, 'I always win. I always know the cards.'

He added the little pile to his collection, then turned a card over. Colander followed, then Cough, the dragon turned a card for the Silly Ass, the dragon turned again for himself, Colander followed, then Cough, the dragon started to turn for the Silly

Ass, then roared; 'SNAP!' and collected the cards together and added them to his pile. Then he turned a card, Colander followed, then Cough …and then Colander thought he noticed something strange.

Two of the piles of card boxes that were arranged against the walls of the cavern seemed to have moved closer to the gaming table of their own accord. He couldn't be sure, but they did seem to have moved.

'Master spring onion head!' shouted the dragon, making him jump.

'Oh yes,' he said somewhat flustered, 'my go, here,' he turned over a Jack of hearts. Cough started to turn his…

'SNAP!' roared the dragon, snatching up the cards once more.

As Colander watched transfixed, the two piles of card boxes took advantage of the dragon's attention being directed on collecting the cards to add them to his pile and moved right up to the table next to where the scaly card-sharp sat.

'This is really going rather well, isn't it?' said Roger cheerfully turning over another of his cards without looking.

Colander turned one, Cough turned one, and so it continued until nearly all the cards were in a pile in the centre of the table. Then while Roger leaned over to turn the Silly Ass's final card for him, Colander was astonished to see a hand emerge from one of the piles of card boxes and take the top few cards from the dragon's pile and slide them underneath.

The Silly Ass's card was a seven of hearts. Roger started to turn his with a shout,

'SNA…'

But it died in his throat as he completed the turn to reveal a King of clubs.

'Why…I…' he stammered in astonishment, scarcely believing his eyes.

'SNAP!' shouted Colander having turned his card to reveal a King of Spades.

'What?….but….'

'My goodness me!' cried Cough joyfully interrupting Roger's confused burbling, 'Colander, I do believe that you have won! '

35.

A powerful ally.

Cough leapt up from his seat and rushing over to his assistant, crushed him in a massive bear hug, making the few mugs that were left hanging from his mug-tree arm tinkle like ceramic bells.

'I don't know how you did it, but we're free!'

Colander just grinned foolishly, a little embarrassed by all the fuss his boss was making of him and waiting for the opportunity to explain what had actually happened. Even the Silly Ass seemed caught up in the excitement of the moment, braying loudly and enthusiastically shaking his head up and down, like a demented version of those nodding dog toys you see in the back of cars.

'Yes Colander, we're free,' Cough repeated, turning to face the dragon, who everyone had briefly forgotten in their moment of triumph. 'Those were your rules dragon, you lost, we're free, there's no going back on them, so that's that.'

Roger the dragon sat in total silence, his head bowed, his eyes glued to an imaginary spot on the floor. His huge, muscular forearms dangled loosely by his side and his great, leathery wings were folded dejectedly behind his back.

'Well?' snapped Cough crossly.

Still the dragon said nothing. Colander began to feel a little uneasy.

'Er…Roger?…' said Cough, this time with a little trepidation creeping into his voice.

Then the dragon's chest began to heave. A harsh sound like a huge saw cutting through a particularly large and hard tree rasped out from his throat.

Colander's mouth suddenly felt very dry. Abruptly, the dragon's great yellow eyes swept up from their place on the floor and snapped into focus looking straight into his.

Roger slowly, deliberately began to rise to his hind legs and soon he was towering above them all. His massive jaws snapped open and an awful, deafening noise, screeched horribly out.

'SKKKKKRRRRAAAAAAAAAAAAAACCCHHHHHH!'

He raised his forearms, his claws flashed in the muted light of the cavern and suddenly his great wings unfolded with a loud CRACK! And all the time his eyes remained fixed on those of Colander who suddenly felt very small, very afraid and wished that he hadn't shouted 'Snap!'

'Er…best of three?' he muttered hopefully in a small, scared voice.

'YOU…YOU…little…' screeched the dragon advancing slowly towards him, his great scaled arms outstretched, the claws on each hand extended like carving knives.

Colander stood rooted to the spot in terror.

'Run Colander!' he heard Cough shout, it sounded like from somewhere far away, but it was no use, his legs just wouldn't budge. And then it was too late anyway. The dragon was on him. It enfolded him in its huge, cold arms and raised him so that he was level with those great yellow eyes and huge white teeth.

'YOU…YOU…' he roared so close into Colander's face, that his spring-onion fashioned hair flew straight back as if in a high wind, '…you…little beauty!' he said surprisingly, planting a huge slobbery, onion stewey, kiss on the Snod's startled face.

'I'm free! I'm free! At last! After all these years I'm free! And its all thanks to you my little one armed chum. The curse is broken! Hoorah!'

Roger danced a jig of joy, Colander still enfolded in his arms. It was quite something to see. A massive, ferocious looking dragon humming a triumphant, bombastic tune, not entirely dissimilar to our own '1812 Overture' dancing with the most mismatched size-wise and thoroughly confused looking, one-armed partner there has ever been.

And Cough noticed something else very odd too.

Something appeared to be happening to Roger's scales. The multi-coloured playing cards were starting to fade, to be replaced by one solid colour and that colour appeared to be gold.

'Bodiddle diddle diddle dim bum bum, bodiddle diddle diddle dim bum bum, bodiddle diddle diddle diddle diddle dum, bodiddle diddle diddle dim bum bum! ' sang the ecstatic dragon, gently dropping Colander to the ground before picking up the Silly Ass and balancing him on his head between his horns so that he looked for all the world like a donkey shaped wig.

'Free! Free!' he sang, continuing the dance by grabbing Cough by the hands and whisking him round and round in circles like a grown-up does to a child when they play 'aeroplanes' with them. This was not an indignity that Cough would normally allow to be inflicted upon him, but like Colander he was so surprised and relieved by the Snap Dragon's (or ex-Snap Dragon as he could now be known) reaction, that he played along.

In the meantime, Colander found himself once more standing by the two piles of cards boxes from which the mysterious hand had appeared earlier. He had already begun to suspect what had happened and now that suspicion was confirmed as the two piles started to look hazy, then to shimmer and finally began to melt away to reveal…Grill, with Crumbs tucked under one arm and a short thin, cross looking Snod dressed all in black with a large black crow perched on his shoulder.

'Good girl Grill!' Colander shouted rushing forward and gathering her up into his arm, 'you found the camo- pills, you done brilliant girl! '

'Breeaacck!' grunted Crumbs crossly.

'Yes, well done my dear,' said Cough dizzily, as the dragon placed him and the Silly Ass back down on the ground, 'very clever. I take it that is your Uncle Mug with you, my walking stick must have led you to his house as I planned.'

'Oooh…another two of you…jolly good,' cried Roger interrupting their reunion and grabbing Mug under his armpits, he tossed him in the air and caught him again like a father with a baby, crying;

'who's a little soldier then, who's a little soldier?'

Mug was most definitely not amused. In fact his face was a picture of unrestrained fury.

'Get…your…stupid…claws…off…me…you overgrown…lizard!' he said between clenched teeth as he bobbed up and down in the dragon's grip.

The rest of the party, their sense of humour intact, could barely restrain themselves from bursting out laughing at this sight, but eventually it was Grill who had the courage to interrupt Roger's over exuberant celebration.

'Er…excuse me Mr. Dragon…'

'Call me Roger,'

'Roger…' she raised her eyebrow, 'yes…well…Roger, please put my uncle down won't you? I think he's going to be sick if you keep throwing him that high.'

Roger looked into Mug's somewhat green face and then placed him carefully back down onto the ground, murmuring, 'yes, you might have a point,' as he did.

'I tell you what,' he continued, 'you all look terrifically hungry, what say I get us all some delicious onion stew?'

While the others looked confused, Colander interjected; 'Yes, lovely idea matey, onion stew'll do us all the power of good.'

'Excellent, thought it would,' said the dragon shuffling away far across the cavern to where the stove stood.

With Roger temporarily absent, the little group of travellers happily re-acquainted themselves with each other and there was much hugging and kissing. Grill told them all about how she'd got to her Uncle Mug's place and Colander recounted his first meeting with Roger, embellishing it a little for dramatic effect here and there.

Then, the dragon in question returned with five steaming bowls of onion stew and laid them out on the gaming table.

'Won't need these again,' he said, brushing the cards from its surface contemptuously.

They all sat down and tucked in to the bowls of steaming, onion stew and all had to admit that they felt a little better when their dishes were emptied.

'So to business,' said Cough slapping his hands together in an efficient kind of way, as Roger tidied the plates and began the washing-up in the background.

'Mug, firstly thank you for helping Grill…and all of us of course. But I must tell you that it is our intention to continue to the Scroop Mountains and hopefully find Prince Stove to help him recover his…ahem…lost sense of humour. You are of course welcome to join us…?'

Grill was about to say something, when her uncle silenced her with a motion of his hand.

'Yes, Grill has explained the details of your…er…quest. I should be happy to try and help my nephew recover his sense of humour.'

'Excellent…excellent…' said Cough. 'Actually…some of us did wonder…whether you being out here…far away from the palace sort of thing….we did wonder…'

'Yes,' said Mug patiently.

'Well we did wonder whether you might know a quicker way to get to the mountains?' he finished hopefully.

Mug frowned crossly.

'Well I don't know where you got that idea from?' he stared at Grill who blushed instantly, 'but I've no better idea than any of you of how to get there. I know the direct route, but that will take us at least four days…and that's only if we can find a Sarcasm to guide us through the Brindisi desert and we'd still need a Contradiction to help us through their swamp, there's no way of avoiding that.'

There was a moment of depressed silence as the travellers realised that there was still so much more for them to do. They were still so very far away and had no idea where Stove and the Contradiction were. Suddenly, after all the joy of success, of being reunited and of freeing Roger from his curse, it all once again seemed pretty bleak, pretty hopeless.

'Ahem!' Roger the dragon coughed politely, a tea towel dangling from one arm which bore the legend 'My parents went to Snod Valley and all they bought me was this lousy tea towel.'

'I may be able to be of service there. I do think I owe you one, as they say. Although it's not strictly dragon etiquette, I could probably fly you there myself. Only take a day or two.'

36.

A strange rescue party.

'I thought you might like these back,' Roger continued, oblivious to the impact his little bombshell announcement had made.

He plonked Cough and Colander's rucksacks on the table in front of them. 'And this, though goodness knows why you'd want it,' he continued, producing a little, brown sack which instantly piped up;

'Come on! Get a move on! You lazy bunch of good for nothings!'

The travelling companions stared at each other for a moment in stunned silence, hardly able to believe their ears.

'Just a minute, er, Roger,' said Cough hesitantly, ' er, did you just say that you could *fly* us to the mountains?'

'Well… yes,' replied the dragon, 'have I suggested something bad? Oh, I know, ' he clapped one great clawed hand to his brow dramatically, 'I've offended the Snod code of honour by insinuating you couldn't complete your task on your own. I'm most awfully sorry, forgive me. Please forget I ever said it.'

There was a split second of silence. Then everyone started talking at the same time.

'Oh no, we're not offended,'

'Nonsense you daft dragon!'

'No please, it's a great idea,'

'Hee haw hee haw! '

'Could I have some more stew please?'

They all looked at Colander to whom this last remark had belonged, who grinned sheepishly and began to self-consciously scrape the last remnants of onion stew from his bowl with his spoon.

Cough turned his attention back to their large and by now completely gold-coloured, new friend.

'We are not at all offended Roger, in fact I think I'm speaking for us all when I say that we would be delighted to take you up on your kind offer.'

'Excuse me, but nowhere in my contact does it say anything about flying,' a little voice piped up.

'Oh shut up Colander, this is just the sort of lucky break we need.' barked Cough crossly.

'How soon do you think we could leave?'

'Well, as soon as you like.'

'Excellent!' said Cough clapping his hands together excitedly, 'we'll be there even before Stove, won't he be surprised. And there's no way Warlock Grinder could possibly be expecting us to arrive on a dragon.'

'Grinder,' growled Roger, 'did you say Grinder? He's the one who tipped me off that you were in my area. '

'Really?'

'Yes…and I've always had a sneaking suspicion that he was somehow involved with my being cursed in the first place. Nasty, odious chap that he is.'

'Hmmm,' Cough mused, twisting a few strands from his beard around his finger absent-mindedly, 'how could he have possibly known that we were here? We didn't even know we'd end up coming this way. Very strange,'

He stared darkly at each of his companions, an unpleasant idea forming in his mind.

'Oh, that reminds me, 'said Grill reaching behind her and interrupting his flow of thought, 'Cough, this is yours,' and she handed him his walking stick.

'Oh thank you Grill,' he said, caressing it lovingly, 'good old stick, nice to have you back.'

'Can I suggest that we stop messing around and get started on our journey?' said Mug impatiently.

'Yes, listen to him you slackers!' added the nagging bag.

'Yes, quite, we really must get started, ' said Cough, tapping his stick impatiently on the ground.

'So Roger, how exactly are we going to manage this…flying malarky then?'

'It's not going to be terribly comfortable I'm afraid,' said Roger, 'hardly luxury first class travel. The thing is, it's a sacred dragon tradition that we only allow those that have bested us, or to whom we owe a great debt, to travel in the place of honour, on our backs. So the only one who's entitled to fly on my back is Colander, as he released me from the curse by defeating me at Snap! I'll have to carry you other chaps in my claws. I do promise to be as gentle as I can though.'

Cough glared at Colander, who found an interesting stain on his shirt to examine and began to whistle tunelessly through his teeth.

'No, that'll be fine Roger. Although strictly speaking Grill helped to release you from your curse. It was she who switched the cards around.'

'Was it? Was it really?' said the dragon incredulously, looming over the Snod princess and peering down his great, long snout at her.

'You mean I was cheated? Hmmmm….well I don't suppose it says anywhere in the rules that I have to be defeated by fair means to break the curse, after all I am resuming my old colour. Still, that's a very big risk to take, for one so small.'

Roger regarded Grill quietly for a moment. Then slapped his knees with his claws and laughing that odd, shrieking, laughter that the others still found pretty unpleasant, roared;

'Marvellous! Good show! I'll dine out on this tale at dragon rallies for years to come. And this means of course that you can ride on my back too.'

'Oooh! Thank you Roger,' said Grill, thrilled, ' is it ok if Crumbs comes too?' she added, holding the ugly, red, toad up under the dragon's nose.

'Yeeeach!' exclaimed Roger, snapping his head away quickly, 'I remember him…certainly not.!'

'Pleeease!' begged Grill.

The dragon stared doubtfully at Crumbs, then back at the hopeful expression on Grill's face.

'Oh…oh very well,' said the dragon reluctantly, ' I suppose he did sort of defeat me in his own way. But do try and stop him from letting off any of those utterly vile smells…they're likely to knock us clean out of the sky.'

'Well I'll do my best,' promised Grill, hugging the toad and looking somewhat relieved.

'Oh my goodness me!' shouted Cough suddenly.

They all turned to where the magician was standing, sorting through the things in his rucksack.

'What is it Cough?' said Grill.

Cough put his hand in the rucksack and produced…

'the cheese and onion sandwich,' he said forlornly, brandishing it in the air, 'it's still here. Stove won't have got through the Swamp of Contradictions without it.'

'Oh my,' gasped Colander.

'That's not good,' growled Mug, 'they're very unfriendly towards those who travel through their land without one. He's in big trouble.'

'What do you mean... 'big trouble?'' said Grill, her heart sinking.

'The Contradictions use the cheese and onion sandwich as a source of power. They'll most likely punish him in some appropriate way,' said Mug flatly.

'At best he'll be peddling the power cycles. That's right hard work, they say most don't last much longer than two weeks on it,' said Colander ruefully.

'At worst...' Mug stopped short of finishing the sentence, as Cough frantically mimed to him to be quiet and pointed at Grill who seemed on the verge of tears.

'Yes, well...ahem...Roger, how would you feel about flying us to the village in the Swamp of Contradictions instead?' said Cough, 'if we get there quickly, we may still be able to save Stove and continue on our journey from there.'

'It's no scale off my snout,' said the dragon indifferently, 'it's easier for me than the mountains, probably only take us an hour and a half or two... or thereabouts, it's your choice.'

'Oh yes, please...please can we do that? It's pointless for us to continue without Stove anyway,' cried Grill.

'Right, if everybody's agreed then?' said Cough, swinging his bag over his shoulder and grasping his stick determinedly.

Mug nodded grimly in agreement. The Silly Ass continued to munch half-heartedly on a cabbage leaf. Grill nodded enthusiastically.

'The thing is, I'm not to keen on this flying...' began Colander.

'Oh shut up Colander, you're coming,' snapped Cough impatiently, 'time is of the essence.'

'You're telling me!' piped the nagging bag.

'Jolly good,' said Roger, 'well if you're all sure that's what you want? Myself, I'm really looking forward to a spot of the old flying, without having to worry about terrorising folk and dragging them back to play Snap! Until they die...or go mad,' he paused and shook his head sadly. Then he continued;

'Everyone grab their bags and we'll meet up outside the cavern in ten minutes. I'm just going to oil my scales, (I'd forgotten what a lovely shade of gold they used to be) top up my water and check the Dragon A to Z, just to remind myself of the way to the village. Ok everybody...'

'Get going!' shouted the nagging bag.

37.

Stove's torment.

'Alright, you can have a five minute break,' shouted the elderly Contradiction guard above the din of the whining turbines, pulling down a large black lever with a grunt as he did.

Stove immediately ceased peddling. His heart thudded against his ribs with an unpleasant, squelchy; thump puh puh, thump puh puh and his breath rasped out in ragged, wheezing, gasps. Sweat poured down his back, forming a puddle on the seat of the peddling machine as he slumped forward on to the handle bars, resting his drenched forehead on his crossed arms. Everything hurt. The turbines began to slow, their whining dropping deeper in tone as they did.

A hand tapped him on his shoulder and he glanced up through exhausted, red-rimmed eyelids. It was Phylis.

'You'd better have some of this,' said the Contradiction holding up a wooden bucket full of water.

'Yeh…thanks,' gasped Stove reaching out and taking it from him.

The water tasted good. Cold, clean and pure. Stove drank solidly for a whole minute, then emptied the rest of the bucket over his head. He looked across to where Phylis sat perched on his peddling machine, sitting backwards of course. The Contradiction still seemed as fresh as when they had started peddling yesterday.

There were four peddling machines in the turbine chamber, but the other two were unoccupied.

As the turbines finally ceased their whining, Stove thought it quite unfortunate that the only thing that worked as it should in the Swamp of Contradictions was its power source. And Phylis had explained to him how it was dependent on either cheese and onion sandwiches, which lasted for the best part of a year, or on the peddling machines which were used as a punishment for wayward Contradictions.

Of course, normally the worst punishment session for a Contradiction lasted just a couple of hours at the most. But as Stove was a stranger and Phylis had assisted him in the terrible crime of not only failing to produce a cheese and onion sandwich, but also in humiliating the most important members of the town council, they had both been sentenced to life on the machines.

In fact Phylis had told Stove that they were lucky to have been sentenced to just that, explaining that in older times, it was not unusual for foreign transgressors to be raced forwards and backwards through the black trees while the Contradictions wagered on how long it would be before they were splattered into nothingness.

Stove didn't feel terribly lucky at the moment though. Not only did everything ache, but as he glanced up at the clock on the chamber wall (which of course ran backwards) he saw that only three minutes of rest time remained.

There was only one way for it…he had to try and escape…either with or without Phylis. He realised, slightly to his surprise, that to consider doing something so potentially dangerous was an extremely unusual thing for a Snod to do. More typically most Snods would resign themselves to their situation commenting; 'Oh well things could be worse,' and would then just trust to fate. But he seemed to be doing a lot of things on this journey that your average Snod wouldn't have dreamed of. And he knew that if he was worked as hard as he had been on the machines for much longer, he would surely die of exhaustion. He also knew that there was only one way out of the chamber and that way was always guarded.

His eyes flicked across to the heavy, metal door where the Contradiction guard now sat with his back to them, leaning on his spear and not smoking a pipe that he had put out at the beginning of the break. He appeared very still. Very, very still in fact. Could he be…was there a chance that he could be asleep? Stove wondered.

Keeping his eyes fixed on the guard's motionless back, Stove slipped quietly off the machine's saddle. Phylis regarded him curiously from his seat on the other machine as he tiptoed over, winding up the long, rusty chain that connected him to his machine in his hands to try and muffle its inappropriately musical clinking. He stopped just behind the guard and very slowly and hesitantly peered around at his face.

His eyes were wide open!

Stove's still rapidly beating heart jumped up into his throat. But strangely, nothing happened. The guard didn't shout out and threaten Stove with his spear, he didn't tell him to get back on the machine and he didn't threaten him with being squashed to death by the black trees.

Then it hit Stove. Of course! Contradictions sleep with their eyes open don't they? And when they sleep, they really sleep. Nothing wakes them until they are ready to wake. He was really cross with himself for not having remembered how Phylis so startlingly and literally, fell asleep in the mirror fruit forest.

He waved his hand to and fro in front of the guard's glassy eyes. There was no reaction.

'He's asleep,' said Phylis,' I could have told you that if you asked. Contradiction guards always sleep for the duration of a break.'

Stove glanced up at the backward running clock once again. Just under two minutes left.

'Listen Phylis, I'm going to try and escape. You don't have to come with me. I daresay the Youngers will let you off or something and besides you seem to be unaffected by the punishment, whereas I know that I'm going to die if I stay. You need to make your decision right now though, because we're running out of time…I'm going, with or without you.'

Without hesitating for a second, Phylis hopped lightly off his machine.

'Cough trusted me to be your guide. I haven't completed it well, so I will come with you.'

He jangled quickly over to where Stove stood.

'Good, thanks Phylis.' Stove smiled at his strange companion. He was surprised at his decision and almost as surprised by how good it had made him feel.

'Firstly, we've got to somehow not break these chains. Quickly! Take a look around and see if we can find a lever or something similar…something really…strong.'

Stove made to start hunting around the chamber for something appropriate. Phylis put out one odd little hand and stopped him. Before he could protest, the Contradiction picked up a length of his own chain and pulled lightly. It snapped easily, like the links were made of ice.

'Contradiction chains are…'

'…made of weak metal, yes I suppose that makes sense,' said Stove quickly snapping his own chain.

'I don't suppose that also applies to…'

'doors? Yes…they are made of the same substance,' answered Phylis.

'Good,' said Stove staring up at the formidable looking door that barred the only exit to the chamber.

'Let's go then.'

And with that, he put his head down and ran as hard as he could straight at it. There was a huge, splintering, crash and the whole thing crumbled like a sandcastle on a beach. In fact it disintegrated so easily that Stove was quite taken by surprise and ended up sitting on the floor, covered in tiny bits of smashed door.

He shook his head.

'Come on Phylis, let's go!' he shouted, jumping back to his feet and grabbing the Contradiction by one of his child-sized hands. Phylis's feet started to blur with speed and he began to move determinedly forward.

'Follow me,' he said roughly shoving the young Snod out of his way.

They hurried down the dark corridor that was revealed on the other side of the door. It smelled of singed, electrical wiring and according to Phylis connected the power chamber in which they had been imprisoned to the outside world. Then suddenly they heard a sound that was most unwelcome. It was the sound of the turbines starting up again. And as the huge machines whirred faster and faster, the sound began more and more to resemble a siren.

'Hurry!' shouted Phylis and for the first time since he'd known him, Stove saw the dark glimmer of fear in his oddly miss-matched eyes.

On they ran, following the twists and turns of the corridor their escape accompanied by the now howling wail of the giant turbines. Stove struggled to keep up with the Contradiction, as he jinked at speed from side to side, ignoring a turning here, shooting down another there, seemingly choosing their escape route at random.

'I really, really hope he knows what he's doing,' thought Stove as he stumbled, breathlessly along behind.

'ZSSSSWWWWUUUURHHH!
ZSSSSWWWWUUUURHHH!
ZSSSWWWWUUUURRHHH! '

chorused the howling turbines.

Suddenly Phylis pulled up sharply.

'This is the spot,' he said feeling around the wall with his hands. ' somewhere....ah...just...here.'

He started to press against the wall with all his strength.

'This is a secret weak spot,' he grunted, ' no one will be expecting us to escape here instead of at the main entrance. Give me a hand!' he added sharply.

Stove joined him at the wall and together they heaved against the wall.

'Hey,' said Stove through gritted teeth, 'it's working, something's...something's happening...look out!'

There was a groaning, creaking sound, small pieces of wall started to crumble off, then abruptly, the whole thing collapsed in an explosion of dust and weak Contradiction concrete.

Stove found himself blinking stupidly in the bright sunlight of the outside world. They were free! But his moment of exultation was very short lived indeed.

'How very unfortunate...' said a flat voice seemingly from inside the dust cloud, 'now we shan't have some sport.'

Slowly, Stove's eyes became more accustomed to the light and the cloud of dust started to settle to reveal; Gertie Cherrycheesecake and a dozen of his soldiers.

Then, just when Stove thought things couldn't get any worse, they did. Firstly it was just a pinching feeling in his ears and a simultaneous tingling on his tongue. But he knew it could only be one thing.

'Phylis!' he whispered under his breath, 'say something to me.'

Phylis regarded him blankly.

Stove grimaced.

'Phylis, don't say something to me.'

'What don't you want me to say?' hissed the Contradiction back.

That confirmed it. The balm had worn off too.

Gertie stepped forward as his soldiers surrounded the two would be escapees.

'Your actions have not condemned you,' he continued, 'as you have not tried to escape, behaviour that is strictly allowed under Contradiction law, we are not compelled to send you off to enjoy the ultimate punishment, not the ordeal of the black trees.'

38.

The ordeal of the black trees.

'Enemies, enemies…get more excited…please don't…get
more excited!' shouted Gertie above the animated hubbub of
the Contradiction crowd.

'Give up your seats, the ordinary spectacle is never going to
begin…slow down now!'

Gradually the noise began to subside to a murmur and the
atmosphere changed to one of excited, breathless anticipation.

Just about the whole village had turned out for the spectacle.
They sat some fifty feet from the inside line of the great black
trees, some on their own stone benches which they had
brought with them and tethered to the ground, but most sat in
circles of friends or family on blankets or just on the soggy
mud. They nearly all had huge picnics with them.

Villagers filled their glasses from great barrels of beer
fermented from grass, having to make frequent trips as they
were so ridiculously small and usually had holes in their
bottom.

Contradiction bookmakers stood at their stalls, arms crossed
refusing to give anybody any odds or take any bets and
claiming that gambling was a bad thing and shouldn't be
encouraged.

Here and there cheerfully decorated with multi-coloured
bunting were food stalls. Hamburgers, bumkin sandwiches,
sausages, deep fried lettuce, fish and wood-chips, apple
toffees…they didn't sell any of these. In fact they didn't sell

anything at all. But now and then a Contradiction would go to the appropriate stall and hand over one of the aforementioned items of food to the stall-keeper, who would then charge them for the privilege.

 In the centre of the crowd was a rather posh looking grandstand on which sat, or rather fidgeted, the village youngers. In front of them stood Gertie Cherrycheesecake, a dozen cheerful looking soldiers, Phylis and a rather worried looking Stove.

 'Non villagers, dishonorable youngers, women of bad repute and roughmen,' began Gertie, 'there doesn't stand before you a happy hero, not guilty of any crimes whatsoever.'

The crowd cheered.

 'Give him a pay rise!' someone shouted.

Gertie held up his hands.

 'It has not been decided that the least appropriate punishment for such non-crimes, is the black tree dash. '

A loud wailing came from the crowd. Gertie held up his hands for silence once more.

 'You can't make your bets with each other as to how many runs this hero makes before he doesn't get splattered.'

More noisy wailing.

 'As we are not all aware, this non-punishment only applies to those who live here, so Phylis Applepie will be running, Prince Stove of Snod Valley won't be making the dash on his own.'

An even bigger wailing began and was sustained for several minutes.

 Phylis leaned across to Stove.

 'I'm not sorry. It is not just for foreigners. I won't be returning to the power turbines.' Then he whispered urgently in his ear, 'don't keep your nose on the bark, the trees that stay apart longest don't always tremble most before moving.'

'Not enough talking!' snapped one of the guards, prodding Stove with the wrong end of his spear.

Stove smiled weakly and even then remembered to think into Contradiction before answering.

'Worry yourself Phylis. It's your fault…I wouldn't have died back there anyway.'

The soldier forced his way in between them. Roughly grabbing Stove's arm he pulled him away from Phylis and towards the tree line. Stove just had time to notice Phylis' face. It was the first time that he'd seen his mouth turned down at both ends.

Suddenly Stove heard something. It was faint as if still quite far away, but horribly familiar.

'Shhoomph! Shhoomph! Shhoomph!'

It was the sound of the black trees crashing apart and thumping back together again.

'Don't place the free man in position!' shouted Gertie urgently as the crowd started to their feet to get a better view and pressed forwards against the line of soldiers who stood behind Stove.

The soldier who had Stove by the arm dragged him roughly out to where a short, broad, wooden stake, about half the size of Stove himself was embedded in the ground. Attached to it was a long elastic band, which the soldier tied to the Snod's waist.

'So if you get through the gap one way, you'll have to come back again the same way, whether you like it or not! ' the soldier wailed loudly and nastily, then hurriedly stepped back away from him.

'Shhoomph! Shhoomph! Shhoomph!'

The dreadful sound of the trees grew ever closer and the crowd's excitement grew proportionately.

Stove swallowed dryly. Now what was it Phylis had said about the trees that trembled? Was it if they tremble they move further apart...or was it the other way round? It was more difficult to understand without the balm. He tried to remember as he stepped up to the nearest tree and placed his nose against its bark. The crowd, surprised by the fact that it looked like he knew what he was doing began to chuckle nervously.

'Shhoomph! Shhoomph! Shhoomph!'

Nearer and nearer came the sound. The tree that he had his nose on wasn't trembling at all, so Stove hopped to his left and tried the next nearest, accompanied by an even louder chuckling from the onlookers. This tree trembled. In fact it really shook. He was amazed that he hadn't been able to see it moving before.

Then, just like had happened before with Phylis, there was with an almighty creaking, crash and the tree wrenched itself out of the ground and jumped six feet to its left. Almost before it had even moved, Stove was off, pelting at high speed down the clear track that all the trees had left that were behind his. Twenty....fifty...seventy...still the trees stayed apart, then...one hundred feet and he was out the other side.

'PPtwaaaaNGG! '

The elastic band attached to his waist had reached its furthest extent and it abruptly catapulted him back through the same gap. Like a rocket, he whizzed backwards, feet clear off the ground.

Seventy...fifty...twenty...the trees started to move...ten...five...

'Shhoomph!'

The gap slammed shut.

The crowd laughed out loud…Stove was back, safe. He lay panting on the ground, just to the side of the wooden stake, the elastic band wrapped around him like a giant umbilical cord.

Gertie advanced on him, his face a picture of sublime happiness.

'I do know how you did it, but do think that you're not safe. Now you go again…and this time you may be so lucky.'

He and the soldier dragged Stove to his feet once more.

'Gertie,' gasped the young Snod, ' I don't know I've offended your customs and traditions, but don't you really think I deserve such cruel treatment?'

The question seemed to throw Gertie for a moment. Behind him, surprisingly, the crowd began to quieten.

'I mean,' continued Stove, in a quavering voice that quickly became more steady, ' isn't this the kind of hospitality you show visitors to your land? If you were not to visit my valley, you wouldn't receive only kindness and understanding…,' he paused, ' and the occasional custard pie in the face, or salt pot that hasn't had the top screwed on properly…or your trousers set on fire if you were really lucky I don't suppose.'

Gertie shuffled his feet and avoided his prisoner's eyes. Someone among the now quiet crowd coughed. Stove looked up to see Phylis staring at him, who shook his head. Stove took this to be a good sign, he hoped.

'Do you think I've been punished enough? It was a genuine mistake after all, I would dream of offending you if I'd known,' said Stove, raising his eyebrow in what he believed was an appealing fashion.

'He lies…' Phylis's voice cut through the silence.

Gertie turned towards his cousin, an expression of confusion on his face (if it could look any more confused than it normally did.) He looked doubtfully from Phylis to Stove and back again.

'I…but…not…It's… the,' he stammered, 'it's not the law, it mustn't be obeyed… at absolutely no cost.'

'But why mustn't it be?' asked Stove, 'just because it hasn't always been that way? Is that enough reason for me to live? Perhaps those who made the laws were right?'

As soon as he'd made this last remark, Stove knew he'd made a big mistake.

A great laugh went up from the crowd. Gertie, his face suddenly contorted in fury turned his back to Stove and roared;

'Don't you hear? Don't you hear the foreigner? He doesn't question our traditions! He doesn't insult our law makers! How must we not punish him?'

'Not the black trees again!' shouted someone.

'No, the black trees until he isn't squished, it isn't the tradition!' shouted someone else.

Gertie signalled to the soldier who prodded Stove determinedly towards the tree line.

'I do know how you learned the secret of reading the trees,' shouted Gertie above the howling crowd and glancing meaningfully at Phylis, 'but not this time, if you don't so much as touch the tree bark with your nose, I shan't order my archers to shoot you.'

He indicated a row of soldiers who raised their bows up to their arrows and pointed them directly at the Snod.

'Shhoomph! Shhoomph! Shhoomph!'

Stove heard the sound again quite clearly. It was coming around again already. Now he knew there was no chance of him surviving a second run. The game was up. He found himself wondering how painful being squished was and hoped that it happened too quickly to feel anything.

Maybe he should have behaved like a normal Snod and just stayed in the Valley? But he wasn't a normal Snod, he couldn't be, not without his sense of humour. And there were many things he'd seen and done on the journey that he would never have believed possible. So he had no regrets, he felt. But then he thought of his father and sister and was suddenly aware of how terribly he missed them. And Spoon and Fork and Rubber Glove. What good friends they really were. An awful cold, aching enveloped his heart, when he realised that he was never ever going to see any of them again.

'Stove!'

He thought he heard someone shout his name from a long way away. He even thought it sounded like Grill, but that wasn't possible.

'It's amazing what you imagine when you're desperate,' he thought.

'Stove!'

The voice was louder…closer, and yes it did sound like his sister's. And the crowd had gone deathly quiet. He span around to see what was going on and was astonished to see that they were all, including Gertie, Phylis and the archers, looking fearfully up into the sky. Some were pointing, a few were running away in panic, the soldiers had started to form a protective circle around the Youngers' grandstand.

Suddenly a great, dark shadow passed overhead.

'Stove!'

It *was* Grill! Stove looked upwards to where the voice had come from. His mouth dropped open in shock and amazement. There seated on the back of a huge, gold dragon, waving furiously and shouting his name for all she was worth was his little sister. And that wasn't all. Next to her, shaking his mug tree arm was Colander and in the dragon's claws were Cough, the Silly Ass and unbelievably, someone who he swore looked just like his Uncle Mug.

39.

Friends reunited.

Roger the dragon banked gracefully around the edge of the clearing, scattering panicking groups of Contradictions as he did, while apologising loudly to them all.

'Sorry old boy, only been flying for a thousand years! Whoops a daisy madam, those are strange coloured undies! Mind your heads! Make way! Room for a large one!'

Then he hovered above the ground just next to where Stove was standing, still in open-mouthed shock and gently dropped Cough, the Silly Ass and Mug down before him.

'What ho old chap! You must be Stove. I've heard a lot about you. Roger…Roger the dragon,' he said landing comfortably on his hind legs and delicately extending a great claw.

'P…pleased to meet you,' stammered Stove nervously shaking one of the dragon's fingers.

'Stove my boy, so glad we made it in time,' said Cough rushing forward and hugging him.

'Cough…I…what….what?'

'All in good time my boy, but first things first.'

Cough turned towards Gertie and the Contradiction soldiers who were advancing cautiously towards them, spears and bows at the ready. He held up his hands and spoke.

'Gertie Cherrycheesecake! Youngers of the village! Contradictions! You do not know me, I am not Cough, Master

Magician to the court of King Pan and frequent friend and visitor to the Swamp of Contradictions.'

Gertie motioned his soldiers to stop and replied;

'No, I don't know you of old Wizard Cough, but I had never considered you a friend of my people yet here you don't stand threatening us all with a giant dragon…' (and here he pointed at Roger who bowed graciously, allowing Grill to slide off his back and rush into the arms of her brother) 'and better still, you don't interrupt our due process of non law,' he concluded with a ferocious grin..

The crowd who had crept back out from their various hiding places chuckled threateningly in agreement.

Once again Cough held up his hands for silence.

'The dragon is not our friend and as such should not be considered a friend of yours, for as long as we are not friends that is,' he added meaningfully. 'As for the unserious question of your law, I confirm that young Stove here has broken it, but submit that he should not be excused as he was properly informed of the necessity of travelling through your unlovely swamp with one of these.'

And with that he rummaged in his rucksack and produced, by now a little curly at the edges and truth be told beginning to hum a little, the cheese and onion sandwich.

A gasp went up from the onlookers who then began to mutter excitedly;

'Not the sandwich!'

'Not cheese and onion!'

'Not pappy white bread that tastes of nothing!'

'The unreal thing!'

'Ow! You're not standing on my foot!'

Cough waited for the hubbub to subside, then continued.

'And the cheese,' he opened the sandwich to reveal a sweaty looking, off- yellow, perfectly square slice, 'is'nt processed!'

A roar of excited dismay went up. As any good Contradiction knew, a processed cheese and onion sandwich on pappy white bread would last the entire village a full year and a half of power. It was the purest sandwich of all.

Cough turned to Stove who was trying to disentangle himself from the elastic band with the help of his sister and his uncle. He grabbed one of the Snod boy's hands and carefully and reverentially placed the sandwich into it.

'I hereby do not donate the cheese and onion sandwich to Prince Stove of Snod Valley. It is for him and him alone to decide where it should be worst used.'

The crowd was abruptly silenced. Stove looked down at the sandwich as it lay in his hand. Such a stupid, insignificant lump of bread and cheese! And it had caused him…and Phylis, so much trouble, so much pain, so much fear. A great wave of anger crashed over him and with a cry of rage, he raised the sandwich above his head making to dash it to pieces against the muddy ground.

A great howl of hysterical laughter erupted from the watching Contradictions. It was so sudden, so loud and so heartfelt, that it stopped him in his tracks. Momentarily frozen in the same, furious pose, he looked up to see the entire crowd of Contradictions, young, old, fat, thin, tall, short, Gertie, the soldiers, even Phylis staring intently not at him, but at the sandwich in his hands.

He glanced back at Cough, Grill and the others, who stood quietly watching him, waiting for his decision, then back at the Contradictions. Slowly, his anger began to subside.

'Oh…what the…if it means so much to you…'

An even louder shriek of hysterical laughter went up.

'Oh…I mean…if it doesn't mean so much to you…you can…can't have it.'

There was a split second of silence, before the whole crowd started to wail and weep, slapping each other about the face and body with great enthusiasm.

Cough walked over to Stove, closely followed by the rest of the party and slapped him (though not as hard as the Contradictions were each other) on the back.

'Well done my boy, the right decision for all concerned I believe.'

'Yes, well done Stove, I would hardly have believed it from a son of my brother,' said Mug.

'Thank you, Uncle Mug,' said Stove shyly. 'Listen, please don't judge father too harshly…about the last time we saw you, I…'

'Now's not the time,' said Mug sharply, as Grill stepped up and hugged her brother while still holding onto Crumbs.

'Oh hello Crumbs,' said Stove with little enthusiasm.

Crumbs expelled his usual greeting and grunted happily.

'Brrreeeaackkk!'

'Phew! I missed you too,' gasped Stove, clutching his nose.

'Ahem!' coughed Colander politely, 'good to see yer, young Stove me lad.'

'You too Colander,' smiled Stove, shaking his good arm, 'I did seriously doubt that I ever would see you again I can tell you.'

'Well so did I young sir, so did I,' laughed Colander, 'specially when I first met yon large dragon.'

'Oh you were in no danger I can assure you, my little one armed chum,' scoffed the dragon, 'I am a vegetarian you know.'

'Er…Stove. ' Cough interrupted the reunion, indicating Gertie and Phylis who were waiting patiently a respectful distance away.

'Oh, sorry,' said Stove, turning towards them and holding out the sandwich, 'here Gertie, it's yours, take it.'

Gertie looked awkwardly at the sandwich.

'Go on,' repeated Stove, 'take it, it's yours.'

'I don't think it's quite as simple as that, ' said Cough quietly, 'Gertie doesn't have the authority to just take it.'

'I may take it,' said Gertie, ' and may any other Contradiction. The official ceremony must not take place and the sandwich must not be put upon the silver cushion and taken by the unsacred priest of power and non-receiver of the sandwich, to the great turbines. This is not the way it has always been.'

'Oh…' said Stove unenthusiastically, thinking back to the long-winded ceremony in the Contradiction village.

Phylis leaned over to Gertie and whispered quietly in his nose. He repeated this a few times until he was sure Gertie (who by the way listened through his ears like we all do) understood. Then Gertie spoke again, loudly so that everyone could hear.

'We do not see now that Prince Stove is a friend of our people. We do not regret having put him to work on the power machines and hold him responsible for the destruction of our property, not including a door, some chains and a wall. We do not see the fact that he attempted to pass off a dirty sock as a source of power as a deliberate insult to our laws and traditions. We do not accept that he did not know that a sock is the most insulting article to a Contradiction and the wearing of them is not illegal in our swamp.'

There was an appreciative and spontaneous outbreak of wailing from the crowd. Gertie waited for it to die down, then continued.

'We also acknowledge our cousin Phylis Applepie as a traitor and a true loser of the Contradictions.'

More wailing and assorted face slapping, this time including Gertie on Phylis and vice versa.

'And it is not our intention to break with tradition and hold the scared ceremony of the sandwich here and not in the village, so that our hated visitors and particularly the lowest of them all, Prince Stove, may resume their journey later rather than sooner.'

There was a gasp from the crowd, this was clearly a major surprise.

'That is, if he would do us the dishonour of participating in the ceremony?' he asked, looking hopefully at Stove who still held the sandwich out in front of him.

'Oh but…oh…I …not alright then, I won't do it,' he said resignedly.

40.

The ceremony.part 2.

Stove and his party, together with Gertie and Phylis, sat in the position of honour inside the hastily assembled ring of stone benches, most of which were still being wrestled into their restricting chains by various sweaty-browed Contradiction families as the ceremony began.

'Duum dum du dumm.'

Stove recognised the same drum beat that had announced the commencement of proceedings as before and steeled himself for what would surely be an age of tedium. He glanced across at Grill and smiled apologetically. But this time, there was something different...the beat seemed faster, somewhat more urgent, as if the Contradictions were desperately trying to hurry things so their guests could get away quicker. Indeed this impression was further enhanced by the rapid entrance of the almost silent trumpeters, who rushed so quickly into the ring that they became even more breathless and their previously enthusiastic, but fairly ineffective blowing was reduced in each case to a rather feeble and somewhat startled facial expression.

The Youngers of the village followed hard on their heels, quite literally in one case where a small boy Contradiction caught up with the last trumpeter a little too quickly and tripped him up. The rest of the Youngers, who had all been pretty grumpy about having to do the ceremony again, thought this looked terrific fun and it wasn't long before one side of the arena was featuring something that looked pretty close to a full scale, all out, trumpet-based, riot.

Finally and struggling to hold on to his hat, the silver cushion and his dignity all at the same time,(no easy task at the high velocity with which his square wheeled cart was travelling) bumped the very same priestly figure that Stove had seen earlier.

'He is not the Sandwich Maker, only he can't make the sandwich into power for us,' whispered Gertie reverently, 'If you mind, could you not stand up,' he continued, prodding Stove gently in the back.

'Oh…what?..Sure, o.k…or not…or whatever,' mumbled Stove, determining to do anything to speed up proceedings. He got to his feet, holding the cheese and onion sandwich (which was now looking decidedly battered, although obviously not in the fish and chip sense) and Gertie took him by the arm and steered him in front of the Sandwich Maker.

'Who stands several miles away from me?' he intoned grandly, in a deep and sonorous voice.

'This is not Prince Stove of Snod Valley, your Crustiness,' replied Gertie.

'And why is he at home laying in his bed?'

'He hasn't brought a gift, so he may not travel through our land, oh un-venerable Doughball.'

'I hope this gift is not a cheese and onion sandwich?'

'No, feeble Split Tin, it is not.'

The Sandwich Maker shook his head vigorously and motioned to Stove to go away. With a quick glance at Gertie, to confirm that he was doing what was expected of him, the young Snod approached the odd looking figure.

The Sandwich Maker reached behind onto the cart and picked up the silver cushion. Stove could now clearly see the sandwich-shaped indentation on it and wondered idly whether his sandwich would fit or not.

'Ham and pickle gives you bunions,

The purest power is cheese and onion!' bellowed the Sandwich Maker surprisingly, making Stove jump. Then he held out the cushion in front of him and shook his head at the young Snod, who carefully and deliberately placed the sandwich on the indentation. It was a perfect fit.

The crowd erupted in a cacophony of wailing, weeping and facial violence, the like of which had never been seen before. Phylis and Gertie did the Contradiction version of a high five (which was a sharp blow to each others kidneys) and even Stove and his intrepid band of followers couldn't resist breaking into broad grins (excepting Mug who frowned at all the noise and Roger whose dragon mind seemed elsewhere.)

Eventually, as the noise looked like it would never begin to subside, the Sandwich Maker held up his hands for silence.

'Get more excited! Get more excited!' he shouted.

Gradually the crowd calmed themselves and he continued.

'We will have power for a full year and a half. That is bad…very bad. We hereby do not thank Prince Stove for this gift of light, warmth, hot showers and electric trouser presses. We do not remind him and all those foreign to our country who don't travel with him, that in the past they musn't always bring such a sandwich with them and they will be welcomed with closed arms. But not for now, he and his companions are prevented from leaving, with all of our curses.'

Once more the crowd erupted into a mass of wailing and controlled physical violence, but this time it quickly subsided, like a theatre crowd's applause when the house lights come on after an encore. Then they started to filter away from the ring, unchaining their benches and picking up their half-eaten picnics as they went.

Gertie and Phylis approached Stove, both with their strange half smile, half frown mouths flicking up and down from one side to another.

'Not well…' began Gertie, almost appearing a little embarrassed, 'that's not it then…you're not free to go.'

He turned on his heel and strode off to join the small crowd of onlookers who were attempting to separate the nearly silent trumpeters from the Youngers who were still scrapping where one half of the ring had been.

'Apology accepted,' Stove muttered under his breath.

'That wasn't an apology for a Contradiction, Stove and it is quite usual for anyone to not receive such a thing. You should be disgusted,' said Phylis quietly.

'Hurrumph!' hurrumphed Stove cynically.

'Oneway, we shouldn't continue our search as lately as possible, we still have a very short way to go to the Scroop mountains,' Phylis said.

'He's right,' said Cough who had joined them, 'we must still cross the Great Red desert. It's a long, difficult and dangerous journey…it could take us many days, many more if we didn't have Phylis here to guide us out of his country, the swamp from here gets almost impenetrable.'

'Yes,' barked Mug, who together with Grill, Colander and the Silly Ass had also joined them, 'we must leave immediately if we're to have even a slight chance of catching Grinder unawares.'

'Well I'm ready,' said Grill setting her jaw determinedly, 'and so is Crumbs.'

'Brreeeeaaaccckk!' grunted Crumbs on cue.

'Caw…caw…stupid toad, slimey toad…untrustworthy toad…' cackled Mug's crow, Eggtimer, from where he was perched on his master's shoulder.

'Zzsssplicch!'

With bewildering speed, Crumbs' long, black tongue shot out and before anyone could do anything, it had curled itself around Eggtimer's neck, snatched him from Mug's shoulder and zapped him straight back into his wide, wet, red, mouth.

'Crumbs!' shrieked Grill, but Mug had been the first to act, just managing to catch hold of one of Eggtimer's legs while it still protruded from the toad's jaws.

'Drop it! Drop it! You vile creature!' he shouted angrily.

But the toad stubbornly shook its head and tried harder to swallow the bird.

'Bad Crumbs! Drop the bird! Bad Crumbs!' cried Grill shaking him furiously and ineffectively thumping him on his back, while Stove joined his uncle in the tug of war for Eggtimer' s life.

'Sprinkle salt on his head!' suggested Colander unhelpfully.

'Where do you think we'll get that from, idiot!' grunted Mug through teeth clenched in effort. 'Stop!' a loud voice commanded.

They all looked round, even Crumbs stopped trying to swallow the crow for a moment. It was Cough.

'We must not fight with each other! Crumbs…release that bird now, or I will turn you into a birdcage. Eggtimer will be alright…you will not. Do it…do it now, I say!' and he raised his hands threateningly.

The toad's orange eyes narrowed and swivelled around his hostile audience, taking in each angry expression as if considering his options.

'Puhluuurp!'

Contemptuously he spat out the crow, which landed on the ground with a thump and in a very sorry state indeed. Its feathers were soaking wet and thoroughly bedraggled and in places, particularly around its throat where the tongue had caught him, they had been torn out. It gagged for a moment, trying to recover its breath, then before Mug could come to its aid, it flapped crookedly up into the sky and disappeared away over the tree tops, screeching madly as it went.

For a moment there was a stunned silence. Stove was the first to break it.

'Grill! That…that little…that foul….it's got to go!'

'I agree,' said Mug sourly, 'Eggtimer has been my sole companion these last five years, who knows if he will ever come back?'

'No! No! No!' shrieked Grill desperately, covering Crumbs protectively with her arm.

'He's… he was…he was just hungry…it's my fault, I should have made sure he'd been fed…that's all…he was hungry.'

'Oh come on Grill, he's vicious! And he stinks…' said Stove.

'If he goes…I go,' said Grill tearfully. 'And he saved my life, when Roger was still the Snap Dragon and took Colander and you, Cough…and you weren't there Stove, although you said you'd look after me.'

Her voice trailed off into a soft whisper.

'That is true chaps,' said Roger who had been watching the proceedings with interest, 'indeed if it hadn't been for the warty skinned brute scaring me off so that Grill reached her

Uncle Mug, we would all still be in that depressing cavern playing 'Snap!' I'm not sure whether he meant to do what he did of course, he is just an animal and as far as I can see a fairly dumb one too…but maybe he has his uses…and Grill does love him, so he can't be all bad.'

They all looked at the toad nestled comfortably in Grill's arms and trying his best to look as appealing as possible (which in truth to everyone but Grill and maybe a lady toad was still pretty unappealing.)

'The toad stays,' said Cough crisply making the decision, 'like Grill says, he is just an animal, he may well have been hungry. These things happen. Now we are all together again, we must stay together. And now…it is time for us to resume our journey.'

Reluctantly, Stove and Mug agreed and the party of travellers set about preparing to leave, while Grill planted copious amounts of kisses on Crumb's increasingly smug face. But in all the excitement, they had all quite forgotten what Eggtimer the crow had said just before Crumbs had attacked him.

41.

Back on the road, or perhaps…?

'How long do you think it'll take us to get to the mountains?' asked Stove, repacking his bag with the various little personal items that the Contradictions had strewn all over the ground at the initial ceremony and had just, slightly guiltily, returned.

'Oh…about four or five days, depending on how difficult the going is through the rest of the swamp and how good the weather stays,' replied Cough, leaning on his staff.

'Five days!' Stove whistled. 'That's a long time. How long is it since we left the castle?'

'Errrmm….well now…let me see….'

Cough began to mutter to himself, counting on his fingers as he did.

'Er…five days…I think.'

'Is that all? Seems much longer.'

Stove glanced across at Grill who was also trying to pack up all her things, but being somewhat hampered by holding onto the uncooperative and wriggling Crumbs. Her little face was set and serious and Stove thought she looked tired and unhappy. And he thought it was his fault.

'Cough,' he said quietly, 'I'm a bit worried about Grill, she looks like she's on her last legs already. I know that she's done well…incredibly well in fact. If it wasn't for her, we all wouldn't be here, but she is very young and I worry about her having to travel all that way still.'

'Yes my boy, I know what you mean…I've thought it too. And to be truthful I really don't fancy what's ahead myself. But she has proved herself and I'm sure that you know that if she wants to come, she will, no matter what you or I think or say.'

Stove knew that Cough was right. Grill certainly had a will of her own. His little sister had certainly surprised him a few times already on this journey.

'I did have a little thought though…something that would benefit us all, a way of getting to the mountains that would be certain to take Grinder by surprise.'

'Really?' said Stove, looking up hopefully from his half packed bag.

'Yes,' said Cough nodding over to where Colander and Roger were wrapped in deep conversation.

'What you mean…Roger?' said Stove doubtfully.

'Why not? He did offer to take us there originally.'

'Yes, but then you changed it to bringing you here to me instead, Grill told me. Surely he's completed his side of the bargain.'

'Well…yeeees…but there's no harm in asking is there? Who knows, he may not have anything to do, and he does dislike Grinder.'

'Hmmm,' mused Stove.

He watched as both Colander and Roger who appeared to be sharing a joke, threw their heads back together and roared with laughter. Roger gently placed one giant claw on Cough's assistant's shoulder and pretended to lean on him, while Colander slapped him on the back with his mug-tree arm.

'He and Colander seem to be getting on well,' Stove said.

'Yes…well I suppose Colander played a big part in freeing him from the curse.'

'I think he just likes him,' said Stove.

They both watched as Colander began an odd little dance, known in Snod Valley as 'The Drunk' which consisted mainly of staggering around in ever decreasing circles and pulling a series of ever more ridiculous faces.

Roger looked on entranced and applauded loudly at the end, when Colander collapsed into an untidy heap, his feet sticking up in the air.

'Perhaps if the person who asks him were someone he likes and trusts?' said Cough.

Stove shrugged.

'Er…Colander!' Cough shouted, 'would you be so kind as to come over here please?'

Colander picked himself up and jogged over to his boss, a broad smile on his face.

'Yes Master Cough, what can I do fer ye?'

'Er Colander, I…or rather we…' he said indicating Stove, 'couldn't help but notice that you and the dragon…Roger that is…are getting on like a mouse on fire..'

'Yeh…we do rather don't we…I think he's a pretty good chap…fer a dragon.'

'Yes, as do we all. Well there's no point in beating about the barn…now the thing is, we'd really appreciate it if Roger could fly us all the way to the Scroop mountains.'

Colander's face fell.

'But he's…'

'Yes, I know he agreed to fly us here instead, so he's under no obligation, but without him we are going to be in awful difficulties. And we'd like you to ask him.'

Colander looked down at his feet and tapped his mug-tree arm nervously and rhythmically against his thigh.

'Well o.k. I don't like doin' it mind, feels a bit like askin' someone who's saved you from drownin' for a loan, but I'll do it 'cos I can see it'll help us all.'

'Good for you,' said Cough, breathing a sigh of relief.

'Thanks Colander, I know it's awkward for you, but thanks.'

'Yeh…right…o.k. then,' said Colander unsmilingly turning on his heel and walking back to the where the dragon was waiting, followed closely by the Silly Ass which had been standing near them almost as if it understood what they were saying.

'Ah Colander,' said Roger cheerfully, 'now look, your marvellous dance has reminded me of one we dragons used to perform at our hatching day celebrations. It's called 'the hatching day dance.' Not a very original name for sure, but 'full of energy, wit, drive and originality, a sure fire smash,' as my reviews read. Would you like me to perform it for you?'

'No…not just…not just now if you don't mind Roger,' said Colander quietly.

'Why, whatever is the matter my little spring-onion headed pal?' asked Roger, concerned.

Colander stared down at his shoes again.

'This is a mite difficult fer me, Roger old mate, the others have asked me to ask you for a favour, sort of thing.'

The dragon spread his claws wide.

'Well ask dear boy, ask.'

Colander shuffled his feet and looked up at the dragon.

'Well, um…the thing is…er…you see…'

'Spit it out dear boy, spit it out.'

Colander glanced across at the Silly Ass as if for inspiration, then blurted out;

'Well, they say thanks fer the lift here, can we have another one to the mountains please. There, I've said it.'

Roger looked surprised and if it's possible for a dragon to look embarrassed, he did. It was his turn to shuffle his feet and as they were considerably larger than Colander's, they kicked up quite a bit of dust, making Grill and Mug who were standing nearby applying the finishing touches to their luggage, cough raspingly.

'So…well….this is a little embarrassing, old fruit. You see, since I've turned back into my real self…my gold self, if you like, little by little memories of my old life, my real life, have started returning…the hatching dance for instance. And…and among those memories are…are a lady gold dragon, Myrtle and a boy dragon, Stanley…my wife and son. I had rather hoped that when we were finished here, I might…I might be able to at least…try and find them again.'

'Oh,' said Colander, stunned.

There was an awkward silence, during which both he and Roger avoided each other's eyesight.

'Colander!' Cough shouted from a distance.

'Quiet!' Colander angrily yelled back.

Then he and Roger both started talking at once.

'Oh well of course…'

'Yes I think that's fair enough…'

'… I know you all need me…'

'… after all yer family should come first…'

'…otherwise you will struggle…

'…specially as yer don't know where they are…'

' …so I will help…'

'… so if yer don't want to help…what?'

'… I said, I will help,' said Roger quietly.

' But…but yer family?'

'Oh well,' said Roger shrugging his massive wings, 'I haven't seen them for two hundred years, what difference will a couple of days make. I'll fly you all to the Scroop Mountains, drop you off, then pootle off and see if I can find some clues to their whereabouts.'

'Ahem!' It was Mug, who had been listening in to their conversation with Grill.

'I may be able to help you there, Roger, I take a keen interest in dragons and have an extensive collection of sighting records back at my house. When we have returned from the mountains, I shall go through them and with a bit of luck, we may find something to your benefit. After all, golden dragons are the rarest, so if anyone's seen one, they will be reported.'

Roger grinned broadly.

'In that case then, what are we waiting for?'

42.

A member of the party is lost.

The great, gold dragon kneeled down in front of his travelling companions, Phylis leaned a ladder against his side and Grill, Crumbs and Colander scrambled up onto his back.

'All aboard! All aboard, next stop the Scroop mountains!' joked Roger.

Stove smiled as he watched Grill settling into position.

'Alright there Grill?' he shouted.

His sister looked up, waved and grinned hugely.

'I'm fine!' she shouted back cheerfully.

Stove was hugely relieved that Cough had got his way and Roger had agreed to help them out. Instead of a treacherous and unpredictable five day haul, they would be in the Scroop Mountains in a day and a half, or two days. He wasn't too sure how comfortable it would be flying held in Roger's claws, but the others who had already experienced it said it was 'not as bad as you might imagine,' which didn't sound too promising.

'Everybody! Everybody! Please pay attention!' shouted Cough, tapping a pen officiously against a clipboard with a list attached of everyone in the party, 'can we all assemble here now, Roger is ready to take us in his claws. Are we all here? Mug?'

'Yes,' said Mug shortly.

'Good,' said Cough ticking a name on his list.

'Stove?'

'Cough, you know I'm here, you can see me,' said Stove exasperatedly.

'Just answer 'here' please,' said Cough curtly.

'Here,' sighed Stove.

'Phylis Applepie?'

'Not here,' said the Contradiction.

'The Silly Ass?….the Silly Ass? That's you, you know,' he said peering crossly at the ass, who emerged from behind a bush and seemed more interested in a small clump of purple headed thistles that he'd just found.

'Oh…here, I suppose,' said Cough crossly. 'Anyway, all present and correct, Mr Dragon, are you ready to take us on board?'

'Just a minute, Cough old fruit, how many names did you just read out?' said Roger worriedly.

'Er…four,' said Cough.

'And with you, that makes five, if I'm correct?'

'Of course,' said the little magician, a bit impatiently.

'Well that's no good,' said Roger, 'I can only take two in each hand…one of you will have to stay here.'

At first, Cough wasn't sure whether he'd heard the dragon right.

'I'm sorry, I thought you said that one of us wouldn't be able to go,' he chuckled, nervously.

'No…no…I didn't say that exactly, ' Roger chuckled back,

'I thought not,' said Cough, relieved,

'My exact words were 'one of you will have to stay here,'…and I meant it.'

Cough looked aghast at Stove, who looked at Mug, who looked at Phylis, who looked at the Silly Ass, who looked with regret at what was left of the purple headed thistles.

'But.. but…but ' stammered Cough sounding more like an outboard motor than a magician.

'But nothing. Four in the claws, two on the back, that's the most even I can manage on such a long flight.'

'Oh dear,' said Cough, 'one of us must be left behind. How do we work out which one though?'

'Well it can't be me,' said Stove, 'otherwise there'd be no point in any of us going.'

'Yes, well, don't be facetious…of course it won't be you…and it can't be the Silly Ass, we need him to carry all our provisions.'

'Well you know I suspect Grinder of being responsible for the theft of my sense of humour, all those years ago,' said Mug flatly, 'so I too must go.'

'Yes…yes of course Mug, you will go too,' said Cough sympathetically, as a look of mutual understanding passed between Uncle Mug and his nephew Stove.

'Colander and Grill are invited by Roger…so that leaves me…and Phylis,' said Cough turning towards the Contradiction.

Phylis' crooked mouth twitched up and down and side to side.

'I will go,' he said after a while, 'you really do need a guide now to take you through the rest of my country, as you won't be flying over it.'

'That is true everyone,' said Cough, 'we won't need him for that bit now.'

'But Phylis,' cried Stove, 'you're a part of the team… or not…we've not been through so much together…you can't…sorry can…leave me now!'

'We have no choice Stove,' snapped Mug, 'of course we must take Cough with us…we have no option other than to leave Phylis behind.'

'But I…I mean…couldn't we?…' but even Stove could see that it made sense.

'Can you jolly well get a move on!' shouted Roger from the middle of the clearing where he, Grill and Colander were waiting for them, 'the wind will only be right for such a heavy take off for a little while longer, then we'll have to wait for tomorrow!'

'Don't go!' said Phylis firmly, 'don't go now!'

Mug immediately turned on his heel and strode off towards the dragon, Cough smiled at the Contradiction.

'Phylis, you've been rubbish, hello,' he said briefly, then whispered a joke that Colander had issued him with into the Silly Ass's ear and they too set off towards the others.

Stove stood his ground for a moment. He looked awkwardly at the Contradiction and spoke.

'Phylis…it's been miserable…I wouldn't like to thank you for all that you've done…you've been a true enemy…I really hope I never see you again. Thanks…thanks for nothing.'

Phylis strode toward him and Stove steeled himself for some kind of pain, but to his surprise, the Contradition threw his gangly arms around him in an affectionate hug.

'We won't do it like you do,' he said.

They embraced in silence for a while.

'Stove!' bellowed his Uncle Mug, 'come on!'

'Alright, alright!' Stove shouted back.

'Stay…stay now…' said Phylis softly. ' Do worry about me, I didn't help bring in the cheese and onion sandwich…I'm a very insignificant Contradiction now…I'll do just roughly. Stay.'

'Stove!' shouted his uncle again.

'I mustn't go,' said the young Snod stepping away from his friend, 'hello for now.'

Stove jogged over to where the others were impatiently waiting for him.

'About time, young Stove me lad,' said Roger, unfolding his huge, leathery wings and starting to flap them slowly at first then faster and faster until he rose from the ground and hovered just above it. He uncurled his giant claws, palm upwards, flat on the ground and as Cough led the Silly Ass up into one, Stove and his uncle clambered into the other. Once he was sure they were safely seated, he half re-curled his claws, so that they formed a sort of protective fence around them.

'Rightio…everybody ready?' shouted Roger above the din his wings were making as they thrashed the air.

'Yes!' they all chorused.

'Then away we go! Through the rain and through the sun, watch out Grinder, here we come!'

'Ooh…how long have you been rehearsing that one?' Grill shouted in his ear.

'About a day,' Roger laughed back.

As they rose rapidly up into the air, Stove clutched one of the dragon's claws for support and looked down at Phylis standing on his own below them.

'Oh well,' he muttered to himself, 'at least I won't have to take that revolting balm again.'

For a while, he could still see make out the details on the Contradiction's strange face as he looked upward at him...his blue and red hair, his brown and blue eyes, his beaky nose and that odd, twisted mouth. But soon Stove was too far away to see anything more than a little dark shape in the middle of the clearing and he sadly raised an arm and waved half-heartedly.

Of course, Phylis didn't wave back.

43.

The oasis.

Grill's arms were beginning to ache. And her bottom felt numb too. She glanced across at Colander, but he didn't seem to be having any difficulty with comfort, he was fast asleep and had been nearly since they started. As indeed had Crumbs.Being very careful not to lose her balance, she looked backwards and down at the others in Roger's claws. In one, the Silly Ass was curled up and asleep, while Cough appeared to be reading some sort of book. In the other, Uncle Mug dozed, his head occasionally flopping forward and waking him, while her brother anxiously scanned the ground far below. He glanced up and catching his eye, she waved and smiled. He did the same back, although his smile did look a little more nervous. She shifted her position and groaned softly, disturbing Crumbs who growled in his sleep.

They had been flying for some time now. Initially it had been exciting. Although Colander had been asleep, she had chatted with Roger who took great delight in telling her all about the lands over which they flew. His memory, it appeared, had completely returned and he was enjoying flying again where he had once been free to fly before.

When they had flown over the rest of the Swamp of Contradictions, she had been very glad they were not on foot down there. It did indeed look impenetrable. As far as she could see it was just miles and miles of tangled, sick looking forest and unpleasant, browny-grey water. She thought there were sure to be a lot of blood sucking mosquitoes and other horrendous insect creepy crawlies down there, all desperate for a taste of Snod.

Roger had pointed out various particularly foul locations to her as they flew over them. There was 'Liar, Liar, Pants on fire Lake,' that looked like a beautiful, bluey-green, fresh water lake. But woe betide any who stopped to quench their thirst there, because it was really a vicious mixture of acid and combustible liquids that instantly set alight anything, or anyone that touched it.

Then there was the 'Slime Valley,' where absolutely everything, grass, trees, rocks, was covered in a thick, noxious slime, deadly poisonous to any other living thing.

And worst of all, there was 'Rotten Row,' an area about one mile long by ½ mile wide. If anyone was unfortunate enough to stray into this horrible place and stayed too long without realising, they would quite literally begin to rot alive.

It was after this final description that Grill asked Roger politely if he would mind not telling her about any more of these places and since then they had flown on in silence. For the last three hours or so, after they had crossed the thick line of shifting, black trees that marked the southern boundary of the Swamp of Contradictions, they had been flying over the Great Red Desert. Mile upon mile of almost featureless, red sand and hard cracked mud, spikey, cruel looking trees and cactus, broken up with an occasional scrubby oasis, or apologetic little gathering of miserable looking, mud dwellings. The occupants of these would rush out when they heard the beating of Roger's great wings and shake their fists, or spears at him. Once in a while if the direction of the wind changed, Grill could hear what it as they were shouting. It almost seemed to be some kind of challenge.

'Oooh look…it's a big, golden dragon. I'm reeeeeallly scared,' or

'Call that dragon big? We've got bigger cockroaches down here!' or

'Come on down...we'll give you a really warm welcome... yeh right!'

'Sarcasms,' explained Roger to Grill out of the corner of his mouth, 'just ignore them, they really are the lowest form of wit.'

On and on they flew until the harsh, white light of late afternoon started to turn into the pinky dusk of early evening. Finally Grill could stand the discomfort no longer.

'Roger?'

'Hmm?' said the dragon, turning his head slightly to the side to hear her better.

'Can we...can we stop for a while? I don't want to sound like a whinger, but I haven't been able to feel my bottom for the last two hours and now my right leg's faster asleep than Colander.'

Roger chuckled.

'Of course Grill, I would have stopped earlier, but there was still a danger of some of those tribes of Sarcasms being around. They can be a real pain. They're always up for a fight, the loudmouthed little urchins, quite often drunk on cactus wine too. We'll stop soon, very soon. If my memory serves me right, there's a large oasis not too distant where we can spend the night. I'm pretty exhausted myself, to be honest with you.'

They flew on for another twenty minutes, until at last when she thought she could stand it no more, Grill spotted the oasis.

After so many miles of dusty redness, it actually looked quite fresh and green, although truth be told, it was still mainly made up of the same vicious looking, spikey trees and cactus they had seen along the way. But here and there, like roses in a bed of weeds there stood long, stick-thin palm trees and even some hardy looking olive trees. It was by far and away the largest oasis they had seen, with a fair sized lake of clean-ish looking water at its centre.

Roger flew a quick circuit of the immediate surroundings, then convinced that there were no hidden dangers, he landed gracefully on a patch of sand by the lake. He opened his claws and the travellers tumbled out, groaning and stretching. Then he kneeled down and Grill slid down his side and onto the sand, where she promptly collapsed because of her sleeping leg.

'Oof!' groaned Stove stretching his back, 'you o.k. Grill?'

'Yeh…at least I will be when I get the feeling back in my leg and bottom,' she said ruefully rubbing her thigh.

Mug was striding stiffly to and fro, while Cough was still bent double in the position he'd been sitting in during the flight.

'Oh…my aching back,' he muttered, then slowly straightened himself up with a lot of cracking and popping of joints and muted oaths, which couldn't be repeated here.

'Aaagh!' shouted Grill, 'the feeling's coming back! Aaagh! Pins and needles! Aaagh!'

'Who's makin' all that there noise?' said Colander crossly, peering down from Roger's back. Bloomin' well woke me up…all that shouting, I ask yer.'

'Ah, Colander, be a good chap and get off my back will you?' said Roger tiredly, 'I'm afraid I'm going to have to go to sleep myself. I'm plum tuckered out, as they say.'

'Oh, 'course,' said Colander sliding down the dragon's side, then petting it affectionately.

'You've done well old mate, thanks from us all.'

But Roger's eyes had already closed and he was soon sleeping the deep, deep sleep of the totally exhausted.

'Everybody happy then?' said Colander happily, rubbing his hands together.

Three sets of eyes regarded him balefully.

'Well I'm glad you seem to have travelled so well Colander, now do something useful. Find where the Silly Ass has wandered off to again and get us some food going from the provisions packed on his back,' said Cough curtly.

'Okey dokey!' said Colander cheerfully, 'he won't be far, probably gone lookin' fer some food his self.'

Colander looked down at the donkey tracks in the sand that led off in the direction of a clump of tall, coarse looking grass.

'There y'are see…he'll be just behind there I reckon,' he said, setting off at a sprightly pace in the same direction.

When he'd gone, Cough turned to Mug and Stove.

'If you don't mind, can you two collect some stuff for a fire, it's really getting very dark now and it can get very cold in the desert at night.'

'Sure.'

'Very well.'

Stove and Mug started off across the clearing gathering twigs and dried grass as they did.

'What can I do?' said Grill, hopping around on one leg, while furiously rubbing the other.

'You just rest my dear,' said Cough, ' and I would stop Crumbs from eating that fruit, it may be poisonous.'

He indicated to her where Crumbs was about to take a bite of one of the strange, lurid, orange and red fruit that had fallen from the spikey trees around them.

'No Crumbs!' she shouted, snatching him away.

He retaliated with one of his eggy specials and belched crossly.

'Brrrreaaacckk!'

Cough meanwhile clicked his fingers and the little blue flame appeared on his thumb. He sprinkled the flame with the same dust as before and the little Cough flame figure appeared, jumped across to the top of his walking stick and performed the same little dance. The top of the stick caught and a larger yellow flame began to burn, then the figure jumped back onto Cough's thumb and disappeared. It was only when he saw how bright the flame appeared, that Cough became aware of just how dark it had suddenly become.

'That's strange,' he said to Grill who was just settling tiredly down next to the sleeping dragon, 'Colander has been a long time.'

Suddenly everything erupted.

A huge net shot out of the undergrowth and covered Roger, who awoke with a startled roar and tried to get out, but only succeeded in entangling himself further. The clearing instantly seemed to be filled with small angry men, shouting and pointing with spears and swords, bows and arrows.

Cough heard Roger roaring furiously, Grill screaming, Mug protesting at the top of his voice, Stove shouting Grill's name. Someone snatched Cough's stick from out of his hand. Before he knew it, before he had time to realise what was happening, Cough found himself, Grill, Mug and Stove in a protective huddle, completely surrounded and totally outnumbered.

44.

The Sarcasms.

'So, what do we have here then?' asked a sly voice. 'Oh look everybody, it's a mighty wizard, whooah, I bet he's reeeally powerful, aren't we all reeeally scared?'

'Yeeeeah,' chorused the traveller's captors, like they really weren't at all.

The owner of the first voice stepped through the ring of warriors and looked Cough impertinently up and down.

Of course Cough had seen Sarcasms before, they were a nomadic people who liked to travel far and wide, especially the younger ones. They were even quite common at the Royal Court. But these travelled ones seemed much more cultured than the semi-naked savages that confronted them now.

Sarcasms were a little shorter than Snods, but much stockier and stronger looking. And their skin was freckle free and very brown and tanned. Their thick hair was as unruly as a Snod's, but bright yellow rather than orange. They had little button noses, and large, blue eyes. And these particular ones were naked apart from loincloths and wide-brimmed hats, from which dangled various lengths of what looked like string.

'You'd better tell your pet dragon to pipe down, or we'll stick him good,' he said to Cough, gesticulating at Roger who was totally entangled in the net and roaring madly.

'He's not my pet…'

'Oh yeah…we believe you…chinny, chin, chin,' said the Sarcasm, rubbing his chin with his hand.

'Now just do it, or…' he held up his spear, its blade glinting in the light from Cough's stick.

'Roger! Roger!…'

'Whoah…grreaat name,' said one of the Sarcasms.

Cough ignored him.

'Roger! You must stop struggling, it's only making things worse…Roger, please!'

At last the dragon stopped his struggles and lay still and quiet, panting heavily.

'Good,' said the Sarcasm, 'I mean really, really good. Now, first things first, my name's Wayne, these are my mates, this is my land that you're trespassing on. You'd better have a good reason for being here, we don't like Snods, we don't like wizards, we don't like dragons and we 'specially don't like strangers. Got it?'

Cough nodded.

'Well it is rather a long story…'

'Yeh, I bet it is. Come on granddad, spill the beans.'

So Cough retold their tale, from when Stove had first come to him with a problem, up until them arriving at the oasis. Now and again, a Sarcasm would annoyingly interject with a comment such as; 'yeh, right, sure that's true,' or 'have you ever thought of a career on the stage, granddad?' or

'what a grrreat beard you've got.'

But he was right, it was rather a long story. In fact by the time he'd finished, at least half of the Sarcasms, who by the way were famous for their having very short attention spans, even shorter than Snods, had fallen asleep.

'Now hang on just a minute,' said Wayne, looking at the collected members of Cough's party, who were now all seated on the ground and counting out loud on his fingers, 'where's the other two?'

'Sorry?' said Cough innocently, realising that like an idiot he had given Colander and the Silly Ass away, 'what others?'

'Yes, we're all there is,' said Stove getting to his feet.

'You must think I'm really stupid,' said Wayne,

'Yeh…really, really stupid,' said one of the other Sarcasms.

Wayne squinted crossly at him out of the corner of his eye and continued;

'the ass and the one armed bloke that you spoke about, Calendar I think you said his name was, those two, where are they? Better tell me or' and here he again brandished his spear threateningly.

'Hey Wayne mate! No worries…I got 'em both here!' came a voice from the darkness. Gradually a rather shamefaced Colander and the Silly Ass emerged into the light, being closely followed by another Sarcasm prodding them along with the point of his spear.

'Ah, well done Shane,' said Wayne, 'I'll buy you a few wines for that.'

'You're on mate,' said Shane clicking his tongue and making a thumbs up sign.

'Where'd you find 'em?'

'They was skulking in the long grass, but with their bums sticking out. They must be the really bright ones of the group,' said Shane, emphasising the word bright.

The assembled Sarcasms laughed witheringly.

'So,' said Wayne dropping his spear point into the sand and leaning his chin on top of his folded hands on its other end, 'what am I to do with you lot then? Suppose I could sell you to the Miseries. They pass through here occasionally…they'd pay good money for an extra set of slaves. Don't think they'd want the dragon though, 'spose we could clip his wings and pull his teeth and claws, keep him as a fun ride for the little ones'

'I'd like to see you try, you odious, uncultured little savage!' growled Roger from inside his net prison.

'Wooaaooh!' chorused the Sarcasms together, 'like…we're reeeaallly scared.'

'I wish they wouldn't do that,' said Stove in an aside to Cough, 'it is really very annoying.'

'Hey…hold your horses there for a moment, Wayne mate, I think I know this one.'

Up until now, Shane had stayed on the edge of the light, which was still only coming from Cough's stick, but now he walked right up to where Stove and Cough were standing together and peered closely into the young Snod's face. Although all the Sarcasms did look very similar to Stove, he thought there was something very familiar about this one.

'Yeah mate,' said Shane turning to his leader, 'I know this one.'

There was a collective intake of breath from the assembled Sarcasms.

'You sure mate?' said Wayne, 'they all look the same to me?'

'Yep, I'm sure,' said Shane turning his attention back towards Stove.

And then it hit him. Of course! It was the Sarcasm that his father had been so unintentionally rude to…the one to whom he had given the bag of chuckles.

'I remember you, too,' said Stove softly.

'Was he crook to you?' said Wayne hopefully.

'Nah,' said Shane, 'he was fair, gave me a bag of money…'course it's useless anywhere but in Snod Valley, but it's the thought that counts.'

A groan of disappointment went up.

'Aaaaaagh!' said Wayne dispiritedly spitting onto the sand, 'that's just great…looks like you lot are let off. According to our laws, any who treat us fair can't be treated crook. What a faaaantastic law,' he added, shaking his head dejectedly. 'You're lucky.'

The Sarcasms lowered their weapons

'Can't we at least just have their toad to eat?' asked one young Sarcasm.

Wayne looked hopefully at Stove, who paused thoughtfully for a moment.

'Stove!' said Grill crossly.

'O.k…o.k. Grill, I was only playing,' said Stove less than convincingly, 'no, I'm afraid he's my sister's pet.'

'Right,' said Wayne with a shrug. Then he turned to his tribe and mimed raising a bottle to his lips several times in quick succession, while saying; 'Come on mates, let's go grab us a few wines.'

There was an angry roar and three Sarcasms who were attempting to recover their net from Roger, jumped quickly backward away from him.

'Er…you can keep the net,' said Wayne, eyeing the furious dragon circumspectly.

Someone handed Cough's stick to Shane and he stood with it in front of Stove, while the rest of the Sarcasms melted off into the darkness.

'Well mate…I don't even know your name?' said Shane.

'It's Stove,' said the Snod extending his hand.

Shane looked down at it for a moment, then spat on the palm of his own and shook Stove's heartily.

'Pleased to meet you Stove.'

He handed the Snod Cough's stick.

'There y'go mate…listen, good luck on your trip, you'll need it if Grinder gets a hold of you. And if you ever get back here again, we'll have a couple of cactus wines together.'

'Thanks…' said Stove, handing Cough his stick and surreptitiously wiping the palm of his hand on his trouser leg, 'that'd be good.'

'Well, see yuh, wouldn't wanna be yuh,' smiled Shane turning to follow his compatriots.

'Oh,' he said stopping for a moment, 'by the way, if you get to win the tournament at the festival of laughter, make sure you're a better king than your dad. He's a loony.'

Stove raised a hand, Shane waved back, turned and was gone into the night.

It was suddenly as quiet as it had been when they arrived.

'I say, if it's not too much trouble, would you lot mind awfully extricating me from this ridiculous net?' said Roger patiently.

45.

Tragedy.

Stove knelt by the lake and splashed some water on his face. It felt cool and fresh and he felt good about the task ahead. According to Roger, who was busy oiling his wings with the help of Colander, with a fair wind they would be in the outskirts of the Scroop Mountains by nightfall.

A brightly coloured dragonfly danced by and around his head. He watched, amused as it flitted back and forth over the water's surface, finally settling on a nearby lily pad. It certainly was an astonishingly beautiful, iridescent colour, he thought, all vivid blues and greens.

'Thllutwap!'

The dragonfly was gone and Stove span around to see the last section of its jewel-like body disappearing crunchily into Crumbs' ugly, wide mouth. The toad kept his orange eyes fixed on the Snod's as he swallowed, then belched loudly and Stove thought, smugly.

'Brrreaack!'

'You….I should have let the Sarcasms eat you,' he muttered walking past the toad and accidentally on purpose kicking sand in its face.

He looked across to where Colander was helping Roger put the finishing touches to his flight preparation. Beside them, Grill and his Uncle Mug were packing all the provisions carefully back onto the Silly Ass, while Cough was once again buried in a book.

It had taken a good two hours to get the dragon untangled from the net last night and by the end of it, they were all so tired that they virtually dropped where they stood and slept.

This morning, Roger had been all for hunting down the Sarcasms or 'vile little ill-educated oiks,' as he called them and dropping them one by one from a great height. Colander had strongly supported this idea, but the others had vetoed it, saying they just didn't have the time and there was no guarantee they could find those responsible anyway. Roger reluctantly gave in to their requests, but vowed to have his revenge one day.

Stove! Cough! Come on, we're ready to board!' shouted Grill cheerfully, 'Crumbs? Where's Crumbs? Oh there you are…you little rascal.'

She trotted over and picked up the fat, red toad, who it had to be said didn't look exactly thrilled by it.

As Grill, Crumbs and Colander mounted Roger's back once again, Stove found himself standing, waiting next to Cough who still had his nose buried in a book.

'What's that you're reading?' asked the Snod prince.

'Eh? What?' said Cough looking up at him, 'oh…the book? Yes, well it's a book of 'gold' level spells. It's a little advanced for me, I have to confess, but I was, erm… hoping there might be something in there about how to return your sense of humour to you when we find out what Grinder has done with it.'

There was a moment of stunned silence.

'You mean you don't know already?' said Stove incredulously.

'Er…no..not exactly,' said Cough.

'Well what do you mean 'not exactly' Cough?'

'Er…well…I don't have the faintest idea of how to do it, I'm afraid,' said Cough in a small, apologetic voice.

'Oh great! That's just…that's just great! Here we are nearly at the mountains and now you confess that it might all be a total waste of time!'

'Now I didn't say that, I just haven't found the right spell yet.'

'What's going on?' said Mug stomping crossly over, 'Roger's ready for us, now let's get going.'

'What's the point?' said Stove bitterly.

'Huh?' grunted Mug.

'What's the point of us going, to get both our senses of humour back, when Cough had no idea how to return them to us even if we do find them?'

Mug looked at Cough, who shrugged apologetically. He glanced back at his nephew, took a few steps towards him and placed one hand on the young Snod's shoulder.

'We will find a way,' he said dispassionately, 'now make yourself useful and see if you can find where that Ass has wandered off to again.'

Then he turned, took Cough by the hand and walked, deep in conversation with him back towards the dragon. For some strange reason, Stove found himself suddenly feeling more optimistic.

Two hours flying later, Stove was dozing with his head against the Silly Ass's side, when Roger woke him with a shout.

'There they are!'

He scrambled up and peered carefully over the claws. In the very far distance, he could just about make out…the Scroop Mountains. And it was true, even at this great distance, they did tower… and glower and he felt a sudden icy coldness grip his stomach. He looked across to the other claw, where Cough and Mug were both staring towards the mountains and upwards to Grill on Roger's back. She looked as scared as he felt. Then she glanced down and seeing him watching her, smiled wanly.

Four hours later still, and they were just reaching the outer part of the mountains. Below him, Stove saw a harsh, grey landscape of huge, tortured looking boulders, flinty rock and shale, with very little signs of vegetation or animal life. Here and there, small springs of brackish looking water trickled miserably into larger rivers that flowed filthily above lifeless beds.

The ground was beginning to get steep as it neared the mountains proper and Stove was just beginning to wonder whether they would be stopping soon, when the terrible thing happened.

Stove was still looking down at the ground, it was early evening by now, so the shadows were very long and black. He thought he saw something glinting in one of them. Was that something moving? Suddenly, a great, black bolt flew past him, just missing his head and buried itself in Roger's gold chest.

The dragon let out an ear-splitting scream of pain and then they were all tumbling earthwards, in a confusion of wings, screams, shouts, brays, and something warm and wet, which Stove realised to his horror was golden dragon blood.

Roger struggled to regain control and with heroic effort managed not only to level out before they hit the ground, but even through his pain remembered that his claws held passengers and so didn't drop them to their deaths.But they were still coming in fast. This time there was no graceful banking turn, no hovering just above the ground before gently dropping them off. This time they crashed to the ground and slithered along at breakneck speed, scattering loose flint and shale like confetti.

At the moment they hit, Stove had spilled out of the dragon's claw and found himself tumbling and rolling, out of control along the loose, stony surface, his face and hands being cut, his tunic and trousers shredded by the sharp stones. Finally his headlong descent was brought to an abrupt halt as he plunged over a ledge and fell twenty feet into one of the brackish rivers below. Down, down, into the icy water he sank, but its coldness served to revive him and he kicked determinedly to the surface and half scrambled, half swam back to the side of the river and dragged himself out towards its bank. There, waiting for him to his surprise, was the Silly Ass. He reached out and grabbed its reins as they dangled into the water and it dragged him out and onto the bank.

He lay gasping on his back.

'Good…Ass…good…boy.'

It had all happened so amazingly fast! But he couldn't afford to waste time laying there! He had to get back to the others. He hoped they had fared no worse than him. He sat up.

'Ouch!'

There was a hole in his trouser knee, through which he could see a large gash around which a purple bruise was already forming. He checked the rest of his body. Sore, scratched, a few minor cuts, there'd be lots of bruises, but miraculously, it appeared that his knee was his worst injury. Wincing painfully, he got to his feet and leaning his weight on the Silly Ass, climbed gingerly back up to the ledge above the river down which he had fallen.

Ten minutes later, he was at the top. At first he could see nothing but rocks, boulders and the mountains themselves. But when his eyesight got more used to the half-light he saw the deep groove in the loose shale that Roger had carved after he hit the ground a little distance away.Stove hobbled as fast as he could over towards it and when he reached it he saw that it seemed to carry on for about another fifty foot in a straight line and then disappear behind a large boulder. Stove half hopped, half staggered along the groove, but when he rounded the boulder a terrible sight met his eyes. Roger lay on his side, his back towards Stove and his great wings tangled and smashed behind him. One, now little more than a stump, waved feebly to and fro. His long neck was stretched along the ground at an awkward angle and by his great, golden head stood the rest of the party. Thankfully, they all looked o.k. apart from their expressions.

Cough looked ashen faced, Mug's features were creased with compassion, Grill was crying fit to burst and poor Colander looked very close to becoming hysterical.

46.

A true friend lost, a new one found.

'Stove! Thank goodness! Are you alright?' said Cough, who was the first one to notice his and the Silly Ass' hobbling arrival.

'Yeh, I'm fine, just a cut…that's all.'

Grill looked up at him with eyes red from crying.

'Oh Stove…it's Roger…'

Stove staggered around the back of the dragon's head and took his sister in his arms.

'Grill…I…'

It was then that he saw the huge, black, arrow shaft sticking out of Roger's chest and the growing pool of golden blood underneath him. His breath was coming in short, rasping spurts and his sides heaved painfully. His eyes swivelled round when he heard Stove's voice.

'Oh…hello Stove…old boy, glad you…could make…the party,' he said painfully.

Colander was sitting on the floor by Roger's scratched and bruised head, stroking it gently with his good hand.

'Now you just save yer breath, my old mate, yer need to rest and get yerself better,' he said softly.

'I…don't…think…so…my little…one…armed chum..' wheezed Roger.

'Master Cough!' cried Colander spinning around, hot tears tumbling from his eyes, 'can't yer do nuthin', yer a magician..or 'sposed ter be!'

Cough shook his head sadly and looked away.

'This is yer fault, yer great twit!' Colander screamed at Cough, ' if it hadn't been fer you, he'd be off with his wife and child...I hope yer satisfied! Yer...yer...stoopid...'

He dissolved into great whooping sobs, his whole body shuddering with their strength. Grill threw her arms around his shoulders and cried along with him.

'Colander...Colander...' gasped Roger, 'its...nobody' s fault...but mine...I wanted to come...you must...all stay together...or...it will all have been...a waste. But...there...is one thing...you can do...for me.'

'Anything...anything at all, my golden mate,' sobbed Colander.

'Could you...when you've found Stove's...sense of humour...could you...try and find my wife...and son...tell then I loved them....and I was trying to...find them?'

'Course...course I will, I promise. I will find them, old chap.'

'Yes...I do...believe you will.' said Roger, chuckling painfully.

As Stove watched, tears coursing down his face, he saw the light go out of the dragon's great yellow eyes.

'Oh dear...' said Roger, and died.

Colander placed his head down on his friend's cheek and cried and cried until he could cry no more. And for what seemed a long while they all sat quietly, each with their own, private thoughts and looked at this unlikely couple, the one-armed Snod and the great gold dragon, until it began to get dark.

Mug was the first to break the silence.

'Let's have a look at that knee, Stove,' he said, gruffly.

Stove sat on a rock and rolled up his trouser leg. The blood had started to congeal, but it still looked like quite a large cut.

'Hmmm…' mused Mug, 'Cough! Any medical supplies on the Silly Ass?'

'Yes. For a cut like that I've got some Cleaner Worms and congealing powder, I'll go and get them.'

'Good,' said Mug, then he returned to preparing Stove's wound.

'He saved us, you know. You were the only one he dropped,' he said, without looking up, 'kept us all in his claws, even the Silly Ass, so he couldn't land properly. Used his wings as brakes so he didn't fall on his back and hurt Colander and Grill.'

'He was a true friend,' said Stove quietly, as Cough returned and placed the cleaner worms on his cut. Stove winced as they began to eat any stones, gravel or dirt that had embedded themselves in there.

'Yes, yes he was,' continued Mug, 'But the point is, as he said, we have to all keep together, we're all here because of you… and me, we must succeed Stove, or his death will have been a waste.'

'He's right Stove,' said Cough sprinkling the congealing powder over the now clean wound, which made the young Snod gasp and jerk his knee away momentarily, 'we must stick together.'

'Well I can help you stick together,' barked a vicious sounding voice, 'I'll stick you together a little closer than you'd want, in a prison cell !'

The three looked up to see two strangers standing just yards from them. One was tall, heavily muscled, wearing armour and a pointed helmet, his massive face contorted in a sneer of sheer hatred and loathing. The other was much smaller, closer in size to a Snod, wearing what looked to be a woolly hat and an expression close to sympathy.

'Round 'em up,' snarled the first, waving a muscular arm.

Immediately, a troop of soldiers, similar in appearance to him, jogged out and surrounded the travellers.

Colander looked up, bleary eyed from where he was laying on Roger's head and sighed resignedly. Grill took him by the hand and pulled him towards her and Crumbs.

'Come on Colander,' she said gently, 'We'll look after you.'

Mug, Stove and Cough joined them, and together with the Silly Ass they were slowly forced into a tight, little circle around Roger's body by the soldiers.

The two characters that had first appeared stepped forward through the line of troops. They looked down at the huge, dead dragon.

'You were only meant to wound him, I told you not to shoot to kill Slimetooth!' said the smaller of the two angrily, 'the Master will be furious, he said to take them alive!'

'He didn't mean this one,' said Slimetooth kicking at Roger's claw, 'he didn't say nuthin' about no dragon. Good shot if you ask me.'

Suddenly, Colander leapt forward in a flurry of arm and mug tree straight at Slimetooth's face.

'You muderin' swine…I'll do fer you…!'

Unfortunately for him however, Slimetooth was not only very strong, but very fast. He easily avoided the clumsy onslaught and brought his mailed fist crashing down onto Colander's head, knocking him senseless.

'Colander!' shouted Stove, starting towards him.

'Any body else fancy some?' asked Slimetooth mockingly, holding up his bloodied hand.

'You foul bully,' cried Grill.

'Heh, heh, missy, well you sure don't scare me,' he laughed nastily.

'Right, round 'em up and pick up that scum too!' he indicated Colander's prone figure.

'Leave the dragon body for the stone wolves.'

With that, the soldiers closed the circle they had formed and started to force Stove, Cough, Mug, Grill and the Silly Ass away from Roger's body and towards what looked like a cave some way further into the mountains. Two of them stopped to roughly pick up the comatose Colander and dragged him along behind cursing at his dead weight as they did.

Before long, they were at the entrance to the cave, and Stove realised that it was in fact the beginning of a long tunnel that looked like it went a very long way right into the bowels of the mountain. There they passed another half a dozen soldiers who saluted Slimetooth smartly and who were standing by a huge, fixed crossbow, now armed with a fresh, evil looking, black shafted arrow.

They marched on in unhappy silence for an hour, their way gloomily lit by smoky, oily, torches dug into the walls, until Slimetooth suddenly called out 'Halt!'

He turned back to his captives.

'Right you pathetic bunch of losers, get in here.'

He stepped forward and opened a heavy wooden door that had been very well camouflaged against the rocky walls. As he did so, a dank, unhealthy smell seeped out from the dark cell within.

'Encourage them in boys,' mocked Slimetooth and the soldiers prodded the party in to the cell with the sharp points of their spears and then flung the still unconscious Colander in after them.

'Take a good look around at your new home,' he sneered, 'and take your time, that's certainly something you've got plenty of. I think you'll particularly enjoy the hot and cold running water…running down the walls that is…ha ha ha!'

The door boomed shut.

It was very dark inside, but as their eyes started to become accustomed to the light, they realised that they were not the only ones in the cell…there was someone else in there too.

'Who's there?' came a weak voice.

47.

The mimic comes in to its own.

'Hello?' said Stove nervously.

'We're travellers,' said Cough, pulling Stove behind him and away from the unknown captive.

There was a brief silence. Then after a brief fit of unhealthy sounding coughing, the mysterious voice spoke again.

'I... ken that voice…is that ye…Cough?'

Cough's jaw dropped open in surprise.

'Why….yes…yes it is…and who's that?'

A figure shambled towards them out of the gloom.

'Do you no recognise me my friend? Well I suppose I have been imprisoned here for the best part of a year, so even my voice will have changed,' he croaked.

Slowly an old man with a long, wild beard and masses of tangled white hair emerged into the feeble light.

'Why…Wheeze…Wizard Wheeze! My old friend!' gasped Cough rushing forward and embracing the ragged figure.

'Oh ho ho ho! Steady old man…ye'll clear break me in half!' chuckled Wheeze, slapping Cough's back with his scrawny hands,

'it's good tae see ye…so good.'

'You too, but what's happened to you, you look…awful.'

'Well so will ye when ye've been here as long as me,' he said crossly. 'By the way, got any food? They're supposed to feed me some slops every day, but they quite often forget. I have nay eaten since the day afore yesterday.'

'Of course,' said Cough, 'everybody, this is my old and closest friend, Wizard Wheeze.'

They all said hello, then Stove got some food and water from the supplies that the soldiers had rather surprisingly left on the Silly Ass's back and they all settled down to eat and rest. Mug tended to Colander and slowly brought him around with nothing worse than a slight cut and a headache, while they told Wheeze the tale of their journey and he in turn explained to them how he had come to be imprisoned for so long.

It appeared that he had received an invitation from Grinder to visit him in the Scroop Mountains, in his capacity as Chief reporter on 'Witches, Wizards, Warlocks and Insurance Salesmen's Weekly. ' Grinder said he had a hot exclusive for him, but when he'd arrived, the warlock had angrily brandished an article that Wheeze had written earlier, criticising Grinder's wickedness and blaming him for the low esteem in which Wizards were currently held. He had then attacked him with powerful magic and although Wheeze had tried to fend him off with spells of his own, he was no match for him. He ended up imprisoned in this cell, chained to an old radiator which Grinder delighted on turning on to full blast occasionally to further torture him. That was at least a year ago, as far as he knew. Thankfully and rather surprisingly, one of Grinder's men had loosed his chains after a few months, so at least he'd escaped from the boiling radiator.

'But you're a wizard, can't you use your magic to escape from here?' said Grill.

'No wee lassy, I'm afraid not. These cell walls are coated with an anti-magic spell, so I'm as powerless as ye...and so is Cough.'

'Yes…that may be true but…well I might still have a couple of tricks up my sleeve,' said Cough, tapping his nose.

'Colander, Stove, can I have a word?' The three of them went into a corner and a daring plan was hatched.

After they'd eaten, Stove went to the door and hammered on it with Cough's stick.

'Ho there! Ho there! Guard! Anybody!'

After a moment an angry face appeared at the bars.

'Shut your noise, or I'll do you good!' snapped the guard.

'Tell your master, Slimetooth, that I have some important information for him.'

'Tell me and I'll tell him for you,' sneered the guard.'

'No I must speak to your master, the information is for him alone.'

'Well he's not here, he's gone back to tell Grinder that we've caught you.'

This was an early blow to the plan.

'Ask tae speak tae the other one, the smaller one,' hissed Wheeze.

'What about the other leader…the smaller one?'

'McGinty? He's still here, but he's a fool.'

'Yes, McGinty, let me speak to him.'

The guard cursed and stomped away down the tunnel. Some five minutes later they heard him stomping back up, a key rattled in the door and it swung open. In came McGinty and the guard, who placed the key in his belt.

'You wanted to see me?' said McGinty.

'Yes, yes, said Stove, standing in front of him, 'I did, I wanted to ask you….er…where you're from?'

'What?' said the Rudanian, 'what's that got to do with you?'

'Er…everything, you see I wondered how you came to be here?'

As Stove kept McGinty talking, Colander, expert thief that he was, crept around behind the guard and took the key without him noticing.

'What's this all about?' said McGinty suspiciously, 'look I'm sorry for what happened to your dragon, I told Slimetooth not to shoot to kill, but that's what they're like around here. Grinder only recruits the most vicious, unpleasant and sadistic Miseries to become his guards.'

'Thank you kindly,' said the guard proudly.

Colander snuck behind Stove with the key, which he handed to Cough, who dropped it into his bag.

'Er, but you're not like them are you? So why are you here?'

'Well I…I…don't stay here through choice, 'said McGinty defensively, ' I'm as much a prisoner as you.'

'Aye…that would be why ye took pity on me and loosed me frae yon radiator then?' interjected Wheeze.

In the meantime, Cough dipped his hand in his bag, retrieved the key and handed it back to Colander.

'Well…I don't like to see anyone suffer…' stammered McGinty.

'Yes….I thought there was an air of…sadness about you,' said Stove sympathetically.

'Look…if you're just trying to get around me, you're wasting your time!' McGinty snapped suddenly, 'I wish there was something I could do for you, but I can't, it's not in my power.'

Colander crept back behind the guard who was starting to become impatient and delicately replaced the key. But just at that moment, the guard looked down and saw him close by.

'Here you!' he said cuffing Colander away, 'get out of it, you ain't getting no key! Come on fool, can't you see what they're up to!' he said, grabbing McGinty's arm, 'this lot are stringin' you along,' and he dragged him out of the cell, slamming the door shut and locking it.

McGinty's face appeared at the bars for a moment.

'You're as bad as he is! Stringing me along, pretending you were interested in my troubles…I thought…but you're just as intent on humiliating or insulting me as him.' he snarled, 'Well good luck, liars…you'll need it!' then his face disappeared.

The travellers looked at each other in slightly guilty silence for a while, while McGinty and the guard's footsteps faded off into the distance.

Grill pulled a rueful face at Stove and he shrugged as if to say; 'It couldn't be helped.'

When he was sure they could not be heard, Stove turned back to Cough.

'Did it work?' he whispered.

Cough reached into his bag, smiled and produced the mimic's glass jar. He shook it gently, there was a metallic tinkling sound and an exact copy of the key floated up against the side of the jar.

48.

The Scaredy Cat Dog.

'Yes!' hissed Stove excitedly, 'it worked!'

Cough reached in, pulled the key out and handed it to Mug.

'Well done everyone, especially you Colander.'

Colander winked back.

'Now Mug, you open the door, remember to thank the mimic and drop him back into jar, he can't last too long out of it. I'll have to get a spell ready to use as soon as the door is open. Stove, can you see outside?'

Stove craned his face up against the door's bars and peered carefully out.

'There's just the one guard, he's a little way down the tunnel sitting on a rock,' whispered the young Snod.

'Right, Grill put Crumbs on the Silly Ass and quickly tell it a joke. Colander?' he looked across to where his assistant was finally replacing his mug tree arm with what looked like a metal club.

'You come with me. Now, ready?' he hissed. They all nodded grimly. 'Go!' he shouted.

Mug opened the door, it swung open and Cough and Colander charged out. There was only one guard, the same one as before. He stared stupidly, dumbfounded at what was occurring for a second, but then sprang to life and hurried towards them with his spear at the ready. Even on his own, he was more than a physical match for them all.

'Birds fly, lions scare, turn this guard into a chair!' shouted Cough.

Instantly, the guard stopped dead in his tracks. His face began to twitch and tremble, his body to rock and shake, then with an ear-splitting howl, he squelchingly morphed into an easy chair that wouldn't be out of place in the poshest front rooms or cheesiest tv ad.

'You did it!' said Stove excitedly.

'Yes, I did didn't I?' said Cough pleased and truth be told not a little surprised.

'Best get going though, someone may have heard that scream.'

'Get a move on!' squeaked the nagging bag.

'Wheeze are you coming?' said Mug, replacing the mimic in his jar, having kissed and thanked it properly.

'Try and stop me!' said Wheeze, striding out of the cell and into the tunnel, 'besides, I'm the only one who kens where Grinder keeps the stolen senses o' humour, we need tae find the Barrel o' Laughs. Quickly this way!'

'Fools! Fools!' wailed an odd, high pitched voice, 'don't leave the safety of the cell, you're all going to die!'

The entire party stopped dead in their tracks.

'What the…who was that?' said Stove peering back into the cell from where the voice had come.

'I've no idea,' said Mug, 'but I intend to find out,' and he reached up and took one of the smokey, oily torches from its place in the wall.

'Och there's nae need to fear,' said Wheeze chuckling, 'ah should've told yer all, but in the excitement…if yer please?'

And with that, he took the flaming torch from Mug's hand and beckoning them to follow him, strode back into the dark cell.

'Oh no!' the querulous little voice piped up again, 'now they're coming back…furious that we stopped them…we'll all be murdered in our beds! Burned alive! Help!'

'Now, now' chuckled Wheeze softly, 'they'll dae nuthin' o' the sort wee laddie…ye're safe and sound wi' us.'

Then he stopped just short of a very dark corner. The friends could just make out a shape moving, or rather trembling, there.

'Gentlemen, lady, donkey and toad, may I present, Sidney, the Scaredy Cat Dog.'

He held the torch out into the corner and revealed…a tiny dog. It was about as big as one of our Yorkshire terriers, but had long, completely white fur and huge black eyes, which reflected back the torch's light as thin yellow, frightened slivers. It was shaking like a jelly on a washing machine and its bottom lip (if you can say that dogs have such things) was trembling uncontrollably.

'Ooooh!' warbled Sidney fearfully, 'please don't eat me!'

'Heh heh! They'll dae nae such thing…heh heh!'

Wheeze turned his attention back to the others.

'Sidney was already in this here cell when Grinder had me imprisoned, he's a gud laddie, although ye may have noticed…somewhat…ahem…timid.'

Sidney drew his forepaws up to his mouth at the mention of Grinder's name and his eyes, unbelievably, opened even wider.

'Ah dinnae ken how long he's been here, or even why he's imprisoned, but I'd be happy if ye were kind tae him. He's bin ma only friend awl this time. Haven't ye Sidney?' he addressed the scaredy cat dog kindly and reached out a gnarled hand to stroke its head. Sidney responded by half closing his eyes and producing a low burring sound.

'Wheeze, is he…?' said Grill.

'Purring? Aye lassie…but remember he is a Scaredy *Cat* Dog.'

'Well hello Sidney, we're very happy to meet you,' said Cough,

'Yes, and I hope you'll accompany us in our escape,' said Stove.

'Precisely! ' barked Mug, 'much as I appreciate this little bonding session, we are supposed to be trying to escape! Now come on! Let's go!'

'Wah!' squeaked Sidney, 'what a scarey Snod!'

'Yes of course, Mug's right, we must be off,' said Cough.

'No time like the present!' snapped the nagging bag.

'Aagh! Where did that voice come from?' squeaked Sidney again.

'Oh for goodness sake!' said Stove reaching forward and snatching up the Scaredy Cat Dog, 'you'll be safe here,' and with that he popped Sidney into a leather bag among the luggage on the Silly Ass's back, leaving the top open so that his huge eyes could peep out and still see where they were going.

'Happy now?' he said.

'It's very high up here, are you sure it's tied on properly?' said Sidney, his voice now slightly muffled in his new hiding place.

'Just ignore him, he'll be fine. It looks nice n' dark n' cosy in that bag. Now, follow me folks, next stop Grinder's (Woooh! came Sidney's muffled cry at the mention of that name) mobile home, that's where the Barrel is bound tae be,' said Wheeze.

And he shambled off as quickly as he could down the long, dark tunnel, the rest of the intrepid travellers hot on his heels.

49.

Out of the frying pan...

On and on they ran. The two magicians, the rascally assistant, the Snod boy and girl, their Uncle, the Silly Ass and their latest companion, the Scaredy Cat Dog, its black eyes peering fearfully out of its new home.

It was really very dark indeed and the further they went, the less of the fitfully flickering torches there were, so the gloom increased.

Wizard Wheeze seemed to know his way alright, thought Stove, as they ducked down yet another side tunnel. He knew they were putting a lot of trust in him, having only just met him, but Cough had faith in him and besides, they had no other options.

'Just a...wee bit further,' wheezed Wheeze panting hard, 'and then we...should be safe enough ... tae stop a while for a wee rest... I dunno about ye, but I'm fair pooped.'

A little further on, the tunnel opened up into a wide chamber, with two other tunnels leading off from it.

'Right...' Wheeze wheezed again, '...let's rest a while...here.'

Everybody had been running hard for an hour. It had proved exhausting work for Grill and Wheeze in particular and now they both collapsed to the ground on their backs and lay spread-eagled on the floor, sucking in great lungfull's of air. Stove sat down panting on the ground next to his sister and patted her encouragingly on the arm. Colander sat on his own in a corner, he hadn't quite been his usual self since the Roger had died, thought Stove sadly. Cough and Mug stood talking in urgent tones.

'This is all very well Cough,' said Mug, 'but what happens if we do find this 'Barrel of laughs,' none of us has any idea how to get the senses of humour put back in to their rightful owners, do we ?'

'Well I'm willing to try,' said Cough.

'How do you know you won't do more damage than good.'

'I…I…don't know for sure,' said Cough quietly.

'I ken the correct spell,' said Wheeze having just about recovered his breath.

'Hey?' said Mug.

'You do?' said Cough incredulously.

'Aye, that I do. I passed my gold level just afore I came here, did I not write and tell ye?'

'No I don't think you did, although I have had a problem with sofa gerbils eating my mail… but that is marvellous news,'

'Aye, I was quite pleased meself.'

'No, I mean it's marvellous news that you know the spell to return Stove and Mug's senses of humour.'

'It's great news!' said Stove who had joined them.

'It's yesterday's news I'm afraid,' boomed a loud voice sardonically and suddenly a stream of soldiers sprinted in to the chamber from behind them, while even more marched in from the two tunnels at the other end. Soon the little party were once again surrounded.

'How did you escape, you scum!' growled Slimetooth forcing his way to the front, 'I'll teach you to try and make a fool of me!' He raised his spear to shoulder height and pointed it directly at Stove's heart.

'Now, now, Slimetooth, temper, temper,' drawled the same booming voice they had just heard.

The lines of soldiers parted fearfully amongst much whimpering and muttering.

'Silence dogs!' roared Slimetooth.

Stove looked over towards the space that they had made. He could hear a low, electrical hum approaching and a huge, squat black shadow loomed across the tunnel wall. He heard Sidney catch his breath in a high squeak.

The troops dropped down onto one knee…and Warlock Grinder glided into view (sitting on a Sinclair C5.)

'Ah! Greetings sir, I was just expressing my displeasure at nearly letting you down, sir.'

'Relax, Slimetooth, you've behaved despicably…'

'Thank you sir,'

'You needn't have worried, there was really never any danger of our friends escaping, not when I have a secret little ally in their camp, so to speak.'

The friends looked stunned. Then they all started to talk at once. Grinder silenced them with an imperious wave of his hand.

'Silence! You sound like a load of jabbering baboons. I could easily make you look like them too.'

They immediately fell silent.

Grinder's expression changed from furious hatred to one of contemptuous courteousy.

'Welcome travellers, you certainly have come a long way…and a particular welcome to you young Prince Stove.'

Grinder's icily cold blue eyes flitted across the group and settled on those of the Snod boy.

'I am so…very delighted to meet you at last. We shall soon get to know each other well.'

Stove swallowed hard. He felt how he imagined a rabbit does when confronted by a fox.

'Now…' continued Grinder switching his attention back to the rest of the group, 'I'm sure you have lots of questions? One at a time please,' he said over politely.

'What do you mean, ally?' said Cough slowly and deliberately.

'Ah, the mighty Cough, wizard, third class. Incidentally, don't bother trying any of your feeble magic spells, nor you Wheeze, you lying old fool, I shrouded you both in anti-spell blankets as soon as you entered the chamber. Not that I couldn't easily defeat you anyway, but why should I waste my strength?

Now, where were we…oh yes, the secret ally. Yes, I may as well tell you, as it won't do you any good to know and I can't wait to see your faces…a member of your party has been reporting in to me at regular intervals. Since right at the very beginning of your hopeless little journey. So you see, I have been in control all along.'

The friends stared at each other for a moment in dumbfounded silence.

'Crumbs! I knew it, he's the only one it could be!' shouted Stove, advancing threateningly on the fat, red, toad.

'Oh puleease…' drawled Grinder, 'give me a little credit do, I'm hardly likely to go around recruiting pond life, am I? (present company excepted, Slimetooth.)'

'Thank you sir,' said Slimetooth, then looked confused.

'But it couldn't be Cough…Grill….Wheeze has only just joined us… Colander… Uncle Mug? I don't believe that any of them are traitors.' said Stove frantically.

'My dear boy…' chortled Grinder, then turned his attention from Stove towards the rest of his companions.

'What do you say, my treacherous friend, shall we put him out of his misery, will you reveal yourself?'

There followed what seemed an eternity of silence. All the travellers looked at each other. As far as Stove could see, none of his trusted friends were moving, only Crumbs who regarded him balefully and the Silly Ass who'd obviously got bored and was heading off somewhere. But the Ass continued trotting forward and just as Stove was about to call him back, he did the strangest thing… he stood up on his back legs.

As the rest of the assembled throng, with the obvious exception of Grinder watched, open- mouthed in astonishment, the Ass then unbuckled the catch that held the supplies on his back and dropped them all on the floor of the cavern.

'Oooh! he groaned, arching his spine stiffly,' about time, my back's killing me. Anybody got a cigarette?'

'That's clever, my little mate, you…you're….talkin' I never knew you could do that?'

Colander was the first to break the stunned silence. Stove shook his head in exasperation.

'He's obviously not the real Silly Ass, Colander. It's Grinder's magic.'

'It's Warlock Grinder to you boy,' said the warlock curtly, 'but yes, you're right, it is my magic. I've always kept a spy in your unpleasant valley, just to keep an eye on your odious little race of Idiots and to steal the occasional sense of humour. In fact that self same spy had been responsible for administrating the Ignorant Pig shavings to you as you slept and thereby stealing yours.

After you and wizard third class Cough disturbed me at my….ahem…ablutions, I determined that the spy should accompany you on your ridiculous journey, just to make sure everything went to plan. (You freeing my dragon from its curse was an annoying and unpredicted event, but it all worked out well in the end.) Then it was just a case of employing a simple transformation spell, something far above your crude abilities Cough. As I knew any lengthy journey would involve the Silly Ass, I transformed my little helper into him. Easy as the easiest pie to make is. Now, shall we re-transform him?'

Grinder mumbled some words under his breath and pointed his fingers at the Ass. Bolts of blue and bright white shot outwards and enveloped him, lifting him up into the air. Then slowly his features started to change, almost to melt, into something or someone different. From where Stove stood whatever it was looked Snod shaped, but he couldn't see any details, because of the brightness of the brilliant blue and white light.

Slowly the flashing subsided and the figure was revealed.

'Hello Stove, Grill,' it said cheerfully. It was none other than…Trowel the gardener.

'Trowel!' cried Stove and Grill together.

'But why?' said Stove.

'Oh look, I'll be honest, I've always hated your family, I loath your idiotic, boorish father and the servile job I have, or rather, had. Grinder stole my sense of humour some years ago you know and I've never missed it. And of course his Lordship pays well.'

'What've you done with the Silly Ass you treacherous cur,' screamed Colander hurling himself at the gardener and getting in a good couple of blows to his head with his club arm, before the soldiers dragged him off. Stove took the opportunity in all the confusion to snatch up the bag in which Sidney was still hiding.

'I shall be particularly glad to see the back of you, you one armed bore!' Trowel raged, rubbing his sore head furiously, 'you've no idea what agony it's been listening to your dreadful jokes!'

'Oh how funny!' chuckled Grinder, 'I like your spirit, spring onion head, you should come and work for me…I could get that arm back for you,' he added, mumbling a few words and pointing at Colander's club arm. Instantly the metal club clanged to the ground and was replaced by a perfect, real one. Colander was absolutely dumbfounded. He looked down at his new limb and slowly flexed the fingers.

'I….can't believe it,' he said in a small voice, 'better'n before.'

'Good…gooood….' Grinder smirked greasily, 'you see, every Snod has his price…you're not so different from our friend Bowl.'

Colander's face darkened.

'You can keep your filthy arm!' he shouted, 'I'll never work fer dragon murderin' rubbish like you!'

The smile fell from Grinder's lips.

'Pity,' he drawled, raising a finger in Colander's direction. His new arm promptly fell off and as the friends watched in horrified fascination, slowly dissolved into a black mush on the ground.

'Oh well…things could be a lot worse,' Cough's assistant found himself saying hollowly.

50.

The Ignorant Pig.

They'd been marching for two hours now, all the while going deeper and deeper into the bowels of the mountains. Stove and Grill walked side by side behind McGinty, Stove occasionally hushing Sidney who whimpered quietly from the bag on his back. Then came Cough and Wheeze, then Mug and a rather confused Colander, who was still recovering from having a new arm, for just a moment.

'What a horrible man,' said Grill, 'what do you think he'll do to us?'

'I've no idea,' said Stove. And he genuinely hadn't, but he feared the worse. He just didn't want to tell Grill that.

'McGinty….McGinty…' he called in a loud whisper.

McGinty glanced backwards over his shoulder.

'What?' he said crossly, out of the corner of his mouth.

'What's he going to do with us?'

'I…I…don't know,' said the Rudanian.

They continued on in silence.

'McGinty….McGinty…' whispered Stove again.

'What?' he said, even more crossly.

'I don't believe you.…I think you know…but you won't tell us, because you feel sorry for us.'

'Rubbish! Now be quiet or Grinder will be down on you like a ton of bricks…and I can assure you that is not a pleasant experience.'

'Help us, McGinty, please,' pleaded Grill.

'I…I can't. Grinder is all powerful…there's nothing I can do for you….and why should I anyway?' McGinty insisted.

'Leave him Grill,' said Stove, 'it takes real courage to tackle a bully like Grinder,' he added witheringly.

They trooped on in silence. But if Stove could have seen McGinty's face, he would have seen an expression of pure, frustrated, impotent, rage.

Finally, the procession arrived in a large cavern, in which stood a mobile home.

'Ah, home, horrid home,' said Grinder.

The soldiers quickly formed themselves into a parade ground line, with Grinder positioned in front of them and Slimetooth and McGinty just behind him. Their captives stood facing them, collected together on the square of green astro turf in front of the mobile home.

'Mind the furniture!' said Grinder sharply, glaring at Colander as he accidentally knocked over one of the white, plastic garden chairs.

'Now then,' said Grinder, getting up off the C5, linking his hands behind his back and pacing back and forth in front of them, like a general reviewing his soldiers.

'I suppose you're all wondering why I called this meeting?…only joking. What are we going to do with you all? That's the question you must be thinking, I'm sure. Well I'm also sure you'll be relieved to know that I have plans for you all. It goes without saying that I'll take all your senses of humour…those of you that still have them of course. Er…Mug, isn't it?' he said stopping in front of him.

'I believe I've already got your sense of humour, had it for some time in fact.'

Mug scowled unflinchingly back at him. Grinder smiled nastily and moved on to Grill.

'Grill…you lucky girl, you'll be my house…or rather mobile home slave, cooking, cleaning, a little gardening perhaps, for the rest of your life. Needless to say, you'll never see the sky again. And you'll have to get rid of that foul amphibian…someone take it from her will they?'

Slimetooth stepped forward, but McGinty beat him too it and snatched the struggling toad from Grill's arms.

'Crumbs…no!' cried Grill, bursting into tears.

'Don't let him see it matters, he enjoys making us miserable,' whispered Stove, gripping her arm fiercely. Grill forced herself to stop.

'Creep…' muttered Slimetooth under his breath as McGinty resumed his position beside him.

'So…who's next? Ah yes…despite your little outburst back there, one arm, I do believe that given time you will come around to my way of thinking…just like McGinty did…although you strike me as not being as mind-crushingly boring and stupid as he is. Who knows? You may even take his job one day?'

Grinder smiled nastily at McGinty, who looked away, biting his lip.

'Yes…' mused Grinder to himself, 'what a fool he is…'

'Shove yer job!' shouted Colander defiantly.

Grinder ignored him and continued pacing up and down in front of them.

'Trowel!'

The gardener who had been smugly enjoying Colander's discomfort was startled by Grinder calling out his name.

'Yes, your vileness,' he said nervously.

'Look, I'm going to be honest with you. Now your cover's blown, as it were, I'm afraid your job no longer exists…after all, the company is having to downsize. I have asked around the network, but there's really nothing suitable. I have however come up with a generous redundancy package, I'm going to turn you into a moth.'

'A…m…moth?' stammered Trowel, his eyes bulging out of his head.

'Yes, a moth,' said Grinder kindly. 'Think of the money you'll save on food and shoes? '

'But….aaaaaaiiieee….'

Grinder flicked his wrist and where once had been a Snod, now crouched a fair sized moth. It flew straight off and started to madly circle one of the flaming torches, occasionally bashing itself against the wall.

'As for the rest of you,' Grinder continued as if nothing had happened, ignoring the shocked expressions on all their faces, 'I have a very special plan for you Price Stove, don't you worry, very special and highly profitable for me. But then I'm afraid all positions of employment in my team are now filled. So you two idiot magicians, and you, er, Mug will be delighted to know that I have a particularly special fate planned for you. You are going to meet a wonderful old friend of mine. In fact, you could say that some of you have already 'touched base ' with him,' (here he made the inverted commas in the air sign.)

Stove glanced at Mug, who shrugged his shoulders.

'If you'll just walk this way please,' said Grinder heading towards a small dark tunnel at the other end of the cavern.

Slimetooth, indicated for them to follow, which they did, accompanied by him, McGinty and half a dozen of the soldiers. The rest stayed behind and guarded Grill and Colander.

'Stove!' cried Grill heartrendingly.

('Ooooah!' squeaked Sidney quietly.)

'Be brave, missy Grill, be brave…' muttered Colander, throwing his good arm around her shoulders.

After about a hundred feet, the small tunnel opened up again into a larger cavern. In the corner of which was a hole going into the wall. It was about Stove's height, and a little wider than Slimetooth's shoulders. Grinder, who led the way, had to stoop to enter it, as did Slimetooth. Stove, Mug, Wheeze and Cough followed in single file, with McGinty bringing up the rear.

'You won't be needed,' said McGinty to the troops who were behind him, 'go and wait by the tunnel entrance with the others, back at Warlock Grinder's residence. Make sure we're not disturbed. And here, take this…toad thing, make sure you don't harm it.' Under normal circumstances, the soldiers didn't like taking orders from McGinty, he was just a Rudanian after all, but as they were very dim and their leader Slimetooth was no longer there, they reluctantly obeyed him.

Immediately inside, the hole opened up into an enormous pit-like cavern. The walkway they were on became a narrow bridge, with the ground falling away to a depth of at least one hundred feet on each side. Half way through the pit, at a distance of some two hundred feet, the bridge ended in a small dais, just about big enough for three, or at a push four. Great, dripping, stalactites hung heavily from the ceiling of the cavern high above, looking like at any moment they could break away and crush the little party. There was a foul stench, sulphurous and diseased. A sickly orangey, red light, from what appeared to be molten lava which flowed sluggishly in a river completely encircling the cavern, was the only illumination. Here and there the constant heat had created pockets of crystals embedded into the walls, which reflected the light like hundreds of vicious little red eyes.

The noise was deafening, an awful crackling, whooshing, accompanied by a high pitch whining, that sounded horribly like the tortured shrieking of thousands of lost souls.

Stove could feel the terror rising in him as he neared the dais, on which Grinder and Slimetooth were already standing facing them. The red light reflected in their faces made them look even more demonic and terrifying, especially when Grinder grinned malevolently, staring straight into Stove's eyes.

'Gentlemen…he said, his voice rising with sadistic excitement, 'may I introduce you to…'

at this point, he paused and he and Slimetooth moved to either side of the dais to reveal just below them on the floor of the hellish pit, the stuff of Stove's worst nightmare…the Ignorant Pig.

Stove could hardly breathe, he heard a ringing sound in his ears, his vision shrank to a dot, he was fainting. And he would have fallen, straight into the Pig's lair, had Mug not caught him by the arm and guided him safely to the floor of the bridge.

Grinder's face was contorted with wicked glee.

'What's the matter boys? You three will be seeing him in close up in a minute! Ha ha ha ha ha! You see I'll get your senses of humour and he'll get his lunch! Oh and don't bother thinking you can try any of your little spells on him…I've made him invulnerable to any kind of magic. Hee hee! Slimetooth! Our first contestant please!'

Grunting with anticipation, the burly Captain of the guards started towards Cough, leering nastily. Suddenly, the Ignorant

Pig roared. It was a horrid sound. A sound of death and despair… a sound so unexpected and so startling that even Grinder and Slimetooth had to turn at look at its creator, shuffling closer to the edge of the dais to get a better view. It was then, while their backs were turned… that McGinty acted. He rushed forward, nearly knocking the two wizards and Mug flying. Years of pent up rage and hate gave him strength and he rammed into the backs of his two tormentors and sent them tumbling down into the Ignorant Pig's vile lair. He would have fallen with them, but Mug, reacting with astonishing speed and agility, dived forward and grabbed his ankle. For a moment he hung there, only yards from the great, black, slavering head of the Ignorant Pig, while Grinder and Slimetooth lay stunned on the floor of the pit. Wheeze and Cough rushed over and slowly, desperately they hauled McGinty back up onto the dais.

'Run! Get out!' he screamed, 'you should have left me! Get out!'

The others needed no further prompting. They turned on their heels and half dragging the still woozy Stove with them, they raced back up the bridge the way they had come.

'Yes run! Run for your lives! We're all doomed, oh help!' yelped Sidney unhelpfully as he bounced around on Stove's back.

McGinty struggled to his feet. He looked down into the pit and saw an awful sight. Slimetooth's legs were sticking out of the Ignorant Pig's slavering jaws. An instant later, accompanied by a dreadful soggy, crunching and slurping sound, he had been completely swallowed.

Grinder in the meantime, had come to his senses and was circling the pit, desperate searching for a way out.

McGinty thought it was probably a wise time for him to leave and he span around to follow the others. He had nearly made the entrance to the cavern, when he heard Grinder bellow.

'McGinty!'

He couldn't help himself, the Rudanian stopped and turned.

'You treacherous fool! I'll get out of here and when I do, you will know what real misery is!'

The warlock raised his arms and a bolt of blue and white shot out towards McGinty, who turned and ran like the devil was after him (which he sort of was.)

The others had reached the outside of the cavern, Stove now fully recovered called back to him, 'McGinty! Run!'

The bolt hit the entrance just above McGinty's head as he emerged from the pit. There was a massive explosion. Stove, Mug, Cough and Wheeze were tossed trough the air like rag dolls by an angry child. It seemed like half the mountain was falling down as rocks, boulders and stones crashed to the floor in a huge, choking, cloud of dust. Stove lay where he had landed, covered his head with his hands and held his breath.

Slowly, the sound of the rocks falling began to slow, until it became just an occasional, rattling trickle. Stove coughed the remaining air out of his lungs. He still couldn't see much apart from dust.

'Cough? You o.k?' he gasped throatily.

'Yes…my boy…' coughed the wizard.

'I'm alright tae,' came Wheeze's appropriately wheezy voice.

'Me…too,' said Mug, emerging through the fog of dust and helping Stove to his feet. Stove saw that his Uncle was completely grey-white with the dust and thought that under different circumstances, he would look quite comical.

'Oh I'm fine, no need to worry about me, nobody cares about me,' whined Sidney peeping out from the leather bag where Stove had dropped it a few yards away.

'Sorry Sidney, I didn't mean to drop you. Are you ok too?' asked Stove apologetically.

'Yes…I believe I am,' said Sidney somewhat snottily, 'thanks for asking.'

Slowly the dust settled and Stove could see that where the entrance to the Ignorant pig's lair had been was now a huge, impassable, pyramid of rocks. He looked closer. Just sticking out of the corner underneath the massive pile was something small and white… it was McGinty's hand.

51.

A dreadful thing happens.

'Oh dear,' said Cough emerging out of the still foggy cloud of dust.

'Aye,' said Wheeze sadly, peering at the motionless hand 'he was nae a bad sort…fer a Rudanian.'

'Poor McGinty…he saved us all. That is, I suppose we're safe…?' said Stove, nervously.

'Oh yes, we'll be safe now. It would take even Grinder a lifetime to get through that huge landslide…that's if he survives the Ignorant Pig…remember he made him immune to magic, that could apply to his own too,' said Cough confidently.

Stove felt almost sorry for the Warlock…trapped in there with that…thing.

'Well, we can do no more here,' said Mug gruffly, 'we must try and free Grill and Colander… and we still have the soldiers to worry about. Let's go.'

He turned and walked towards the tunnel entrance, closely followed by Wheeze and Cough. Stove stood for a moment, remembering McGinty's unexpected act of heroism and wishing he could have got to know him a little better.

'See you, McGinty,' he sighed, ' thank you.'

Just as he turned away to follow the others, something caught his eye. He looked again at the small, buried hand. Surely not, he thought. It couldn't have moved. Nobody could survive being buried under a fall like that. But as he watched, it did move. Just a slight twitch, but definite movement.

'Cough, Wheeze, Uncle Mug! He's alive!'

The others rushed back to him.

'But he can't be…there's a least a ton of stuff on him,' said Mug incredulously.

Once again a finger twitched. It was enough. Without wasting any further time, they started to frantically dig.

'Are you sure you want to do that? It looks very dangerous.' widdled Sidney, but they all ignored him.

As Mug and Stove removed the smaller rocks, Wheeze and Cough used their magic to carefully remove the bigger ones and gradually they uncovered McGinty's face.

'Water!' Stove called, and Mug handed him a flask.

Stove tore a rag from his sleeve and tenderly wiped the worst of the dust from McGinty's face. His eyelids flickered…and opened.

'Phew!' he coughed, ' just as well I'm used to this happening to me.'

'McGinty, you're alive!' said Stove delightedly.

'Oh, am I? Thank you,' said McGinty weakly.

They redoubled their efforts and after a while had cleared enough to drag him out from the debris.

Remarkably, apart from some slight cuts and bruises he appeared unharmed, a fact that the others marvelled at.

'Be careful he's not a zombie!' cried the Scaredy cat dog, shrinking back into his leather bag. Once again, the others ignored him.

'Well,' said Cough, 'I have no idea how you survived, but it is good to have you back McGinty. Astonishing…quite astonishing. I wouldn't have believed it, if I hadn't seen it myself.'

Cough paused for a moment and plucked absent mindedly at his beard, as if in a dreamy trance. Then he pulled himself together and went on;

'But listen everybody, our troubles are not over yet, we must still deal with Grinder's soldiers and we must still find the Barrel of Laughs, it's what we came for, after all.'

'Ah, that won't be as big a problem as you think,' said McGinty, coughing and brushing himself down, 'follow me.'

And before they had time to question him further, he strode off down the tunnel, pausing occasionally to produce a huge and dusty sneeze.

Cough frowned at Stove who pulled a face and shrugged, but with no idea what else to do, they trooped diligently off back through the tunnel behind him. Stove paused for a moment to sweep up the bag that still contained Sidney on the way, noticing with little surprise a muffled shriek as he did so.

They were soon back in the main cavern, where Grinder's mobile home was situated. Ominously, the soldiers were still there, standing in a smart parade line. Sidney let out another quiet shriek.

'We're doomed, we're all doomed,' he piped breathily, trying to force himself even further down into the bag on Stove's shoulder.

But strangely, the soldiers didn't react to their entrance at all.

Colander and Grill were sitting on the white, plastic garden furniture on the astro turf in front. Grill leapt up when she saw them, looking like she couldn't believe her eyes.

'Stove!' she cried joyfully, rushing across to him and bypassing the line of troops, who again surprisingly didn't react. In fact they didn't even move a muscle.

She threw her arms around her brother and he hugged her back, smiling delightedly.

A happy scene followed as all the friends were reunited and McGinty's role was explained, after which Grill kissed him and Colander slapped him on the back with his good arm (causing much embarrassment and another other fit of coughing.)

'I don't understand…why don't the soldiers do anything?' asked Mug waving a hand in front of the nearest one's eyes.

When he'd finished his coughing fit, Mcginty explained to them that the soldiers were incapable of making a decision on their own and would stay where they were until they starved to death if no one in authority told them to do otherwise. Colander was all for leaving them as they were, but Grill insisted that this shouldn't happen, so McGinty strode out in front of them, pushed out his chest, threw back his shoulders and barked a command.

'Soldiers! Stand at ease! Now listen up. Grinder and Slimetooth are dead. That makes me in charge. You are hereby dismissed. Return at once to wherever your tribes and families are. Do not return here ever again. Leave your weapons. That is all.'

The soldiers stood for a moment, looking confused, then by dribs and drabs started to drift away down the main tunnel. Grill stepped up and took Crumbs back from one of them, who handed him over without protesting.

'Brreeeaaccckkk!' belched Crumbs happily, seemingly pleased to be with her again.

Eventually, all the soldiers had all gone, leaving a pile of discarded helmets, spears and armour.

'Simple as that,' said Mug, sucking his teeth.

McGinty would have smiled if he could.

'Now, the Barrel of Laughs...Mug, I think I may need your help?' he continued.

They disappeared into Grinder's mobile home.

After a few minutes, and with much grunting and gasping, they re-appeared struggling to carry a dull, black, metal barrel between them. Stove's eyes widened as they lay it down on the Astroturf in front of the mobile home.

'Ooooh, dangerous, dangerous,' gasped Sidney.

Stove decided he was getting a bit fed up with his little passenger, so he laid the bag carefully on one of the plastic chairs and Sidney retreated further inside again.

'Is that...?' Stove said in awe, looking back at the container.

'The barrel of laughs?' said McGinty, '...yes...it is.'

Stove felt a great relief flow over him. They had made it. All that way, after all those adventures. But they had made it....or nearly all of them had anyway.

'Right,' said Wizard Wheeze, 'as I said earlier, I ken the spell tae return yer lost senses o' humour... Stove....Mug and if ye'd like... ye too, McGinty.'

The Rudanian looked alarmed.

'But I don't remember ever having had one,' he spluttered, 'maybe I won't like it...I'll be the weirdo back home amongst the other rude, Rudanians...mind you they already thought that about me anyway,' he added a little forlornly.

'If yer sense o' humour was stolen, it'll be in here and so will those of all yer countrymen.'

Suddenly a wild thought occurred to Wheeze.

'Ye could take the barrel back with ye...I could even come wi' ye and...and help ye wi the spell...ye did save all our lives after all.'

McGinty frowned thoughtfully and rubbed his chin.

'So…I….me….Alec 'Bonkers' McGinty….I could change my entire country? I could make it a better place, make it how it once was?'

'Aye.'

Wheeze smiled encouragingly.

'Well…in that case…why not?' he turned to Stove.

'You know, if someone had told me when I first set off to the mountains all that time ago, that I would be able to bring back such a treasure for my people, I *buzz…bizzz…*'

Stove looked at McGinty incredulously.

'Sorry?' he said.

McGinty frowned.

'I said I *buzz….buzzzy..bizz..*'

McGinty pursed his lips crossly.

'I *buzzzip,,,buzz…*'

As Stove recoiled in horror, McGinty's head started to swell up out of shape like a balloon and his eyes began turning completely solid black. His nose became longer and longer…and then his entire body began to shrink as his buzzing became ever more frenetic.

'What is it Stove?' said Grill in a small, frightened voice, 'what's happening to McGinty?'

'I don't know…it's like he's…he's turning into…some kind of insect!' said Stove trembling.

'He's what?' barked Mug, 'how can that be *buzz…buzzzip…*'

Mug clapped his hand to his mouth and his eyes widened in fear. Stove span around to look at his uncle. To his dismay, he saw his features start to distort in the same way as McGinty's had.

'This is magic!' shouted Cough, 'powerful, bad magic! Wheeze! We must try and fight it! We must...
....*buzz...whizzzz...bizzzz...*'

Stove looked in panic back and forth between the two Wizards, as slowly they too started to transform before his very eyes.

'By cracky! *Zzz...zzzip...*what's happenin' to us!...*buzzzzip!* shouted / buzzed Colander.

Scarcely able to register the horror he felt, Stove's eyes flitted rapidly from one of his friends to the other and then back to McGinty. But now instead of where the Rudanian had stood a moment ago, there now hovered a fair sized blue bottle. Then suddenly Grill began to wail.

'Stove! Stove! It's happening to me!'

He span around to see his sister staring at him in wide eyed terror. She held out her hands to him...only they were no longer hands, they were insect's legs.

52.

Grinder's apprentice.

'You fools! Did you really think a little act of treachery and a few tons of rubble would get rid of me? Now you'll pay!'

Stove dragged his attention away from the awful image of his transforming sister and towards the source of the booming voice. There, in the entrance to the cavern stood the terrible figure of Warlock Grinder.

He was caked in a thick dust that obscured the cheery colours of his Hawaiian shirt, his hair hung around his face in a tangled and bloodied mess and his raging eyes stared out of a furious mask of dirt and died blood.

'Grinder! Please stop this…please!' cried Stove.

The warlock turned his blazing gaze on Stove. Suddenly as if switched off, his rage abated.

'Oh you needn't worry Stove,' said Grinder, his voice suddenly assuming a creepily kindly tone,

'I'm not going to turn you in to an insect, just the others. Oh no my boy, I have far too important work for you to do.'

Stove's mind was a confusion of questions. But the important thing right then was to save his sister.

'Grinder I don't care what you do to me…I don't care what you want me to do…I'll do it! Only please…please take your spell off my sister!'

'Alas, it's too late my dear boy. Take a look at your sister now.'

Stove reluctantly turned around. Now in the place of his sister was a brightly iridescent dragonfly.

It flitted up until it was level with his eyes and hovered in front of them. Stove's eyes filled with tears and he reached out a tremulous hand towards it.

'Oh Grill…' he whispered, 'I'm so sorry…'

'Yes…pity,' drawled Grinder, limping over to stand beside him, 'she would have made an excellent addition to my staff.'

Stove turned to face him in fury, as the Grill dragonfly made a hasty exit.

'Grinder! You….you….'

'Now, now my lad…calm down do, all is not lost. All I ask for is a little cooperation and you can get your sister back…'

'What do you mean?' asked Stove, trying to stay as calm as he could.

'Yeeees,' continued Grinder, 'and your other friends too…McGinty aside, I have other plans for that treacherous cur,' he spat, the rage flitting across his face again for a fraction of a moment like a shadow, before resuming his creepy charm.

'What I did, I can just as easily undo.'

'You…you can change them back?'

'Naturally…as long as they don't get eaten, or squished. You wouldn't want to see them transformed back if that happened…all that yeuky mess…though it might be amusing…'

Grinder stroked his beard thoughtfully for a moment, then continued.

'So of course it would be better if I did it sooner rather than later,' he said craftily, regarding Stove out of the corner of his eye.

Stove quickly scanned the cavern. The Grill dragonfly had settled on a rock in the corner. Mug had become a wasp and he fizzed angrily around the mobile home. Cough and Wheeze who had transformed into bumble bees buzzed aimlessly around, occasionally knocking their heads against its windows. Colander who had turned into a large, black spider with one of its front legs missing scuttled lop-sidedly into a large hole under a rock. There was no sign of the McGinty fly.

'Well, what do you want?' said Stove.

'It's such a little thing Stove, really, so very easy for you to do and won't actually harm anyone…in fact it will make things a lot better for a lot of people.'

Grinder gripped Stove by the arm and steered him over to where the Barrel of laughs stood on his lawn.

'I'll just have to take a little rest here,' he said groaning, as he rather feebly lowered himself onto the plastic chair that stood between the Barrel and the chair on which Sidney still hid in his leather bag. He reached into his pocket and produced a small candle, which he lit with a wave of his hand and placed carefully on the arm of the chair. A heavy, sickly sweet aroma instantly assailed Stove's nostrils.

'Oh dear me, my aches and pains…this candle's perfume helps a little. I'm just a poor, feeble old man really you see.'

He smiled crookedly up at Stove and sighed sadly, 'and somewhat cruelly misunderstood.'

'I don't think so Grinder,' said Stove flatly, 'you steal people's senses of humour.'

'Do I? Do I my boy?'

'Yes, you do, you know you do! And you keep them all in here!'

Stove strode over to the round, black barrel and pointed at it. Grinder involuntarily half rose from his chair. The expression of weary kindliness fell suddenly from his face to be replaced by one of (Stove noticed rather surprisingly) fear. But before he had time to reflect on this, Grinder quickly regained control of himself.

'Stove, Stove, Stove,' he sighed, shaking his head sadly and lowering himself back into his chair, 'my dear boy, please let me explain. Just come a little closer…come away from that horrid barrel and let me open your mind to the truth.'

Stove stood his ground.

'I'm fine here,' he said defiantly.

'Hmm…very well, if you wish my boy, stay where you like. But if I were you I wouldn't touch the barrel, it has a coating that will make you ill.'

Stove glanced doubtfully down at the barrel and moved a step away from it.

'Now then,' said Grinder, the cloying tone returning, ' let me explain. You say I steal senses of humour, I prefer to think of it as liberating folk from foolishness and from wasting their lives.'

Stove looked incredulous and was about to say something when Grinder held up his hand to quiet him.

'Hear me out. Just look at your own case. Consider where you are now, how much you have done on your journey, the amazing things that you have seen. Ask yourself, would you ever have done as much if I hadn't liberated you from your sense of humour?'

Stove was silent. The heavy scent of the candle seemed to envelop him and make his mind feel fuzzy. But it was true. He had done some things, incredible things that he'd never have imagined doing before.

'Why you'd still be doing the wasteful, pointless things that you've always done if it wasn't for me, you'd think that all life was about was having a laugh and nothing else. But now you know that there's so much more to it. That's down to me,' continued Grinder, wafting his hand over the candle and causing it to flare up momentarily 'and I think that you know that?'

Stove bit his lip. He was beginning to think that Grinder was right, maybe they had all been wrong about him after all…

…While Stove was deep in thought, his mind wrestling with all that Grinder had to say, in the corner of the cavern another drama was being played out that had he been aware of, would have banished any other thought from his mind.

Crumbs had been sitting on the plastic turf where he'd been left when Grill suddenly found herself being transformed. He'd watched with a vague, emotionless, toady interest all that occurred until her transformation had completed and she'd turned into a dragonfly. A dragonfly!

Something stirred in Crumbs tiny brain and he remembered vaguely a time by a pond, a bright coloured dragonfly and how deliciously crunchy and tasty it had been. And here was another!

The fat, red toad watched the tasty morsel fly up in front of Stove's eyes and then flit off into the corner of then cavern. He saw it settle on a rock. Narrowing his glistening, orange eyes, he slowly, quietly, waddled off in its direction.

'Yum!' he thought…

…'And if I can improve your life so much, why should I not do it for others too? Are you the one to deny them?'

Grinder's voice droned on in a low monotonous hum. Stove's eyelids began to feel heavy and he was aware of how strong the candle's scent was becoming.

'Think of your friends. Think of Fork, Spoon and Rubber Glove…think of your father…'

Stove woozily looked up at Grinder.

'Yes…I know he embarrasses you,' said the warlock sympathetically, ' but without that ridiculous sense of humour…well, he'd be a proper king.'

There was a silence…

…By keeping himself right up against the wall, Crumbs had managed to get quite close to the dragonfly without being observed. He could move pretty quickly if he wanted to and the thought of that crunchy body sliding down his gullet made him move even faster. But now came the tricky part. There was a distance of some ten feet between where he crouched in the shadows to where the dragonfly perched on its rock, its head facing his hiding place. Even he realised that if he came out of the shadows, he would be seen and his victim and potential snack would fly off. But if it turned the other way…And so he hungrily watched and waited for the right moment…

… 'Well what exactly is it you want me to do?' said Stove croakily. The candle's scent seemed to make it harder for him to talk now, or to move. It was like he was swimming in treacle.

'Simple my lad,' said Grinder with a nasty chuckle. 'You see, you coming here is so perfect for us both. I unfortunately am the victim of an old and terrible ailment, which means I cannot leave the mountains, otherwise I would have completed my mission of mercy myself. But you coming here means that I now have the perfect apprentice to carry out my good work for me. Just imagine how much better things would be for all your people, if they had the same opportunity to better themselves as you? Who are you to rob them of that chance?'

Stove's legs felt a little wobbly. But he didn't really notice, because at that moment it came to him in a blinding flash of realisation. Grinder was right! Of course he was! How had he ever doubted him?

'What I ask of you is not for me my dear boy…it is for them. I want you to return to Snod Valley. I want you to appear at the Festival of Laughter as you planned. Most of your nation will be there. I will give you a special potion distilled from the Ignorant Pig's trotters (may he rest in peace). When you are announced, you will walk out onto the stage and smash the bottle of potion. It is most powerful, but will not harm your people. It will simply free them all from their bonds of laughter. I will collect all of their senses of humour here, in the Barrel of Laughs. They will be liberated…think of it…a new dawn for your people…and you as their leader…think of it Stove…Will you do it? Will you help me make them better?'

Grinder paused, spreading his arms wide and smiling what Stove now believed was a smile full of love, hope and promise. His head was pounding, the heavy sickly sweet candle scent was making it harder and harder for him to think clearly, but he knew what must be done, what had to be done…how had he ever doubted it?

'Where is your potion Warlock Grinder? I pledge to help you in any way I can, with all my heart and soul.'

53.

The Scaredy Cat Dog finds his courage.

A number of things seemed to happen all at once.

Grinder threw his head back in a triumphant roar of laughter.

With a cry of; 'Stove! Don't listen to him! He's hypnotising you!' Sidney shot out of the leather bag on the chair next to Grinder and knocked over the candle on its arm.

It went out and instantly the heavy, cloying scent disappeared.

The Grill dragonfly, startled by the commotion, turned away from Crumbs allowing him to scuttle out of the shadows towards it.

And Stove's head suddenly cleared.

'You!' howled Grinder turning to face the tiny, huge eyed dog, 'I thought you were dead!'

'Y...y...you l...l...left me for d...d...dead. Y...you ...m...monster!' screeched Sidney, stammering with fear. 'Twelve years I r...rotted in that dungeon, forgotten, unloved, alone, until Wheeze joined me. You used to love me...I was your faithful dog...I did you no harm. And why did you have me imprisoned...j...just because I knew your secret! I wouldn't have t...told anyone...but now...'

'Silence you fool!' roared Grinder, 'I should have killed you back then, but it's never too late to fix a problem!'

Grinder drew himself up to his full height.

'Stove!' shrieked Sidney cowering into a ball, 'it's laughter! Laughter kills Grinder! It's why he has to destroy it! Unlock the barrel, unleash the laughter!!'

Instantly, Stove sprang into action. He dived across to the Barrel of laughs. Grinder who was about to fry Sidney alive, span around towards him.

'No! Stop!' he raged, 'touch that and I will kill you!'

Without pausing to think, Stove grasped one of the large metal clasps on the barrel's lid and snapped it open. There was a hiss like steam escaping. Then he turned his attention to the other. He grabbed it with both hands, when suddenly a huge blast of white heat crashed into him and hurled him violently across the cavern, where he slammed into the wall. The impact took his breath away. His clothes and hair were smoking and singed and he felt sure he must have broken something. But he was alive. He peered awkwardly up at the Warlock through a fringe of blood, as he advanced threateningly towards him.

'Fool!' snapped Grinder, 'that is just a fraction of the power I could have used. I could easily have killed you if I'd wanted, but I spare you to carry out my commands, whether you want to or not. It could have been easy for you, but now you will be my slave. And I will still get all your people's senses of humour. As usual I will get what I want. In the meantime, when I've dealt with this treacherous 'dog' (here Sidney yelped in fear) you will learn all about suffering and loss.'

Grinder turned back towards Sidney who was cringing inside his leather bag once more, desperately trying to hide himself. Then he stopped and turned back to Stove once again.

'He's right, by the way,' he sneered, a really unpleasant grin on his face, 'it is laughter that I fear. It's the only thing I fear in fact. But there's another reason I steal what I steal. It gives me power. You see, the Barrel of Laughs is the source of my power. All the energy coming from those nasty little senses of humour combine together to give me power. Ironic isn't it?'

He barked a humourless laugh.

'I suppose if you had a sense of humour, you might think it funny too.'

He turned towards Sidney once again, his back to Stove.

'Incidentally, I really don't care if you know all this, the fact that you can't do anything at all about it is most amusing…your friends and sister will stay as insects and soon your mind will belong to me anyway.'

Grinder started to walk back towards the Scaredy Cat Dog's rather obvious hiding place, rolling up his sleeves and rubbing his hands together in anticipation as he went.

'Grinder!' called out Stove.

The warlock stopped in his tracks and angrily swivelled to face him.

'What?' he snapped.

Stove held his closed fist up in front of his face. He smiled crookedly, even though the effort re-opened a nasty gash on his cheek that had started to crust over. Slowly he unfurled his fingers. There, in the palm of his hand lay the other clasp from the Barrel of Laughs.

Grinder stared at it aghast. He couldn't believe what he was seeing. The cruel smile fell from his lips.

'But…but…you…I…how did….?' He stammered.

To Stove he suddenly looked like a little old man, no longer the fearsome and all-powerful Warlock.

'But that means…'

He whined in terror and turned to face the Barrel of Laughs.

If he'd been paying attention instead of gloating over Stove's predicament, he may have noticed that the barrel's second clasp was missing. And he'd certainly have noticed that its lid was now floating about six inches above it.

From where he lay, Stove noticed a bright, silver glowing light begin to emerge from the barrel and he suddenly heard a faint, low humming that sounded like thousands and thousands of people talking and laughing at a party.

Grinder just had time to croak, 'No!' before with a huge…

BANG!

…the lid blasted twenty feet up to the cavern's ceiling and rebounded down, smashing a hole through the roof of the mobile home. The silver light swooshed up and out of the barrel like water breaking through a dam and filled the cavern with a brightness so intense that Stove had to shade his eyes. At the same time, the laughter started.

First of all it was just an individual giggle. Grinder winced. Then more and more voices joined in and the intensity of the laughter began to increase. From a giggle, to a chuckle, to a guffaw and finally to a screaming belly laugh. More and more voices made it ever and evermore terribly loud.

Almost painfully loud, thought Stove wincing and covering his ears. But if he was suffering, it was nothing compared to what was happening to Grinder.

The heart of the silver light seemed to settle around him like a shroud. It pulsed angrily in time to the laughter. Grinder crouched in its centre, his hands over his ears, his mouth open in the wordless agony of a never ending screech.

'Aaaaaaaaaaaaaaaaaiiiieeeee!'

The sound was so awful that Stove almost began to feel sorry for him. And then something very strange happened. Grinder began to look younger, Stove was sure of it.

His long white hair began to darken, first at the tips and then all the way to the roots. It was the same with his beard. Before long it was jet black and then shorter, then just a fuzzy mess and finally it was gone altogether. As Stove watched, amazed, he saw that Grinder's face had become that of a young man, then a teenager... and then he began to shrink.

Still the laughter continued unabated. And still Grinder shrank. He was a boy of about seven and his Hawaiian shirt hung around him like a dress. Then he became five and it was more like a bed sheet. Then three, then finally, he seemed to disappear completely. The silver light and the thunderous laughter seemed to intensify for a moment and then as abruptly as when it had first appeared, swept back in to the barrel as if someone had reversed the film on which it had been shot.

Then with a clanging and crashing, the lid burst through the side of the mobile home, span high into the air and slammed down onto its top.

The laughter immediately stopped. All was silent apart from Stove's laboured breathing.

Suddenly, the silence was broken.

'Crumbs!' shouted Grill, 'get off my foot! Why are you biting me you naughty boy!'

54.

What was taken is returned.

'Grill!' shouted Stove joyfully and somewhat painfully jumping to his feet, 'you…you're back, you're ok!'

'Why what do you mean Stove,' said his sister crossly prizing Crumbs jaws from her foot and rubbing it ruefully. 'Naughty Crumbs!' she said again.

Stove looked perplexed, 'well, don't you remember?'

'Remember what?' said Grill, looking blankly at him.

'Ow!' said Cough, interrupting Stove as he was about to try and explain exactly what 'what' was, 'the top of my head is really sore.'

'Ay, mine tae,' grumbled Wheeze rubbing the top of his.

Stove looked around to see the two magicians sitting on the astro turf in front of the now partly destroyed mobile home.

'What on earth?' said Cough noticing the destruction for the first time, 'what has been going on Stove?'

Just at that moment, Mug appeared around the side of the mobile home, looking somewhat confused too.

'How very odd,' he said, 'I was having the strangest dream about flying around desperately wanting to find someone to sting.'

'That's strange,' said Cough, 'now you come to mention it, I was having a rather vivid dream too, about being desperately attracted to flowers and honey.'

'Hmmm, I won't tell you what I was finding myself desperately attracted to,' said McGinty joining the others, 'but it was certainly very unpleasant.'

'Help!' came a muffled cry, 'get me out o' here!'

They all looked across to the corner of the cavern where lay large, flat rock. Peeping out from the cramped space underneath it, looking very cross and red in the face was Colander.

'Oi!' he bellowed, 'who went an' put me in here then? It ain't funny you know…I suffer with the clostra…clostro…closterer…I don't like bein' in small places me. Get me out!'

Trying hard not to laugh, the others hurried over to Colander's temporary prison cell and with a lot of grunting and groaning, a little magic and a great deal of bad language from Colander, wrestled the rock away and succeeded in freeing him.

As they all sat on the ground, puffing and panting (and in Wheeze's case wheezing of course) from their various exertions, Stove recounted the fantastic events that had recently occurred. The other sat in silence, open mouthed. They had no recall whatsoever of what had happened. When he had finished, there was a total, stunned silence for a moment. Then Mug spoke,

'So Grinder survived the rock fall…and what a devious plan he had… incredible. Stove, to say you have done well would be an understatement. My boy, you have saved the whole valley and us all too. We are all so very, very proud of you.'

'Hear, hear!' shouted Cough and Wheeze together.

'Blimey!' said Colander, 'I don't think I'd have fancied meself as a spider for ever. No wonder I was dreamin' about eatin' fly pie.'

'Hmmm…' said McGinty pulling a face, 'let's not talk about that shall we?'

'Oh Stove…' said Grill adoringly, as she stepped forward and threw her arms around his neck.

The others quickly joined her and soon Stove was at the centre of a happy little backslapping, hugging, cheering, crowd.

'Thanks everybody,' said Stove, a little embarrassed at all the attention, 'but it wasn't just me, there is someone else to thank you know?'

'Ay and where is Sidney? Where is the so called Scaredy Cat Dog…Sidney where are ye?' said Wheeze enthusiastically.

They turned their attention to the Stove's leather bag, which still lay on one of the plastic chairs.

'It's alright now Sidney,' called Stove cheerfully, 'you're safe now, Grinder's dead…he's gone, this time definitely.'

'Ooooooow!' came Sidney's terrified howl from deep within the bag, 'I'm not coming out…not while he's still there.'

Stove felt a chill touch his stomach. The cheery atmosphere immediately dissipated.

'Er…er…' he swallowed dryly, 'while…while who's still there? Who Sidney?'

'Him!' shrilled Sidney, 'Him!'

A small, white furry paw emerged trembling from the leather bag and pointed to the pile of empty clothes that had formerly belonged to Warlock Grinder.

'G…G…Grinder!' he shrieked.

Time froze.

The colour slowly drained from Stove's cheeks. He turned, ashen-faced towards the others. They stared back, stunned like rabbits in a car's headlamps. Then slowly, very slowly and taking his courage in both hands Stove edged over towards the pile of clothes. Apart from Sidney's muffled whimpering all was silent…but then suddenly there was a different sound…a stuttering, mewling sound.

Stove's heart thumped as he neared its source. The mewling increased in volume. Then he was standing right by the crumpled, brightly coloured Hawaiian shirt…and it was moving. By now Mug, Cough, Wheeze and Grill had joined him.

'Breeeack!' protested Crumbs from Grill's arms as he struggled to escape.

Cough leaned forward and gingerly lifted up the shirt with his staff to reveal…

'A baby!' cried Grill, 'It's just a baby!'

She stepped fearlessly forward and before anyone could stop her had dropped Crumbs to the Ground (where he promptly let off one of his eggy specials) and swept the new born baby up into her arms.

'Poor little thing, he's hungry.'

'Now Grill, I believe that that baby is Grinder. He may be dangerous, we must be careful…'

'Oh nonsense Cough, he's just a baby.'

And he did seem to be just that.

After a while, they were all happy that Baby Grinder would be no harm to them and once again the atmosphere lifted. Wheeze magicked up a bottle of warm milk and a somewhat odd and old fashioned looking pram and after he had been fed and emitted a happy and full sounding burp, the baby feel asleep inside it swaddled in the Hawaiian shirt.

Even the Scaredy Cat Dog was eventually persuaded to emerge from his leathery hiding place and the little party sat down together to a relaxed (and relieved) celebratory supper of egg and bumkin and liquorice stick tea, that Colander had salvaged from the supplies that had been on the Silly Ass's back.

'Splendid!' said Wheeze eventually, patting his full stomach fondly, 'now then, tae business.'

'Business?' said Stove quizzically.

'Ay lad, business. The business of getting all yer senses o' humour back…it what yer came fer after all.'

'Well yes, of course. But how…? Stove stammered nervously.

'Listen laddie, do yer want yer sense o' humour back or not? There's nuthin' tae be afeared o'. When yon Barrel was opened earlier, it did nae have the proper

spell placed on it afore hand. I ken that spell so ye'll be safe this time. So…?'

'Well of course I want my sense of humour back, it's what we've been through all we've been through for,' said Stove a little indignantly.

'Good,' said Wheeze, 'now who's first?'

Stove looked at Mug, who looked at McGinty, who looked back at Stove, who in turn looked at Mug, who looked back at him. He nodded and smiled.

'I will go first,' said Stove.

'Good,' said Wheeze. 'First, unclasp the barrel.'

Stove did this, carefully prizing the large metal clasps from the barrel's lid once more. Immediately, the lid rose gently into the air of its own accord and as it did so, Wheeze began to chant a spell in what sounded like an exotically strange and different language.

As Stove watched entranced, the lid gently rose higher and higher until it was just above his head. Once again he could hear the same faint, low humming that sounded like thousands and thousands of people talking and laughing at a party. He looked down into the barrel, but there didn't appear to be anything there… not even the other end of the inside of the barrel…just an inky, blackness. Then suddenly, there was. A tiny, white spark, like a single bright star in a black, midnight sky.

As Wheeze's chanting continued, it began to sound to Stove less and less like the words of a strange language and more like a distant and heavy rumbling. If we'd been there, we would have thought it sounded like the sound of an approaching train. Then slowly, the miniature star started to rise up towards Stove's head, until it was level with his eyes. There it hovered for a moment. Above the rumbling, Stove could hear a single chuckling voice coming from it. It started to circle his head. Then it began increasing its speed. Faster and faster and faster and faster it circled, until Stove had to give up trying to look at it because it made his eyeballs ache to do so. And as it circled, so the noise of the chuckling increased accordingly. Then it stopped abruptly, right in front of Stove's forehead and…

'Puuurlipp!'

…it hit him straight between the eyes, like a hard little pebble and vanished inside his forehead.

'Ow!' cried Stove, 'that hurt!'

He looked crossly around at the others. Wheeze had ceased his chanting. They all looked anxiously at him. Grill held her breath. Then slowly he began to chuckle.

'I…ha ha ha…I didn't expect that! Ha ha ha!'

And he laughed and laughed like he'd never laughed before.

55.

The Festival of Laughter.

Their journey home was a lot easier than they had feared it would be. Helped not a little by Wizard Wheeze summoning the giant Leaping Lizard, upon which he assured them they could all fit very comfortably, especially as the Silly Ass was no longer with them.

And on that subject, Colander pointed out that if they had all turned back into themselves from the insects into which Grinder had transformed them, then it meant that 'that swine Trowel' must have reverted to Snod form when Grinder's power had disappeared too. He was keen to try and find him and treat him to a taste of 'old whippy' as he referred to his latest arm attachment which was fashioned from a birch tree.

The others agreed that they must at least try and find him, if only to return him to the Valley to face some less 'old fashioned' justice. But after a good day's searching the treacherous gardener was nowhere to be found.

'P'raps somethin' ate 'im,' muttered Colander hopefully.

McGinty was particularly enjoying having a sense of humour as he'd no recollection of ever having one before. This did result in him constantly playing what he thought were tremendous practical jokes on Wheeze in particular (with the enthusiastic encouragement of Mug, now also reunited with his sense of humour) until the Wizard could stand it no more and threatened him with removing his sense of humour again, if he didn't calm down a bit.

McGinty was keener than ever to return to his native country with the stolen senses of humour and true to his word, Wheeze agreed to accompany him together with Sidney the Scaredy Cat Dog, of whom he had grown rather fond.

For a while they were all at a loss for what to do with Baby Grinder, but then it was decided that it would be best if he too accompanied Wheeze who would act as his guardian and tutor and bring him up 'wi' a proper respect fae others.'

They re-sealed the Barrel of Laughs and packed it onto Grinder's Sinclair C5. And after much hugging, kissing, promises of staying in touch and a little crying (in particular from Sidney and Baby Grinder) set off back through another tunnel through the mountains towards Rudania (very slowly.)

The others began the long trek in the opposite direction back out of the cavern, down through the tunnels and out of the cave into which they'd been dragged by Slimetooth and his men what seemed like a very long time ago.

Eventually, they emerged, blinking into the sunlight just as the giant Leaping Lizard arrived. And he certainly was a giant, even a little bigger than Roger had been.

Cough read out the magical incantation given to him by Wheeze and the lizard flicked out his black tongue in what Stove hoped was a friendly manner and lay down on the ground so they could board. Then he, Grill, Colander, Cough and Mug mounted their ride and holding on tightly, they were off!

There was a sad and quiet moment as they passed the spot where poor Roger had died, although surprisingly, there was no sign of his body. Stove was most perplexed by this and he craned his neck to look behind at the spot for as long as he could. Where could it have gone? A horrid thought occurred to him.

'Leave him to the stone Wolves' was that what Slimetooth had said?

He shuddered. And yet, surely if…if he had been devoured by them, there would be something left there still. Bones…or something. But there was nothing. Not even dried golden blood. It was as if he had never been there. Irrationally, Stove found this thought somewhat comforting.

On and on they travelled, giant leap by giant leap along the route by which they had come.Grill had fashioned a small harness from Grinder's net curtains that she used to tightly strap Crumbs onto her lap. This was an indignity that he found hard to put up with so frequently peppered the unfortunate travellers with dreadful, eggy smells for the duration of the journey.

On they bounded, into the Great Red Desert past the occasional Sarcasm homestead, whose occupants would angrily shake their spears, or just their fists at them, as they flashed by.

'Call that a giant lizard! My kid's got bigger tadpoles than that!' was one shouted insult they managed to catch.

Then before long, they were confronted by the line of great black trees that marked the beginning of the Swamp of Contradictions once again. The Lizard paused and crouching down a little further than usual, propelled itself even higher over the top of their strange, upside down, tangled roots.

Their progress through the thicker, wilder part of the swamp was slowed by the lizard having to be very careful about where it landed. His leaps became more erratic accordingly, some shorter and higher, some longer and more shallow. This resulted in his passengers and Colander in particular suffering a certain amount of travel sickness.

But as the swamp became less impassable, so their speed increased again. They bounded easily over the Contradiction village and as Stove glanced back he could just see Gertie dashing across the village ring with a troop of his soldiers, shouting 'don't give us another Cheese and onion sandwich!' desperately at the top of his voice.

Soon they had passed the spot where Stove had been tied to the wooden stake in front of the other boundary of black trees, which the lizard cleared without difficulty once again. But as they arrived at the ruined outskirts of the Great Mirror Fruit forest, they suddenly veered to the west and continued towards the huge plain instead.

The change of direction was because Mug wanted to go home and no matter how hard Stove tried to persuade him to return with them to the Royal Castle and make peace with his brother, he remained adamant that he would not.

'There's been too much water under the bridge, Stove, I'm afraid,' he said.

So they arrived at Mug's scruffy, little farm… and a pleasant surprise was waiting there for him.

'Caw!'

'Eggtimer!' Mug cried delightedly, embracing first Stove and then Grill and jumping down from the lizard's back.

The crow, looking a little thin and still pretty ragged around the neck where Crumbs' tongue had snared him previously, waited until his master had moved a good distance away from the toad and then flapped down and perched on Mug's shoulder.

'Caw! Good to see you sir!'

'Good to see you too,' said Mug stroking the side of the crow's head affectionately.

Crumbs meanwhile, regarded him balefully and hungrily from his undignified position on Grill's lap.

Then with a wave and a blown kiss and many promises to return to visit as soon as possible, the remaining group of adventurers continued on their way back to the edge of the Mirror Fruit Forest.

This was as far as Wheeze had told them the Leaping Lizard could take them, owing to the denseness of the trees and lack of good landing places. They dismounted close to the spot where Stove and Phylis had last rested before emerging into the dead place where the forest met the swamp. There, to their surprise and delight, they discovered one of Stove's glowing, green, Gloworm blood markers.

'What a bit of luck!' said Cough, 'that'll save us at least a day knowing the short cut that Phylis took you on Stove my lad! We'll be home even sooner. Excellent! Well done!'

As it turned out Cough was a little out in his guess, it actually took them another day and a half to reach the Castle and when they arrived it was already getting dark.

The first thing Stove and Grill did was to search out their father who was, not surprisingly, relieved and delighted to see them. Stove's letter, it turned out had only served to worry him further and since receiving it he had been in a most uncharacteristic state of gloom and despair. But his spirits now lifted completely and it wasn't long before he was back to his old self, doing the famous dance he had invented called 'The penguin being chased by a fox dance' and yodelling his greatest hit songs at the top of his voice.

So it was that finally the day of the long awaited Festival of laughter arrived and Stove found himself standing in the wings of the stage, nervously waiting his turn and watching as Cough announced him to the crowd.

'Thank you...thank you ladies and gentlemen...' he said as the polite applause died slowly down, 'that was Cakeknife and his ... 'interesting' joke about...er... weasels and platform boots. And now… for the delight and delectation of your funny bones…tonight's favourite to win the crown…you know him…you'll love him. He's the son of our King, who we all know as the funniest man in the land and twenty times winner of the festival…ladies and gentlemen, will you please put your hands together, make sure you keep a tight grip on your sides to stop them splitting… and give a great big festival welcome…to the one…the only… Prince Stove!'

Cough turned and smiled encouragingly at him, beckoning to him with his outstretched arm. There was an out of tune fanfare and a blinding flash as one of Cough's magical fireworks went off alarming close to Stove as he strode out on to the stage. The crowd went wild. They cheered, they stamped, they chanted his name.

'Stove! Stove! Stove! Stove!'

He looked down into the audience. Sitting on the front row next to Fork, Spoon and Rubber Glove and smiling proudly up at him was his sister Grill, with Crumbs on her lap. Next to her was Colander, brandishing his shiny, new, articulated metal arm and cheering at the top of his voice. Then his father, beaming with pride and with his arm around him, a surprise…his Uncle Mug, grinning from ear to ear and laughing at the comments his brother shouted at him over the din.

And finally, another surprise…

'Go away Stove! You're rubbish!' Phylis shouted, smiling his odd, up-down smile and whistling loudly through his nose.

Slowly, the noise abated. Stove took a deep breath…and began.

THE END.

(or if you're a Contradiction, The Beginning.)